"Open your eyes,"
Nathan whispered

"Who do you see?"

"You," Emily answered.

"That's right. What do you feel?"

"Your warm hands on my arms."

"Do you see or feel anyone else?"

"No," she said softly.

"That's right," he whispered. "I'm the only one here. Now close your eyes and tell me the first thing that crosses your mind."

Her lashes fell, and she saw stars twinkling against the black backdrop in front of her eyes. "Stars," she whispered. "I see stars."

"So do I." His voice was raspy. "Every time I look at you, I see stars. Open your eyes and look at me, Emily. I'm the one who needs you. I don't want *anyone* on your mind except me."

ABOUT THE AUTHOR

The middle child in a family of seven, Charla Cameron grew up in a small town in the panhandle of West Florida. Married for twenty years to her high school sweetheart, she is the mother of a teenage daughter and son. After living in Alabama and Connecticut, Charla and her family returned to Florida when her husband went into business for himself.

After becoming a devoted romance reader, Charla wrote her first novel in 1983. *Diamond Days* is her debut with American Romance.

**CHARLA
CAMERON**

DIAMOND
DAYS

Harlequin Books

TORONTO • NEW YORK • LONDON
AMSTERDAM • PARIS • SYDNEY • HAMBURG
STOCKHOLM • ATHENS • TOKYO • MILAN

To my husband, Floyd,
for all the Diamond Days he's given me

Published June 1991

ISBN 0-373-16396-7

DIAMOND DAYS

Chapter One

Flashbulbs exploded in her face. Microphones were thrust under her chin. Emily blinked but hurried on, with two reporters scrambling to keep up with her. Although they barked questions, she kept her head erect and her lips pressed tightly together. Other reporters, clamoring for the attractive brunette's attention, their shouts canceling out the sense of each other's words, joined the trio in a headlong dash down the courthouse hall.

She'd cut her hair. She had gone back to her maiden name. She'd even moved to a new state. Still they'd found her.

Emily Clements burst through glass doors and into the muggy heat of a June day in Tallahassee. Outside, a crowd of people surrounded her. The strobe of camera lights intensified. A mike struck her cheek, bruising the flesh. She winced and raised an arm to protect herself.

Emily gritted her teeth as her resolve grew stronger. She'd known this would happen when she decided to block production of the movie, but she had hoped to have a couple of days before the story broke.

She pushed a photographer out of her way and started walking once again, determined not to let the reporters get the best of her. If she could make it down the steps, her car wasn't far away. The crowd moved closer, as if sensing they were about to lose their prey before any questions were answered. Their flailing hands and arms stripped her gray leather purse from her shoulder, but she caught it before it was lost in the badgering crowd that engulfed her. The questions didn't stop, but neither did she as she struggled toward the refuge of her car.

When at last she reached the bottom of the steps, the mob blocked the sidewalk. Trembling with anger, Emily searched the group of reporters for an opening through which she could dart. In the midst of the maze of mikes and flashing cameras pointed at her she saw angry eyes, moving mouths, bits and pieces of unfriendly faces.

Suddenly a hand grabbed her arm and began pulling her through the crowd. Fear gripped her, and she tried to twist free of the person who held her so firmly, until she realized he was clearing a path for them both. Her head struck something hard—a camera, another microphone—she wasn't sure. She covered her forehead as she was unceremoniously hustled to a waiting car. The door was open and she felt desperate. Quickly she slid into the front seat and someone shut the door. With trembling hands she reached up and pushed the lock.

Briefly Emily closed her eyes and took a deep breath. She had escaped from the reporters, but what about the man sliding behind the steering wheel of the car? Was she safe with him? Who was he, and why had he helped her?

Her ears rang from shouts and cries of frustrated newsmen as the car sped away from the curb. That scene was over, but now she had to contend with the stranger sitting next to her. Her stomach twisted with nervous knots and her mouth felt as if she'd stuffed it with cotton.

"What a close call," he said. "I thought that mob was going to have you for dinner."

His voice had a teasing quality and a smile played on his lips, but Emily was too apprehensive to respond to either. Her hands clenched in her lap as she dared a quick look at him. "Are you a reporter?" she asked in a whispery tone.

He glanced at her briefly before turning his attention back to the traffic. "If I was, I'd have left you back there in the midst of them."

For a split second their eyes met, and Emily suddenly felt embarrassed and vulnerable. In her desperation to escape the news media, she had put her trust in a complete stranger. That was a reckless thing to do.

Emily ran an unsteady hand through her short brown hair. "Maybe you should let me off right here," she said, deeply regretting her unwise action.

"Don't be crazy." He glanced toward her. "The reporters would see you and stop you again. Is that what you want?"

The memory of all those men and women poking her with their mikes, yelling questions and shining their bright lights into her eyes flashed through her mind. She tensed. No, she couldn't go through that again so soon. "No," she answered firmly. She'd had enough for one day.

Emily ventured another look at her rescuer. He wore a sophisticated navy blue suit, white shirt and striped tie. His eyes were a rare shade of midnight blue—the darkest she had ever seen. He had a soothing voice and an easygoing smile. He could have been one of the thousands of government workers who thronged Florida's capitol district daily. He wasn't a minor functionary, though—not with the car he drove. The average government employee couldn't afford a Lincoln Continental. What was she thinking? Here she sat, in a car with a total stranger! She should be worried, or at the very least angry with herself for being so impulsive.

"Were you waiting for a taxi?"

She whipped her head back around to look at him. "No, I have my car," she answered.

He didn't appear dangerous, she thought. Still, she should have been more careful. If those reporters hadn't been so boisterous, she would have been in the safety of her home by now. Not locked in a car with a complete stranger. She squeezed the strap of her gray leather purse between her hands and wondered how she was going to get out of this car. The roaring in her ears increased and she suddenly felt light-headed. Her breathing became choppy. What was she doing? If she didn't get control of herself immediately she was going to hyperventilate. She couldn't let delayed shock set in. She laid her head back against the seat and taking deep breaths, tried to calm her breathing.

"By the time I make a loop around the capitol building in this traffic, the reporters should be gone. I'll drop you off at your car."

Emily could barely hear him from the ringing in her ears, but she was relieved to know he wasn't planning to kidnap her. She willed her heartbeat to slow down and her stomach muscles to relax. There was no reason to fall apart now. This man was handsome, well-mannered and certainly not half so threatening as the reporters had been. In all fairness she needed to express her gratitude.

She turned her head just far enough to see his profile. "Thank you for helping me," she said softly. When he looked her way, their eyes met and held for a brief moment. She continued. "I should have waited until Evan, my lawyer, was ready to leave. I didn't know I'd have a problem with the press today.''

A car horn blew behind them, and Emily turned to look out the back window. The rush-hour traffic had crawled to a halt, and someone was definitely unhappy about it. Relaxing a little more, she leaned her head back against the padded seat once again. A tired sigh escaped past open lips and her shoulders pressed against the soft leather.

''Listen, with this backup it'll be half an hour before I can get to your car. There's a diner just up the street. Why don't we stop there and give everyone else a chance to get off the road? Besides, you look like you could use a cup of coffee.''

Emily sat up straight. ''No, you've already done enough. I don't want to keep you from anything.'' She shook her head as she answered, but thought she'd love a cup right now.

He smiled reassuringly. ''The only thing you're keeping me from is an evening alone. Anyway, I could use a little coffee myself. It's been one of those days for me, too.''

She hesitated because she didn't want to take advantage of him, but her need to rest finally prompted her to agree. Her mind was still spinning with too many thoughts and too much anger. If she was going to fight Dreamstar Productions and Tad Aubrey, she had to be strong. Two years was long enough to be silent.

Nathan Burke turned sharply right, leaving most of the traffic behind. Diligently he racked his brain for some clue to this woman's identity. He should know about every big news item that occurred in the state of Florida, in the whole world, for that matter. How had he missed this one?

He stole a glance at her. She was a little older than he had first thought, maybe close to thirty. Because she was petite, from a distance she looked younger. The gray linen suit she wore was expensive, and she had nice legs. Not much to go on, but something had drawn him to her when she stood on the courthouse steps. Maybe it was the way she held her shoulders and lifted her chin, or the defiance that showed when she pushed the reporters out of her way. In either case, he didn't like the idea of one against so many.

He parked the new Lincoln in front of the red-roofed diner. Sometimes he had lunch in this place, especially when he wanted to be alone. No one here attempted to make small talk with him. He liked that. He even liked the grumpy waitress who wore dresses too short and too tight for her large build.

Facing his lovely companion directly he said, "If we're going to have coffee together, I think we should at least exchange names. I'm Nathan Burke."

"Emily Clements," she answered in a hesitant voice as her gaze found his.

Her name wasn't much to go on. Nathan still didn't know who she was, but at least, she'd looked him in the eyes. She was no longer afraid of him. That made him feel better. He quickly checked her hands. No rings, but that didn't mean anything. "Okay, Emily. Let's have that coffee."

It pleased Nathan that Emily waited for him to open the car door. Not a big thing, but nice. He never understood why Michelle hated for him to do it for her. It was strange that six years after the divorce that little quirk still bothered him.

Walking beside Emily, Nathan realized that she couldn't be more than two or three inches over five feet, yet she matched his longer stride. Again she waited for him to open the glass door to the diner and that made him feel good. As they strode past the familiar Norman Rockwell print hanging on the dingy wall, he smiled. No other artist had ever captured American life the way Rockwell did.

Out of habit, Nathan chose a table in the back and took the booth facing the door, leaving Emily to stare at a wall with peeling paint. Since becoming Senator John Merritt's press secretary, he never sat with his back to a door. In his business he didn't like to be caught off guard.

Without bothering to come over to their table, a plump woman in a red-checked apron asked what they wanted. Nathan held up two fingers and said, "Coffee."

For the first time, he had the opportunity to look closely at Emily. Her eyes were a shade of green that would rival any rain forest in the Amazon. Shining waves of brown hair framed her oval face. Too short for his taste—but attractive. She had classic features, which she emphasized with a little makeup on her eyes and cheeks. The gray suit she wore was well tailored, nipping in at the waist and enhancing her feminine curves. The fear he had seen in her eyes when he grabbed her arm had been replaced by fatigue. He could understand that. And even though she looked tired and worried, she was a beautiful woman.

"I don't know why you stopped to help me, but I'm truly glad you did," she said gratefully. "I was at the breaking point." She gave him an appreciative smile, and Nathan noticed a faint quiver in her bottom lip.

Nathan leaned on the red-cushioned seat and returned the smile as the waitress set the coffee in front of them, placing two little containers of cream by each cup. "You looked like you could use a hand. I don't know why those reporters were snapping at your heels, but believe me I know what they're like and how hard they are to handle.''

He noticed that she sipped the steaming black liquid without adding cream or sugar. He also noticed that her hands were trembling, and she looked as if she was about to cry. It bothered him that she was still so obviously upset about something. After she placed the stoneware mug on the chipped table, she lightly rubbed her forehead just over her left eye.

"Headache?" he asked, thinking that if he could get her to talk she'd feel better.

"No, no it's nothing," she murmured.

Her quick glance at him before turning her attention back to the coffee told him she wasn't telling the truth. His gaze traveled up to the place she'd rubbed. Through the wispy strands of light brown hair he saw an angry looking bruise. Damn! A camera must have struck her as he pulled her through the crowd. He should have been more careful.

She looked so vulnerable with her sad, round eyes and beautifully shaped lips. He hated to question her, especially when it was obvious she'd already been through hell. Tears were gathering in her eyes. He watched as she raked a hand through her hair and the curls fell back into place. Late-afternoon sunshine filtered through limp curtain lace to bathe her face in light. He didn't want to be pushy, but those reporters had been after her like tigers going for red meat. If he knew why, maybe he could help.

He softened his voice and asked, "Do you want to talk about what happened today?" His words were undemanding, yet the mug shook in her hand when he spoke. Whatever was wrong had taken its toll on her. He added quickly, "Don't say anything if you don't want to. But sometimes it's easier to talk to a stranger."

The unshed tears glistening in her eyes raced to the surface and spilled over, slipping down her cheek as she whispered, "They won't let my husband die."

Nathan was dumbfounded. He hadn't expected such an emotional reaction to his probing, or such a startling answer to his statement. She placed her elbow on the table and let her forehead fall into her palm, shielding her face from his view. Her shoulders shook as silent sobs racked her body.

He slipped out of his seat and into the booth beside her. Gently he touched her, then carefully pulled her into his arms and held her close while she cried. "Shh—" he whispered. "Everything's going to be all right." To his relief his voice sounded reassuring, even to his own ears. He wasn't any good at this sort of thing. Never had been.

Frustration ate at Nathan as he brushed his hand over her soft hair. This beautiful woman was torn apart and he wasn't doing much to help. Why did she want her husband to die? Who was keeping him from dying? His mind quickly replayed all the big stories of the last couple of years. Either she was talking in riddles or he was slipping. He wasn't any closer to knowing who she was. Exactly who was Emily Clements, and why didn't he know her story?

Within a couple of minutes her sobs turned to sniffles, but Nathan continued to hold her until she pushed away. He reached into his pocket, pulled out a neatly pressed handkerchief and handed it to her. She dabbed the corners of her eyes, not looking at him.

"It's okay to cry," he said. That sounded trite and unfeeling but hell, he'd never known what to say when a woman started crying. Especially one he didn't even know.

Emily didn't look up or acknowledge Nathan. If she'd been embarrassed to find herself sitting in a car with a stranger, she was mortified to have buried her face against his shirt and wept like a baby.

"I'm sorry," she whispered between gusty breaths. "I don't know what happened to me." She blew her nose and wiped her eyes again. It was his fault she'd fallen apart, she told herself. She wouldn't have if he hadn't been so kind, his voice so gentle. Emily squeezed her eyes shut. Why couldn't she have kept control of herself until she was home?

"There's no need to be sorry. You can cry on my shoulder any time."

Emily sniffled and attempted to smile at his effort to lighten the mood. "It's just that it's been two years, and the press still won't leave me alone. They want to know what I think, how I feel. It's none of their business. I hate all this publicity. I just want to be left alone to go about my life, as I did before all this happened." She looked up at him and realized how close he was to her.

Picking up her coffee, she drank again. What was she doing pouring her heart out to a stranger? She wiped her eyes once with the dampened handkerchief. Somehow she had to pick up the pieces of this disastrous afternoon and walk out of here with her head held high.

"The press has been after you for two years?" he questioned.

"Oh, they left me alone for a little while. Until that awful man wrote his book. That's when I moved to Florida and took back my maiden name." Emily laughed nervously and sipped her coffee again. This guy must be a saint to sit quietly and let her cry all over his shirt, then prattle on about herself. She risked a glance at him and was surprised to find concern showing on his features. "Why am I telling you all this? Why are you even listening? Surely I'm keeping you from something. I'll call a cab, or maybe I'll walk back to my car." She kept her eyes on her coffee cup. It was so damn hard to look him in the eyes, even though he seemed to be extremely understanding.

"No, no," he assured her quickly. "Believe me, I'm not missing a thing. I want to hear what you have to say, but I'm not sure what book you're referring to." She came from another state and now used a different name. That could explain why all the reporters knew something he didn't.

She turned and faced him with tear-filled eyes. *"America's Kind of Hero,"* she whispered.

Nathan felt heat rise in his chest. Her words were barely audible, but he heard them and his muscles tensed. Now he knew who she was—and so did every other American who'd read Jeremy Smith's fictional account of Gary Spencer's death. He remembered the story.

Gary Spencer had been killed in South America while trying to subdue a hijacker on a plane. According to witnesses, Gary jumped one of the hijackers from the back and wrestled the gun from him. Just as he did and the passengers roared their victory, a second hijacker shot him. Gary became an instant hero, "America's kind of Hero," as Smith so aptly called him. One who wasn't afraid to die fighting for liberty.

Nathan winced at the thought of the things this lovely woman must have gone through, was still going through. "There was talk about a movie based on the book. Is that why you were at the courthouse today?" He was glad he could finally make an intelligent observation.

Her hands continued to tremble as she finished the last of her coffee. "Yes." She pulled a paper napkin out of the chrome-plated holder and wiped her mouth. "My life had just begun to settle down when I received word that Tad Aubrey was going to make a movie based on Smith's book. I'm trying to keep Dreamstar Productions from making the movie. I've been silent for too long. Gary is dead." She closed her eyes for a moment, the grimace on her face showing how deeply she suffered. "I've buried him, but I won't be free until everyone else puts him to rest. Every time the press tells his story I have to relive his death. Gary did what he felt was the right thing to do, and I'm tired of people taking advantage of it. I want to stop them." Renewed anger gave her strength. Her shoulders straightened, and she looked into his eyes. "It seems every time there's a hijacking now, somebody makes a movie, writes a book or, as in my husband's case, both."

"Why don't you want the movie made?" he asked, knowing she might not want to answer such a personal question.

She stared at him a long moment. His question was typical of the ones the reporters were shouting at her half an hour ago. She might as well learn how to answer them. Emily Clements was no longer in hiding.

"I hated Smith's account of Gary's last few hours. His portrayal of my husband was grossly inaccurate. Many times after the book came out I wished I'd consented to the interview Smith wanted. If I had, maybe Gary wouldn't have come out looking like an irrational hothead who couldn't take the strain and buckled under the pressure."

All of a sudden she stopped. When had she become so militant? She picked up the paper napkin and wiped her mouth again. "I must be going insane. I don't know why I've told you so much. I don't even know who you are."

"I'm a good listener, and I'm also Nathan Burke, press secretary to Senator John Merritt."

Her eyes widened, the fear returned. "You work for the press! You should have told me." She reached for her purse.

"No, Emily," he said calmly, placing his hand on her shoulder. "I'm not a reporter. I don't work for the press, but I deal with them every day. There's a big difference."

She shook off his hand and lifted her chin. Her voice was firm as she asked, "Would you mind taking me back to my car now?" She handed him the wet handkerchief, and he stuffed it in his pocket without taking his eyes off her face.

Slowly, he told himself, *you're going too fast, rushing her. Just get her phone number and call her tomorrow.* Nathan reached into his pocket and brought out a pen, then pulled a napkin from the chrome-plated holder. "Before I take you back to your car, I'd like your phone number."

When she didn't take the pen immediately, he began to worry. There wasn't a reason in the world why she should trust him or want to see him again, but he wanted to see her. If she didn't give the number freely, he knew how to get it. He had never misused his power as press secretary to John Merritt, but if he had to, in order to see Emily again, he would.

He had a feeling that Emily Clements was just the person he needed to bring national attention to CAT. He breathed a sigh of relief when Emily took the pen from his hand and jotted down her number.

THE HEADLINES IN THE NEXT morning's paper were worse than Emily had anticipated. She should have known she'd land on the front page. Closing the front door of her condominium with a bang, she went into her winter white kitchen, threw the paper on the counter and poured hot coffee into her favorite cup. Why should she read the story? She already knew what it would say. Reporters continually rehashed the same story. Would they never tire of it?

As she stood at the counter, tapping her slippered foot restlessly, she stared at the picture of herself being dragged through the crowd by Nathan Burke. The telephone rang, startling her for a second. She glanced at the black-faced clock with white Roman numerals and knew it was her mother. Who but Lacy Clements called before eight in the morning, before the cheaper night rates changed to day rates. It wasn't that her mother couldn't afford the call, she just didn't like waste.

Last night, when she had talked with her parents, she had assured them she was holding up very well. Obviously her mother needed to make sure nothing had happened during the night, and that her youngest daughter was up and going.

Remembering her mother with a fondness that made all the smothering worthwhile, Emily spoke a cheerful hello into the phone.

"Emily, it's Harold Stobey."

"Oh, good morning," she said, a tinge of surprise showing in her voice. Harold was the broker of the real-estate firm where she worked. She cringed when she realized he must have seen the morning paper, too. She had known this would bring her out of hiding, but perhaps she should have told her employer first. It was a sure bet that he didn't want his employees showing up on the front page of the paper.

"I'd like to have a meeting with you at nine-thirty this morning. Can you make it?"

She glanced at the clock again. "Yes, that will be fine."

"Good. We'll talk then."

With the receiver once again in its cradle, Emily picked up her coffee and stared at the picture of Nathan dragging her through the crowd. She had a feeling Mr. Stobey wouldn't be as easy to talk to as the man who had rescued her the day before. When she'd cried from the strain of the day and the insensitive actions of the reporters, Nathan hadn't made a big deal about it, for which she would always be grateful. Why had she told Nathan so much about herself? Because his voice was gentle and his kindness genuine. And she'd needed to talk.

Thinking of Nathan brought him vividly to her mind's eye. She must have been drawn to him. Why else would she have gotten in his car? She'd felt strength and determination in his hand when he grabbed her. His bewitching blue eyes had caressed her face with gentleness. His voice was smooth, caring.

Emily rinsed her empty cup and left it in the drain. The morning paper stared up at her from the counter. Out of all the pictures they had taken, she wondered why they had chosen to print the one of Nathan pulling her through the crowd. She read the caption under the picture. Ah—now she knew. Being rescued by Senator Merritt's press secretary would sell more papers. The longer she looked at the picture, the angrier she became. Emily swept the paper off the counter, wadded it as small as she could and stuffed it in the trash compactor. Nathan

Burke wouldn't get any more free publicity at her expense.

At nine twenty-five she walked into the downtown office of Stobey and Ackerman. For two years she had worked in this office without anyone really knowing who she was. Today she felt as if she was walking in for the first time, because now she was not simply Emily Clements. She was Gary Spencer's widow, the title she'd hidden from for over two years.

"Good morning, Melody," Emily said as she stopped by the secretary's desk. "Any messages?"

"Hi, Emily. You've got plenty of messages. I think every newspaper and magazine in the state has called, but you better go see Mr. Stobey first. He said to send you in right away."

As usual, Melody's blond hair bounced on her shoulders and her blue eyes sparkled as she talked. Emily liked Melody because she was always so perky and vivacious.

"Yes, I know. He called me earlier. I'm not looking forward to our discussion. I think I'll get a cup of coffee first."

Drinking too much coffee had become a way of life for Emily recently, but she was at a loss as to what to do about it. She was just glad she hadn't gone back to smoking, a habit she had given up more than five years before.

"I guess we all were a little surprised to find out you're Emily Spencer. From what I read, it sounds like you're in for a big fight with that production company. I hope everything goes your way," Melody added with a compassionate smile.

Emily nodded slowly. "Thanks. I have a feeling Tad Aubrey is the kind of man who doesn't give up when he wants something. But neither will I." She paused. "Not this time."

Melody handed the yellow slips of paper to Emily. "I know just what you need to take your mind off your troubles. How about a game of tennis tonight? I want to try out a new racket."

"Sure. I'll call for court time and let you know." That was another thing Emily liked about Melody. She was a terrific tennis player. The condos where Emily lived had their own swimming pool, fitness center and tennis courts. Emily often asked Melody over for a game of tennis because she was a good player. Janice, her best friend, would occasionally break down and play a game with Emily, but she didn't like the game.

As Emily poured the dark liquid into the cup, she remembered that Nathan hadn't touched his coffee yesterday. Yet, he had said he could use a cup, that it had been one of those days for him, too. He had been successful in gaining her confidence, and he certainly knew how to get her to talk. Was there an underlying reason for that?

Emily sighed, still thinking about Nathan. She'd been too upset yesterday to notice much about him, but now she remembered that his shirt had smelled fresh even though it was the end of a hot day. The way she'd rubbed her face back and forth across the cotton material was sure to have left makeup stains, yet he'd held her close without flinching. And he hadn't batted an eye when she returned his damp handkerchief.

Taking a deep breath, Emily replaced the glass pot and picked up her coffee. She had to push thoughts of Nathan out of her mind and concentrate on fighting Dreamstar Productions and Tad Aubrey. Evan had assured her there was little chance the movie could be stopped. But that wasn't going to stop her from trying to keep her husband's last hours of life from being shown on every television in America. The thought of it filled her with fury.

Emily turned away from the table and almost ran into Raymond Sanders. Raymond hadn't taken kindly to Emily's rejection of his advances when she had first come to work for Stobey and Ackerman. In order to get back at her, he took every opportunity to be sarcastic and patronizing. Tall and handsome, with light blond hair and blue eyes, he wasn't accustomed to getting the brush-off from women. But the last thing Emily had wanted or needed when she moved to Tallahassee was a man.

"Well, well, well. Look who we have here."

Letting her expression convey a message of irritation, Emily stepped away from him. "Excuse me, Raymond, but Mr. Stobey is waiting for me."

"I know he is, Mrs. Spencer. I've already spoken with him this morning. Why didn't you tell us you were Mrs. Gary Spencer?" he asked as he brushed his well tailored jacket aside and slipped both hands into his pants' pockets.

Emily gave him a cold stare. "My name is Clements." Being called Mrs. Spencer again was more of a shock than she expected. But she wouldn't let Raymond know that. Somehow she had known if anyone was going to give her a hard time it would be Raymond.

"Why? After your husband died wasn't his name good enough for you?"

Emily gasped as his hurtful words cut through her with razor sharpness. Just as her arm jerked to slap his face, Raymond turned away, laughing. Her chest heaved with anger. For the first time in her life she wanted to slap a man. What kind of person was she becoming? Suddenly she was shaking so badly coffee spilled over the cup and on her hand. She winced and quickly set it down, then grabbed a napkin to wipe away the burning liquid. The sting on the back of her hand renewed her anger. She contemplated following Raymond and doing the damage she first intended. But she didn't. She took a deep breath and ran a shaky hand through her hair.

"What a jerk," she mumbled as she picked up the coffee cup once again and walked to the back of the large room. She knocked on the dark paneled door of Mr. Stobey's private office. After hearing a brisk answer, she opened the door and stepped inside.

"Good morning, Mr. Stobey," Emily said, masking her inner turmoil as she entered the sunlit room. Still a nice-looking man, though nearing retirement age, Mr. Stobey's hair showed no signs of gray. The crinkled lines that ran from his eyes belied his hair's dark brown color.

Harold Stobey leaned back in his leather chair as he said, "Sit down, Emily. Make yourself comfortable."

Wiping at the back of her peach-colored skirt with her free hand, Emily eased herself into a brown velvet armchair. The window behind Mr. Stobey's desk showed a perfect hazy blue sky.

"I thought we'd better talk about the article in this morning's paper. Needless to say, I was surprised to read that you're Emily Spencer and you're trying to stop production of a movie about your husband."

Emily cleared her throat and straightened her shoulders. This was one of the things she hated. Why should she have to explain herself to anyone? "There isn't much to tell," she hedged. "Dreamstar Productions wants to produce Jeremy Smith's book, which is loosely based on my husband's death. I want to stop them."

"Yes, the article told me that much. What I want to know is why you kept your identity a secret? Why didn't you let any of us here know you were Emily Spencer?"

He folded his hands together and placed them under his chin. His voice was even, but his words demanded an answer.

Emily moistened her lips. She disliked his inquisitive manner. In all fairness, maybe she should have told him the truth about herself. "I didn't really keep it a secret. Clements is my maiden name, and I use it legally. I've kept my personal life private, not secret."

Harold Stobey picked up his pipe from a crystal ash-tray and stuffed it with tobacco from a leather pouch. Emily knew he was thinking, pondering what she'd said. She watched him strike a gold-tipped match and put it to the packed tobacco. With a sucking noise, he drew on the pipe and brought the tobacco to life, filling the room with a sweet, pleasant smell.

The burn on her hand had reddened but the sting was easing. If she was lucky it wouldn't form a blister. She sipped her coffee while Mr. Stobey continued to adjust his pipe. She made dents in the soft disposable with her fingernail while she waited for him to speak again.

"Why did you feel it necessary to keep your identity private? Did you think we wouldn't understand?" he finally asked when he seemed satisfied the pipe was going to stay lit.

With a sighing breath, Emily prepared to tell as much of her story as she was willing to. "No, that's not the reason. I moved here to get away from it all. In Birmingham, where I lived before coming to Florida, I was called constantly by newspaper and magazine reporters wanting to interview me. Even Jeremy Smith wanted to talk to me about the book he was writing about Gary. I was having a hard enough time coping with my husband's death and the reasons behind it. I couldn't deal with the flashing cameras, the press—people waiting outside my door, the continuous ringing of the telephone, all the questions, the invasion of my privacy.'' Emily stopped when her voice started shaking and her bottom lip trembled. Somewhere she had to find the strength to continue.

Tension mounted in her chest, making breathing difficult. She rubbed the back of her neck and stared out the window for a couple of moments. She wouldn't let herself get worked up over this again. She wouldn't allow herself to lose control the way she had yesterday. Curiosity was natural, and she had to learn to cope with it.

After a moment of silence, Emily continued. ''When I couldn't take the pressure any more, I swore my parents to secrecy and moved without leaving a forwarding address. I chose Tallahassee because my roommate from college lives here. I knew I could have the anonymity I sought without being completely alone.'' Emily took a deep breath and inhaled the distinctive aroma of the pipe tobacco. It was a pleasant scent, and she realized it also had a calming effect.

''Why did you decide to give up your anonymity to thwart Dreamstar's production of this movie?'' Smoke issued from Mr. Stobey's mouth as he spoke.

Emily stiffened. His question asked more than she was willing to tell at the moment. ''My reasons for going after Dreamstar are personal.'' Saying anything else would be giving away too much of herself. She wasn't ready to do that. Smith had taken away Gary's dignity, integrity, and now Dreamstar wanted to put Smith's warped account of the story on national television for the whole world to view. She couldn't let that happen. Not without a fight.

''I see.'' Holding his pipe between his teeth, he reached for his wire-rimmed glasses and settled them over the bridge of his nose before looking at her again. "Emily, you realize that my first concern has to be for this office?"

"Yes, of course." She thought she heard a trace of a threat and her back stiffened again. "I don't believe I've done anything to discredit this firm."

"No, I don't think you have either, but I'd be remiss in my duty if I didn't caution you to be careful. Do what you have to—as long as it doesn't affect your work or reflect badly on this office. If that happens, we'll have to talk again."

Emily let out a sigh, but didn't take her eyes off the older man. "I understand," she answered in a firm voice. She started to let that be the end of their conversation, but for some reason she couldn't. "I'm not doing this for the notoriety, as some people might think."

Mr. Stobey laid his pipe in the ashtray. "I didn't think that for a moment," he answered.

Emily gave him a grateful smile. "Thank you."

Chapter Two

Finding himself once again staring off into space, Nathan Burke tapped his pen on his desk in frustration. Why couldn't he get Emily Clements off his mind? Her dark green eyes haunted him. It wasn't like him to be so interested in a woman so quickly, especially one who had the kind of troubles she did. She'd almost had him crying, too. He knew how rough the media could be and knew they were especially hard with a hot item such as terrorism.

The moment he'd seen her pushing her way down the courthouse steps, he had been drawn to her side. Even surrounded by reporters, she had moved with purpose and determination. It had taken courage for her to answer his probing questions. He admired that. He'd been a stranger, yet she'd risked opening herself to him. He didn't understand his need to protect her when she was doing a fairly good job of protecting herself.

Okay, so she was attractive. Tallahassee and D.C. were filled with attractive women. Women that didn't have to face the kind of problems that she had staring at her every morning when she woke up. He'd been the route of trying to help a woman with hang-ups, and he wasn't going to get caught up in anything like that again, he told himself. He'd just appreciate her from afar while he talked her into working with him on CAT.

He pulled the crumpled napkin from his pocket and looked at the number written on it. He wanted to get her involved in CAT. But would she consider joining a group called Citizens Against Terrorism? That could be a problem. CAT wanted—no, needed—media attention. Emily didn't.

The controversy between Emily and Dreamstar was bound to cause a lot of publicity. He had to find a way to channel some of that toward CAT. The senator wanted to bring national recognition to this new organization. The major problem had been their failure to bring any big-name people into the group. Gary Spencer had become a household name because of his act of heroism. The attention surrounding the production of this TV movie about Gary would be good for CAT. It could give them the break they had been looking for. And that would help John's campaign platform for tougher laws dealing with convicted terrorists.

But he could understand Emily's feelings, too. The man at Dreamstar was exploiting her husband. She had a right to be angry. She'd had enough of reporters and publicity and was entitled to her privacy.

Nathan looked at the napkin again and quickly dialed her number before he talked himself out of calling her. His heart pounded loudly in his chest as a soft hello drifted into his ear. "Hello, Emily, it's Nathan. I called to see how you're feeling."

"I'm fine, Nathan. In fact, I'm glad you called. This gives me an opportunity to apologize. I don't know what got into me yesterday. My only excuse is that it was a difficult day. I don't usually—talk so much about myself."

"Emily, an apology isn't necessary. I didn't do anything I didn't want to do."

"Well, I feel as though I took advantage of your kindness and that wasn't my intention. I know you didn't bargain for my life's story and a soggy handkerchief when you gave me a lift. Thanks for being a good Samaritan."

"Yesterday's forgotten. We'll start over. Are you free to have dinner with me tonight?" Nathan held his breath while he waited for an answer.

"I'm sorry, Nathan, I have plans."

Nathan's pulse raced. He'd waited until it was too late. Of course she had plans. "How about dinner tomorrow night? We'll go to the Ocean House."

"No, I'm sorry. That won't be possible."

Surprised, Nathan realized he was getting a polite brush-off. Why? She had been so nice when he first called. Apologizing for keeping him from dinner and thanking him for his help.

The fear of rejection rose within him and a hint of anger outlined his voice when he asked, "Are you free any night for the next three years?"

"No, I'm not."

Her simple statement said it all. He pulled the phone away from his ear and looked at it as if he didn't believe what he had just heard. She'd turned him down flat. For three years! Just who did she think she was? Hadn't he already told himself he was interested in her only for what she could do for CAT? And here she was turning him down before he had the chance to tell her he only wanted to use her in a political campaign. Could she have guessed?

Returning the receiver to his ear he said, "Emily, there's something I'd like to discuss with you. Could you make an exception?" he asked diplomatically.

"No," was her soft reply. "I don't want to have to go into it with you. Just accept the fact that you caught me at a weak moment, and I used you. I'm not proud of it. I have apologized for my behavior and thanked you for your kindness. That's all I can do."

The fine hairs on the back of his neck bristled. "That's not good enough, Emily."

"That's the way it has to be. Goodbye."

The phone went dead. She hung up on him. He couldn't believe she'd actually hung up on him. Well, it was better this way, he told himself. She was too attractive, anyway. He probably would have found himself caught up in her problems and forgetting about what she could do for CAT. Nathan went back to tapping his pencil. Who was he kidding? He couldn't let her go so easily.

A knock on the door disturbed Nathan. When it opened, a tall, well-dressed redheaded man peered around the door. "Am I early?" he questioned.

"No, right on time, Roger. Come in and sit down," Nathan said as he pointed to the wine-colored leather chair in front of his desk.

Roger was a young lawyer Nathan often called on when he needed someone to do legwork for him. Because of his interest in a political career, Roger was always more than willing to help the senator. One of the things Nathan had liked about Roger when they first met more than three years ago was his easygoing manner.

"You're spending a lot of time in Washington these days. How's it going?" the younger man asked as he

straightened the knot in his tie and brushed at the silk-
ened length of it.

"John's getting ready to announce that he'll be running for reelection next year, so there's a lot happening
right now."

"Why all the fuss? He's a shoo-in," Roger remarked
with all the confidence in the world.

"No one's ever a shoo-in, and I don't want to hear a
comment like that again. John has a good chance of
beating any opponent because he's a good politician.
And don't forget it," he added firmly.

"Sure, anything you say." Roger smoothed a hand
over his perfectly styled hair.

Nathan tapped his pen on the blotter. Roger was
clearly stunned by the reprimand. There was no reason
to take his frustration out on Roger, other than the fact
he happened to be the only one in the room. Nathan
sighed heavily. He couldn't let Emily get to him like this.
She wasn't that important.

"I asked you to stop by because I need your help,"
Nathan answered pushing back his chair, then crossing
one leg over the other. "How long has it been since
you've been in touch with anyone from CAT? Can you
give me an update on it?"

"I'm not sure. It hasn't been on the priority list in a
while. As best I remember, the last count had the membership close to fifteen and they were meeting in Lucy
Morrow's home every other Wednesday. It seems their
intentions are to grow in numbers and financial support.
They also want to be an effective lobbyist group. Along
with federal funding, they hope to influence Congress to
pass stiffer penalties for individuals and groups convicted of terrorist acts here in America, as well as
abroad."

Nathan listened carefully. He already knew what Roger was saying, but it was good to hear the group hadn't lost its focus.

Roger spoke again. "I read the morning paper. Does this have anything to do with the Spencer woman and the movie they want to make about her husband?"

"If you read the paper, you know she now goes by the name of Clements."

"My mistake," Roger answered quickly. "The paper didn't say why she was getting into your car. What gives?"

"We were talking about CAT, remember?" Sometimes Roger was too smart.

Roger shifted in his chair. "All right, if you want my opinion, I think CAT could use a woman like her. I mean her husband's death is big news right now. If we could get her to join we could not only capitalize on the court battle and the production but also bring out that the terrorists were never brought to justice."

Nathan pursed his lips in thought, then looked at Roger. The young man was too perceptive. "I want all this in writing and on my desk tomorrow morning."

"Sure, no problem." Roger hesitated. "Are you going to tell me why? Is this sudden interest again in CAT for the senator or the Clements woman?"

Nathan stared at Roger from under thick lashes. "You ask too many questions."

"Hey, Nathan, I'm just trying to do a good job. I think it will help if I know our long-term goal."

Rubbing the faint trace of beard on his cheek, Nathan studied Roger for a moment. "All right. The more noise CAT can make, the better John's chances of pushing his bill through the Senate. Because of Gary Spencer and the movie about his death, Emily is a big news item right now. The publicity she could bring to CAT would be a big boost to their need for public awareness, which in the long run will help John's campaign."

"Do you think we can get her interested?"

Nathan shrugged. "That could be a problem. Emily would benefit from an association with CAT. With an organization like CAT behind her, I think she'd have a better chance of at least slowing down Dreamstar."

"What's the problem? Is it something we can take care of?"

"I don't know. I have doubts. It seems the press gave her a hard time when her husband was killed. She stays as far away from the media as she can get."

"That happens, but if we play our cards right maybe we can get her on our side." Roger paused briefly, then continued. "What about John?"

"A vacancy is coming up on the Foreign Affairs Sub-committee on Terrorism. John hopes to be appointed. That will put him in a good position to help CAT, and he expects supporting a group like CAT will help get him reelected. Everyone in America is asking for stiffer laws against terrorism. It's a good platform. We can't go wrong with it."

"Looks like we're going to be busy for the rest of the year. Do you want me to talk to Emily Clements?" Roger asked.

Nathan's eyes narrowed. There was a slight twitch at the corner of Roger's mouth. The kid was smart. Nathan liked that. "No, I'll take care of her. I want you to attend CAT's next meeting and report back to me."

Roger's eyes widened. "You're kidding?"

"No, I'm not," Nathan said calmly.

"Uh—look, Nathan, listening to a group of men and women talk about lost loved ones isn't exactly my cup of tea, if you know what I mean.'' There was a nervous chuckle at the end of his sentence and he squirmed uncomfortably in his chair.

"I know what you mean. But do it anyway.'' His eyes were firmly fixed on Roger's face.

Roger lifted his hands in a show of helplessness. "Oh, come on, Nathan, give me a break. I can't take that sort of stuff. Let me talk to the Clements woman and you attend the CAT meeting."

Nathan didn't blink an eye. He continued to stare at him. Roger needed to know just how important this was to him.

"You're really serious about this, aren't you?'' Roger asked.

"Yes, I'm serious. When's CAT's next meeting?''

"Ah—I'm not sure. I'll have to check.'' His voice had a resigned tone to it.

"I want you to find out, then be there. Set up an appointment with me for the next morning.'' Nathan's voice carried a ring of authority.

"Nathan, I—okay. You want it. You've got it.'' Roger got up and left without another word.

Nathan felt somewhat more subdued when the door closed behind the young man. Roger had hit the nail on the head when he mentioned Emily joining the group. The first thing he had to do was get her to talk to him.

"THAT'S THE MOST AGGRESSIVE game you've ever played. How did you ace so many serves?'' Melody asked as she met Emily at the net.

Emily wiped her forehead with the white terry-cloth band that circled her wrist, then grinned at Melody. "I guess you better take that new racket back for a refund.''

"I think I will. That's the last time I'll ask to play tennis when I know you have things on your mind. You used me as a workhorse to get rid of all your frustrations," Melody accused with good humor.

"You're right, I did." The call from Nathan just before she walked out the door bothered her more than she realized. Turning him down hadn't been easy, but with everything else she had going on, she couldn't afford to get involved with a man. "You didn't really mind, did you?" Emily asked seriously.

Melody zipped the Prince racket into its blue leather holder. "Only losing six to three." Melody laughed as she pulled the rubber band out of her long hair and shook it, sending blond curls flying. "Actually, that's the reason I asked you for a game. I had a feeling you needed to get some things out of your system. Feel better?"

"Much better," Emily answered and pulled the sweatband off her forehead.

"Come on, let's go to the clubhouse. I'll be the good loser and buy the diet soda."

Laughing, Emily turned around to head for the exit when she stopped and stared at the man leaning against the gatepost. She was sure her heart skipped a beat at the sight of him. Why was he doing this? Her palms felt sweaty for the first time that evening. She turned to Melody, who looked at her strangely.

"I think that man over there is waiting for me." She pointed in Nathan's direction. "Could I take a rain check on the soda?"

Melody scrutinized the man. "For him I'd give up a diet soda, too. Who is he?"

She took a deep breath. "Nathan Burke. Come on, I'll introduce you."

Emily couldn't meet Nathan's smile with one of her own. She really hadn't expected him to pursue her, and certainly not so quickly. In one way, she was glad he'd come. It meant he cared, and that made her feel good. But it also meant she would have to tell him that she had no room in her life for a man right now. Especially one who worked so closely with the press.

"Hello, Nathan," she said in a controlled voice.

"Hello, Emily." He echoed her words in an equally low voice.

Emily moistened her dry lips. "I'd like you to meet a friend of mine. Melody Youngston, this is Nathan Burke." Emily watched the two greet each other with a handshake and polite words before Melody turned back to her.

"I'm going to take off, Emily. I'll see you at work tomorrow." She faced Nathan with a friendly smile. "It was nice to meet you." With a wave Melody was gone, leaving Emily and Nathan standing quietly, looking intently at each other.

Nathan spoke first. "You have nice legs."

At his surprising statement Emily looked down at her legs, which glowed pink from her previous exertion. She had always considered her legs too short to be attractive, but she could only respond to the compliment the way she liked her compliments received.

"Thank you," she said, and suddenly her heartbeat increased.

Before either could speak again, the next couple was ready for their turn on the courts. Nathan lightly touched Emily's arm and they moved away from the gate and bright lights into the shadows of the evening. They stopped by a bench that overlooked the courts and sat down. A light breeze stirred the muggy air, bringing a brief relief from the humid June night.

"I hate to admit it, but I really didn't believe you when you said you had plans tonight so I decided to come over and confront you. When you didn't answer the door, I decided to just look around the complex. I guess it was luck that I found you."

Because of the bright lights from the courts, Emily could see him watching her. His eyes told her he was being honest. "Why did you come over?" She kept her tone even, trying not to read too much into his action.

"I had something I wanted to discuss with you. I was determined not to take no for an answer. When you hung up on me, there wasn't much else to do."

Emily looked away. "I didn't hang up on you. Our conversation was finished."

"That's a matter of interpretation." He paused and smiled. "I had more to say."

"All right, you're here now. What did you want to say?"

"I don't want to go into it here." He looked around the complex. "I'd like to discuss it over dinner. A business dinner," he added quickly.

What kind of business could a press secretary possibly want to discuss with her? "Does this have to do with politics?" she asked as she pulled a white towel from her tote bag and patted her neck.

"In a way," he admitted.

Suddenly Emily laughed and shook her head. "This can't be real." She looked directly into Nathan's eyes, the smile still on her lips. "I have three major magazines breathing down my neck, begging for an interview. Two newspaper reporters showed up at the office this afternoon and my employer had to ask them to leave. I'm fighting the press, Dreamstar, and on occasions I fight with myself." She didn't let her gaze waver from his face. "And you want to discuss politics with me. You're incredible."

Nathan sighed. "You're right, I am. And I agree it may be unconscionable of me to even suggest it at this time. But I wouldn't have mentioned it if I didn't think you would benefit, too."

In spite of her resolve not to be interested in what he had to say, she found that she was. "How?" she asked, stuffing the towel back in her bag.

"Have dinner with me tomorrow night, and I'll tell you all about it. All I'm asking is that you listen to what I have to say. I'm not asking for any promises."

She was probably playing the part of a fool, but he had told her only enough to pique her curiosity. There was no way she could say goodbye to him now without hearing what he had in mind that would help her.

"All right. I'll meet you for dinner tomorrow night." She rose and picked up her tote bag.

"Seven at the Ocean House?" he asked.

"I'll be there," she said and turned and walked away.

Chapter Three

Emily stepped out of the shower onto the plush green carpet of her bathroom. She rubbed the droplets of water from her gleaming skin and berated herself for the butterflies in her stomach. This was a business dinner, not a date, and would probably be a complete waste of her time. She couldn't even remember now why she'd let Nathan talk her into meeting him.

No, she couldn't lie to herself. She knew why. Nathan Burke was not an easy man to say no to. The concern in his eyes and that disarming smile of his had haunted her. His voice was smooth and as polished as new brass. And why shouldn't it be? He was a press secretary. He was supposed to know how to get people on his side and make them believe whatever he said. And she did.

As she walked over to the mirror, her arm brushed a healthy green fern that hung by the shower. She wrapped a small towel around her dripping hair while her reflection stared back defiantly.

There was so much about herself that she'd changed in the past two years—her home, her hair, her name. In her struggle to forget who she was, she had actually become someone else.

Yanking the wet towel off her short brown hair, she shook her head and let the curls fall into place. She had never liked her hair short and curly. Now was the time to let it grow long again. But she wouldn't go back to the use of her married name. Not out of any disrespect to Gary, but she needed a sense of identity. Maybe she'd look for a different place to live, too.

There were times when she hated this ultramodern condo, with all of its vivid colors, chrome and mirrors. The stark whiteness of the condo, with its accents of vermilion red and canary yellow, was beginning to close in on her. She had chosen it because she had wanted something completely different from the house where she'd lived with Gary in Birmingham.

Determined green eyes stared back at her from the mirror. She'd made some changes, but there were still more to come. She had discarded the shell of anonymity and now she had to learn how to cope with the press, the court system and Dreamstar Productions. She'd never like it, but she'd do it for Gary.

After dressing in a coral-colored skirt and matching blouse, Emily walked over to her dresser. The pearl earrings Gary had given her on their wedding day lay in a china dish beside a collection of seashells. Occasionally she bought other earrings, but the pearls were her favorite. She couldn't help but wonder sometimes what her life would be like today if Gary had lived. Quickly she popped the earrings into her ears and ran a comb through her drying hair. There was no use in thinking about what might have been. Gary wasn't alive, and writing books or making a movie wasn't going to bring him back to her. It only made his death harder to accept.

After refreshing her eye makeup, Emily walked into the living room to get her purse so she could put on her lipstick. She wandered over to the tropical-fish tank and watched the fish lazing under the tank's blue light. "Did I forget to feed you guys today? I think I did. I better take care of that right now."

Taking the lid off a ceramic ginger jar, Emily reached into the vase and took out a generous pinch of the flaky food and sprinkled it into the tank. She watched as the red velvets and the swordtails raced to the top to eat, while the zebra continued to dart back and forth across the length of the ten-gallon tank. "You guys sure lead easy lives," she said with envy, as she checked the thermometer in the tank to make sure the water temperature wasn't too low.

As she replaced the lid, she gave herself a mental reprimand. She couldn't let herself get so wrapped up in her life that she forgot important things such as feeding the fish. She hadn't bought them because they went with the decor. They were a form of therapy. After Gary's death, she'd needed something to take care of. She needed someone or something to be dependent on her, so she'd have a reason to get up in the mornings. The condo association didn't allow dogs and she didn't like cats, so she'd bought fish. She was no longer dependent on them. She had a fight going with Dreamstar and she'd met a man who intrigued her. That was reason enough.

The Ocean House restaurant was in Tallahassee's downtown section and was a favorite of many of the locals. The name of the restaurant belied the location, because it didn't overlook the Gulf of Mexico or the Atlantic as did most of Florida's famous restaurants.

The Ocean House appeared full at first, when Emily met Nathan in the foyer, but a hostess seated them immediately in a room with walls covered in a flocked silver brocade paper. A crystal chandelier hung from the high ceiling.

"Would you like a drink from the bar?" the waitress asked as the hostess handed them the menus.

"I'd like white wine," Emily said and noticed that Nathan ordered club soda. "You don't drink?" she asked when the waitress was gone.

Nathan smiled. "Oh, sometimes, but seldom at a business dinner. I like a clear head when I'm trying to sell an idea."

"Is that what you're going to do tonight?" she asked. "Sell an idea?"

"I'll wait and let you be the judge of that. Why don't you tell me a little about yourself while we wait for our drinks. Where did you grow up? Do you have any brothers or sisters?"

The thought of her two sisters made Emily's eyes sparkle. He couldn't have asked a question that would have pleased her more. "Yes, two sisters. Christina is the oldest, then Rhonda, and I'm the baby of the family. We lived in the Homewood section of Birmingham."

Nathan chuckled, showing beautiful teeth, and crossed his arms over his chest. "I bet your mother had her hands full with three girls. All that ribbon, bows and lace."

"Are you kidding?" Emily smiled easily, pleasantly. Nathan had set a light tone and it infected her. She hadn't talked about her childhood in a long time. "It was more like bicycles, skateboards and skinned knees. We didn't have a brother, and my father encouraged all of us to go into sports."

"So your mother had three little tomboys?"

"And she loved every minute of it. Two of us raced dirt bikes and all three of us played Little League."

"You raced dirt bikes?"

Smiling, Emily answered, "Yes, for a couple of years, but I have to say swimming has always been my first love when it comes to sports." She paused. Whoa! He'd have her telling her life's story again, if she didn't watch him. He knew how to make her forget her troubles, and she liked that. "But we didn't come here to talk about my childhood, did we?"

"Well, is there anything wrong with trying to get to know you a little better?"

"No, but maybe we should get on to the reason we're here," she said as the waitress set their drinks on the linen-covered table.

"Would you like to order now, or should I come back later?" the middle-aged woman asked.

Emily opened the menu and quickly scanned the house specialties. "Mmm—a garden salad and the broiled seafood platter sounds good to me."

Nathan never opened his menu. "Good choice. I'll have the same." He handed the menus back to the waitress and waited for her to walk away before he continued. "Okay, we'll get down to business. Have you ever heard of an organization called CAT?"

The name was unfamiliar. She wrinkled her forehead and shook her head. If Nathan wanted her to be on a committee to save cats this would be a short evening. She wasn't the least bit interested. She picked up her glass and sipped the wine. It was crisp and fruity-tasting just the way she liked. "CAT? No, I don't believe so. Why?"

His face took on a serious expression. "It stands for Citizens Against Terrorism."

Emily felt her smile freeze on her face. Her chest tightened. She pressed the cotton napkin to her lips and cleared her throat. "No, I'm sure I've never heard of it," was all she managed to say.

"I'm not surprised. It's fairly new. Right now CAT is a support group for friends and relatives of victims of terrorist acts, but their aim is to become a powerful lobby in Congress. The group was formed a few months ago and is presently headed by a woman named Lucy Morrow."

Emily moistened her lips and tasted the lingering flavor of the sweet wine. Anything dealing with terrorism used to immediately put her on edge; now it put her on the defensive. "What does this have to do with me?"

"I'm not sure. That's why I wanted to talk with you. I knew the tennis courts weren't exactly the place to discuss this."

Emily nodded but didn't say anything. She had no idea that such a group of people had banded together. Citizens Against Terrorism. The very name quickened her pulse.

"Personally, I think the group would be good for you, and I'd like to explain why." He paused. "First, I'd like to be up-front with you. While it's true I think CAT can help you, there are other reasons I want you to join."

Their eyes met. His were calm, and she thought she heard a ring of authority to his voice. "Go on," she answered.

"John—Senator Merritt is trying to help the group get funding to help start chapters in other states, the lobbying costs and other expenses necessary to run a national organization. The publicity generated from your legal fight with Dreamstar would go a long way in helping to bring national attention to CAT. The way I see it, that will help you and CAT. If CAT was already a national organization or an effective lobbying group such as MADD, and you had their support, you would have a much better chance with your fight against Dreamstar."

The napkin crinkled in Emily's hands. She'd been right about him from the morning she'd seen their picture in the paper. He wanted free publicity from her. With cold eyes she looked at Nathan and asked, "So what you want from me is the publicity that's being generated from this legal fight."

"I'm saying if we work it the right way, the publicity could help both of us get what we want."

"You are no better than Jeremy Smith or Tad Aubrey. They both want to make it big off my husband's death, and so do you."

"Dammit, that's not fair or true." He placed his hands on the table and leaned forward. His breath fanned the flames from the small candle. "What I'm asking you to do is not that cold and heartless. You're going to fight Dreamstar anyway. Why not use that to help the people who've had their lives destroyed by terrorism? Emily, I'm not asking for a few publicity shots. I want much more than that from you. I'm asking you to become involved in a group that can help you and others fight companies such as Dreamstar, fight the way the press covers victims and their families when terrorist acts occur, and help you fight the ridiculously inadequate laws dealing with terrorism." He stopped and sat back in his chair, his blue eyes burning into hers. "I'm asking you to help make a difference."

Emily was shaking by the time he finished. She turned away from him. His words held so much truth it shook her to the core. Yes, she wanted changes in all those areas he mentioned, but her first reaction was to let someone else do it. She had enough fights going on. She sipped her wine again and noticed that Nathan picked up his club soda and downed half the glass before returning it to the table.

"I have all I can cope with right now," she answered and knew it was a feeble excuse when she said it.

"You can't just say no until you've at least checked it out."

"Watch me." Her voice trembled and that made her angry. She wouldn't fall apart on this man again. With an unsteady hand she brushed at her hair and looked away while she willed her heartbeat to slow down.

"Emily, I'm sorry it has to be you." He waited for her to look at him, then continued. "I'm sorry *I* have to be involved. But like it or not, this legal battle with Dreamstar is going to cause publicity, maybe get national coverage, and if CAT can pick up a little attention by being on the sidelines, they're going to do it. Your fight with Dreamstar is just the event CAT has needed to spur them forward."

He sounded so sincere. "Why?" she asked.

"Because each and every one of these people has had someone they know and love killed or hurt by terrorists and they're tired of it. They're ready to fight back any way they can. These people want to lobby for stricter laws, stiffer punishments and international expediency. They want to make a difference."

"What about you? Are you one of them because you've been hurt by terrorism?"

"No, not personally. I believe in what CAT stands for, but other than that, it's a political issue with me. John has agreed to help the group because he believes in their objectives, and the truth is it'll be an excellent campaign platform."

At least he was being honest with her. She couldn't fault him on that.

"Emily, if you want to get anything accomplished in the political world, you have to use publicity. Your battle with Dreamstar has given us the perfect vehicle."

She was losing ground and knew it. She didn't care about his political campaign, but she was interested in a group that wanted to do something about terrorism. What was she thinking? She hated publicity. Where was her resolve? "I don't want any publicity from this hearing."

"Maybe that's because you're not using it to your advantage. Did you ever stop to think about the ways you could use all this attention to help you fight Dreamstar? Don't you think it's time you started trying to find ways to make it work for you?"

He was making sense, but she wasn't sure she wanted to hear it. She was compelled to fight him. "Why can't the press just let me do what I have to do? Why can't I have my day in court without everyone making a big deal out of it?"

Nathan's eyes caressed her face for a brief moment. Comfort issued from him. Although he never touched her, she felt his warmth and concern.

"Terrorism is a big deal, Emily. All I'm asking is that you come to a meeting and see what it's all about. Check out this group. If you decide it's not for you, I won't be upset."

Tired, Emily sat back in her chair. It wasn't like her to be so firm on an issue she hadn't looked into. Maybe he was right. Maybe she should at least look into the organization. She took a deep breath. "All right, I'll consider it. It's a difficult decision and that's all I'll agree to."

"That's all I ask." He sat back in his chair. "I believe our dinner has arrived just in time."

Emily looked at the fresh salad greens the waitress placed before her and wondered where she was going to find an appetite. Nathan Burke had certainly given her something to think about. Citizens Against Terrorism? She could very well be interested in the group, but what would she do about all the publicity? She'd hidden from the press for two years. But hadn't she basically agreed to accept their probing when she decided to fight Dreamstar?

Emily picked up her fork.

AT HER DESK EARLY THE NEXT morning, Emily tried to work on a market analysis for a client. Her thoughts kept returning to Nathan and the caring look in his eyes when he had told her about CAT. Citizens Against Terrorism. The very name of the organization gave her chills. She hated anything to do with terrorists, but she'd found herself calling Evan to ask if he knew anything about the group. He promised to make a few calls and they set up a meeting for late afternoon.

On principle, she had to try to stop Dreamstar. And about the publicity, Nathan was right. It would happen whether she wanted it to or not. She learned a long time ago that she couldn't control the press. But was he right in saying she could use it to her advantage? How would she go about doing that?

Emily looked back at the market analysis she was trying to complete. She had too many things to do other than think about Nathan and his pet project, or Tad Aubrey trying to move up the court date.

Emily was so deep in thought, she didn't hear anyone approach her desk until she saw a cup of coffee placed in front of her. She looked up and into Raymond Sanders's startling blue eyes. Her mood suddenly changed.

"I noticed you didn't have your usual cup of coffee, Mrs. Spencer," he said, a grin stretching his thin lips.

Emily took a deep breath and pushed back her chair. She'd tried to make allowances for his crudeness and immaturity, but she was ready for Raymond to grow up and leave her alone. "I'm trying to cut down, and I'm busy," she commented dryly.

"This is decaffeinated," he said, pointing to the cup.

"In that case, thank you, but I'm still busy." She wanted to end the conversation before it went any further. Raymond never had anything good to say to her.

"So why did you keep it a secret that you were Gary Spencer's wife? I mean he was a big hero. I would have thought you wanted everyone to know." He spoke in a tone of voice that made it clear he thought she was hiding something.

The last person she owed an explanation to was Raymond. "I didn't keep it a secret. I kept it private, so I wouldn't have to answer inane questions from people like you." She never let her eyes wander from his face, but she knew anger glowed in her cheeks.

Raymond chuckled lightly. "Oh, that's a good one, Mrs. Spencer. Your sarcasm is improving." He pushed some papers aside and rested a hip on the side of her desk. "What gives with this big front you're putting up? I don't believe for a moment that you don't want this movie to be made. Just think of all the publicity you'll get, not to mention the big bucks."

Emily's dislike for this man burned like hot coals. "I don't give a damn what you believe. Now get off my desk before I accidentally stab you with my pencil." She smiled confidently and pointed the pencil at his thigh. "I'm busy. I have to finish this for a client."

Raymond stood up straight. A sneer twisted his lips. "You're such fun to be around, Emily," he remarked before he turned and sauntered away.

Emily threw her pencil on her desk and rubbed her forehead. The soreness from the bruise was almost gone. If Raymond continued this form of harassment, she'd have to speak to Mr. Stobey. She refused to take it anymore.

"Does that frown on your face have anything to do with the man who just left your desk?" Melody asked in her usual jovial manner as she approached Emily.

"Yes, it does. When is he going to grow up?" Emily asked her friend.

Melody laughed. "He won't. He'll always be a jerk. I'm told every office has one."

"You're probably right. If you're free tonight why don't you come over for a game of tennis and try that new racket again?" Emily teased.

"Are you kidding?" Melody's eyes brightened. "I took it back to the store. I haven't been beaten that badly since high school. I'll come, but I'm bringing 'old faithful.'"

Emily laughed lightly. "Good. I'll call and see what time the courts are free and let you know later. I feel like I'm going to win again tonight."

The telephone rang and Melody answered it at Emily's desk. "Stobey and Ackerman, may I help you? Just a minute, please." Melody pressed the hold button. "It's for you. Someone named Lucy Morrow. Will you take it?"

Emily tensed. She was the woman Nathan had said started CAT. He sure didn't waste a minute. How dare he ask that woman to call her? Emily bit down on her bottom lip. No, she wasn't ready to talk to her.

"Take a number and tell her I'll get back to her later." Melody gave Emily a questioning look, which she didn't answer, so Melody did as she was told.

THREE HOURS LATER, Emily found herself sitting in Evan's office waiting for him to hang up the phone. Evan Pierce was a successful civil lawyer in the firm of Bryan, Pierce and Hyman. He was a sharp dresser, wearing only the best tailored suits. His hair had just enough silver to make it attractive. His time wasn't cheap but thankfully Gary's estate had left Emily well provided for and she couldn't think of a better way to spend the money. She was certain Gary wouldn't have wanted this movie to be made.

"Sorry that took so long, Emily."

"It's all right. I needed some time to collect my thoughts," she said.

"Well, before we get down to the news about the hearing, I'll tell you what I've been able to find out about CAT. It appears to be an organization that's new on the scene, but gaining a reputation fast. A group of people who have been touched by terrorism in various ways are all banding together. I had my secretary make a couple of calls, and earlier today I talked with the woman who heads the group, Lucy Morrow. She sounds like an intelligent woman, so I suggested she give you a call. My best advice to you is simply to talk to her, hear what it's all about. No one will force you to join a group you're not interested in."

Emily looked at Evan and smiled. So she was wrong. She'd thought Nathan had given Lucy Morrow her number. She'd have to remember not to try and second-guess Nathan. "Thanks for looking into it. You're right.

I have to make up my own mind as to what I want to do about it."

"We may have some trouble as far as the suit is concerned, Emily." Evan opened a folder and flipped through some papers. "Tad Aubrey has asked the judge for a summary judgment."

Emily tensed and moved to the edge of her chair. "What does that mean?"

"Unfortunately it means you don't get your day in court, which is exactly what Aubrey wants."

"Why? I don't understand?" she protested. "Are you saying the judge has ruled against us?"

"No, no. Let me explain it this way. The summary judgment is a petition for the judge to simply read the facts of the case and make a decision. If you don't have the opportunity to get on the stand and testify, it's going to hurt us, and Aubrey knows it. Believe me, the last thing he wants is you up on the witness stand talking about your husband. Your sincerity comes through so clearly the judge and jury would be swayed, and Aubrey doesn't want to chance it. This was a smart move from him."

"But I don't understand. How can they take our day in court away from us? It's not right," she argued.

Evan threw up his hands. "It's the system."

All in a quick, easy motion, Emily stood up and leaned over Evan's desk. "Don't tell me it's the system. Tell me how we can fight it." Her voice was loud and emotional. This couldn't be happening.

Remaining seated, Evan also remained calm. "If we lose, we can appeal. We can keep Dreamstar and Aubrey tied up in appeals for years. That's how we'll fight."

Emily sighed desperately and sank back into her chair. She was shaking all over. Was she willing to have the threat of this movie tied up in the appeals system for years?

Chapter Four

Bright sunlight fell across Emily's face as she stared up at the building that housed Senator Merritt's Florida office. She could no longer put off talking with Nathan about this organization called CAT. For a short time she'd felt anger and resentment that Nathan should even mention such a group to her, but after she thought about it she realized this could very well be something she should be a part of.

She squelched the last bit of reluctance that lingered and took the front steps at a brisk pace. The directory in the building's main entrance told her Nathan's office was located on the third floor. She joined a crowd waiting for the next elevator.

She didn't have any trouble finding his office, several doors down on the right. A well-dressed middle-aged woman with dark hair looked up as Emily walked inside.

"Oh, we're not open yet," the secretary said graciously as she rose from her chair. "We don't open until nine."

Emily glanced at her watch and saw that it was five till. "I'm sorry. I didn't know." She smiled to reassure herself that she'd done the right thing in coming to Nathan's office. "Do you mind if I wait here?" She pointed to one of the padded chairs against the wall."

"I'm sorry, I didn't get your name. Did you have an appointment with Mr. Burke today?" The woman looked down at an open book, scanning the page.

Suddenly Emily realized how hasty she'd been in just showing up at Nathan's office the first thing on a Monday morning, expecting him to be free to see her. Of course she should have made an appointment. She could have even called and told him she'd decided to attend a CAT meeting and ask him to mail any information she needed. It wasn't like her to be impulsive. She didn't know why she felt she needed to talk to him in person.

"My name is Emily Clements, and no, I don't have an appointment. I guess I was hoping he might have a few free moments. Maybe I could just leave Mr. Burke a message?"

The secretary smiled and picked up a pencil. "Certainly. What would you like me to tell him?"

Emily moistened her lips. "Ah—tell him—"

While she was trying to think of exactly what to say, the door opened and Nathan walked in. "Emily. This is a surprise," he said in that soothing voice she'd come to expect.

"Good morning." She smiled, thinking he looked so handsome standing in front of her dressed in his dark blue suit and white shirt, his briefcase clutched tightly in one hand. Suddenly she had the urge to get close enough to him to smell that fresh-washed scent of his shirt and the lemon fragrance of his cologne. She shook her head. What was wrong with her? "I'm sorry. I shouldn't have shown up here without an appointment or calling first."

"It's no problem. I have time." He looked at his secretary. "Hold my calls."

Emily noticed that his secretary started to say something but thought better of it. Nathan obviously didn't have time. "No, I won't keep you. I just stopped by on my way to work to tell you that I've decided to attend a CAT meeting and ask where I can get more information."

Nathan smiled, too. "All right, come in my office and I'll tell you."

She looked at the secretary again, thinking the woman was going to give her a snide look, but she had already found something to do. "All right," Emily agreed. "But only for a moment."

"Would you like me to bring in coffee, Mr. Burke?" the secretary asked from behind Emily.

He looked at Emily. "No, thank you. I'm fine."

Nathan put his hand to Emily's back as they walked into his office. The pressure of his touch was warm and firm, easing some of her discomfort.

His office was tastefully decorated in warm colors of beige and brown. College degrees and certificates covered one wall and a large picture of Nathan and Senator Merritt, with the President standing between them, hung on the wall behind his desk.

"I'm glad you stopped by. I was hoping to hear from you," he said as he laid his briefcase on his desk. "Sit down."

"Really, Nathan, I can't stay. As I said, I'm on my way to work. If you'll just tell me who I need to contact about when and where CAT meets, I'll be on my way."

Nathan pushed a small brass cannon aside and leaned a hip against his desk. "Okay. No small talk. It just so happens that the next meeting is tomorrow night. If that's not enough notice, you can make the next one."

Emily's stomach muscles tightened. This wasn't the time to get cold feet. Now that she'd decided to do this, she wanted to get it over with. In fact, the sooner, the better, she told herself. "No, tomorrow night is fine." She cleared her throat. "What time and where do I go?"

"Why don't I pick you up and take you?" he asked.

"Don't be silly. I can find this meeting on my own."

Nathan folded his arms across his chest and looked into her eyes. "I'm sure you can. But I'm going anyway. Besides, I'm the one who told you about this group, and I'd like to see it through."

Emily realized she was twisting her purse strap between her hands and quickly hung the handbag over her shoulder. She didn't know why the thought of this organization made her so nervous. She looked at Nathan's kind expression and knew it would be easy to start depending on him. He had all the qualities she liked in a man. He was generous, trustworthy and levelheaded. Not to mention good-looking.

"All right. What time should I be ready?" she asked, not giving herself the opportunity to deny his offer a second time.

"Seven."

"That sounds good." Why was she hesitating? She had the information she needed. They had gotten all they could out of this conversation, but she was still standing in front of him.

"I'm glad you were interested enough to stop by. Would you like Lucy Morrow's number? I'm sure she'd be happy to answer any questions."

"No, thanks, I have it."

"Good."

Emily took a deep breath. "Well, I'd better go." She turned to walk out but looked back at Nathan and said, "Thanks."

Nathan nodded and smiled.

"ROGER, COME IN," Nathan said to the fair-skinned young man peering around the open door. "There's been a couple of changes since we talked."

"Okay, what's going on?" Roger settled in the chair in front of Nathan's desk.

"First, you can relax. You won't be going to the CAT meeting tonight, I will."

"That is good news." He smiled. "Great, in fact, but what brought on the change?" He opened his folder and took out a pen, ready to take notes.

"Emily Clements has decided to go, and I'll be taking her." Nathan kept his voice businesslike, even though he knew Roger was too astute not to notice his interest in Emily.

Roger glanced up. "More good news. How did you talk her into it? When we last discussed this you had doubts she'd even consider being a part of the organization."

Nathan pushed away from his desk and rose, stuffing his hands in the pockets of his gray pin-striped slacks. "She's only agreed to go to a meeting and see what CAT is about. There could be half dozen reasons why she won't join. She may not be interested, too busy, or the most probable one, the threat of too much publicity associated with her and the group. In any case, we'll take one step at a time. For now, she's decided to attend this meeting. And that's where we'll start."

"Okay. If she joins, where do we go from there?" Roger asked, jotting down notes as he talked.

"We give her a few months to get involved, and when the time is right we ask for her help with coordinating the senate hearings on terrorism."

"When will it be announced that John is being appointed to the subcommittee?"

Nathan rubbed the back of his neck and rotated his shoulders. "You know how slowly congress moves. It could take another two weeks or longer. In the meantime we have to work toward next spring, when John will be up for reelection. A strong showing in his fight on terrorism will pull him way ahead of any contender."

"I'm with you all the way," Roger said. "What's my next job."

"A difficult one. I want a comprehensive study done on terrorism, and I want it as soon as you can get it."

Roger held up his hand. "Wait a minute. How far back do you want me to go? I mean terrorism must have started way back in the Bible with Adam or Moses or one of those guys."

Nathan laughed. No one could look more stricken than Roger. His red hair and freckle-spattered face lent itself to open expression. "Start with Kennedy and don't overlook people like Sadat and the Beatle that was killed in New York a few years ago. Give me details on all hijackings and bombings in recent years. When I say comprehensive, I mean it."

"I don't think you know what you're asking. This could take months or years."

Nathan walked around his desk and clapped the younger man on the shoulder. "Not if you get to know a few people in the FBI, the CIA or the NSA and get into their computer files."

Wide-eyed, Roger looked at Nathan with disbelief. He rose from his chair. "Do you know what you're saying?"

"I'm saying I don't think it'll be as difficult as you think. The information is available. All you have to do is know where and how to get it. You're smart. You'll find a way."

"Oh, all I have to do is get it." He swore under his breath. "I could probably get the crown jewels from the Tower of London easier than what you want."

Nathan forced back another smile and urged Roger toward the door. "Tell me, is CAT still meeting in Lucy's home?"

"Ah—no, I forgot to tell you. Tonight's meeting is being held in Room 104, Building *D* at FSU. This is their first meeting that's open to the general public. It was announced on the radio and in the newspapers. They're hoping for a big turnout."

"How about press coverage?"

"Not the last I heard. The media is still waiting for something big to happen before they jump on the wagon. If you want me to let them know Emily Clements is coming, I'll guarantee the press will be there."

Nathan rubbed his chin. No, it was better to let Emily have this night to herself. He had a feeling it wasn't going to be easy for her, and reporters could put her over the edge. "Let's keep this to ourselves for now." He open the door for Roger. "Keep me informed on your work."

"Yeah, I'm going to be so bogged down in paper you'll be lucky to see me in the next year."

Roger started to walk away, but Nathan called to him, "Oh, and Roger, you did a good job on CAT."

Roger smiled. "Thanks, Nathan."

Nathan shut the door and walked back to his desk. He didn't know what was wrong with him. He'd had no intention of going to that meeting with Emily until he heard her voice, and then he couldn't keep himself from offering to go along, knowing he had to be by her side. Damn. What was wrong with him? He didn't want to get mixed up with her. Yes, he wanted to eventually talk her into taking a major role in CAT, working on the senate hearings and possibly doing a little campaigning for John when the time came. But he hadn't wanted anything else to develop between them.

Why couldn't he forget the fresh-washed smell of Emily's hair that one time he'd held her? Why couldn't he forget how small and vulnerable she'd felt in his arms that afternoon? All he'd done was hold her, but in that brief time she'd touched him like no other woman, not even Michelle. Wasn't he supposed to know how to keep business relationships separate from personal ones? He didn't mix the two, ever. Michelle had taught him that during his brief political career. So why did he find himself wanting to hear Emily's voice, taste her lips, feel his skin against hers? Why was she so damn tempting?

Memories from the past crowded his mind. When was the last time he'd heard from Michelle? Two years, maybe? He wondered if she still ran that little dress shop in south Florida. Had she remarried? Hell, what did he care! He plopped back in his chair and opened the folder on his desk. He'd done all he could. He forgave her, but she was right—he'd never forget.

A BRILLIANT SUN FLOATED high in a cloudless pale blue sky. Basking in the blistering sunshine, Emily contemplated diving into the pool to cool off. Usually she was at the pool only long enough to do a few laps. Today she felt like taking it easy and soaking up some tanning rays. Because she'd spent the morning showing houses to a couple she had been working with for several days, there was no guilt about taking the afternoon off and being lazy.

She adjusted the strap of her black one-piece swimsuit as she walked to the pool's edge and dipped in one toe. Tepid. Sometimes she wondered if she was part salmon. She liked to swim in cold water, and she seemed to always be fighting her way upstream.

Two major things had happened since her meeting with Evan a few days before. One she'd initiated herself. She'd stopped by Nathan's office and told him she'd like to attend the CAT meeting, which was being held at eight o'clock. When he'd asked if he could take her, she'd agreed without hesitating. She still wasn't exactly sure why. There were many things about him that she found appealing, but she had to keep reminding herself that she wasn't going to dwell on them. This wasn't the time for romance to enter her life. Besides, he certainly hadn't given her any reason to think he was interested in her except on a strictly professional level.

Emily looked around. Only a couple of people were in the water, but several more surrounded the pool deck. They were clustered in intimate little groups, talking and laughing among themselves, their happy, smiling faces animated by their conversations.

Breathing deeply, she turned her back on the chattering groups and sat down on the edge of the pool. She wanted to get hot before taking that first plunge into the water's depth.

The other big thing that had happened was that Evan had called and told her Dreamstar had been successful in having the hearing date on the summary judgment moved up. That didn't surprise her. While she had the money needed to fight Dreamstar, she didn't have connections. Obviously Tad Aubrey did. But if she was truthful with herself, she wanted to get the hearing over with, too.

According to Evan, she had a solid case, but he kept reminding her time and time again that most judges ruled on facts when they read what was written in black-and-white. Their ace had been her testimony on the witness stand. The summary judgment had taken that away from them.

Jeremy Smith's book had been bad enough. His distortion of the facts made her write him a scathing letter. In his reply, he had blamed her. If she'd consented to the interview he'd wanted, no mistakes, real or imagined on her part, would've been made. She was angry with herself for refusing that interview and probably always would be. Because she'd let Gary down on the book, she simply had to stop that movie.

Anger welled up inside her and ran down her spine every time she thought about Gary's last few hours of life appearing on television for all of America to see.

The splashing of cool water on her hot skin caused her to look up. A well-built young man grinned sheepishly and called, "Sorry." She waved to him to show she didn't mind, then, dangling her legs over the side, lifted her face to catch the full radiance of the sun. She wanted to block out all the sounds around her and forget about everything while the hot rays bathed her with their warmth, but she couldn't. Nathan came into mind.

She recalled his clean scent, the firmness of his chest when he'd held her for that brief time in the diner. His voice was soft and deep, cultivated, with smooth tones, and ever so reassuring. The color of his eyes was unusual, but she found warmth in their dark shade of blue.

And she'd liked the fact that he'd been honest about his political interest in her.

Even though Nathan worked with the press, she felt comfortable with him. And she was especially glad he had taken it upon himself to help her that afternoon at the courthouse. Although he hadn't shown the least bit of romantic interest in her, she couldn't keep her thoughts from straying to kisses and caresses. Suddenly Emily stood up and dived into the pool to do laps. Right now she didn't have room for another man in her life. Gary was still too much a part of it.

Three hours later, Emily walked into her living room to answer the door. Nathan was right on time, for which she was grateful. She had a feeling this meeting would not be an easy thing to get through. She had never participated in a group discussion on terrorism, and she wasn't the least bit sure she'd get through the meeting. At this point, she didn't know what to expect, so she wasn't going to promise herself anything.

"Nathan, come in," she said and showed him into the cathedral-ceilinged living room with its two skylights.

He looked around the room, and Emily followed his gaze as it moved from the white leather couch to the glass-and-chrome tables and over the brightly painted pictures hanging on the walls. His gaze lingered for a moment on the fish tank. "Do you like living here?" he asked as he turned to face her.

Funny he should ask that, she thought. "I really liked this place when I first moved here. It was different and I was making some radical changes in my life, so it seemed to fit. Now, I'm not so sure. I think I prefer more traditional homes."

"So do I," he said, not allowing his eyes to leave her lips. "But like you, I live in a condo. I do it because it's easier with all the traveling I do between here and Washington. No time to take care of a home."

Emily took the opportunity to really look at Nathan while he told her where he lived. His midnight blue eyes had a nice shape and seemed to always have a teasing light shining in them. She found that extremely attractive. His lashes were a darker shade of brown than the hair that showed faint signs of silver along the crest of his ears. The bridge of his nose was narrow, and his lips full and finely shaped. When she looked back into his eyes, his intense gaze tightened her stomach muscles.

She cleared her throat and picked up her purse. "Well, I guess we should go."

"Are you nervous?" he asked as they walked out to his car.

"Yes, I am. Very nervous, in fact." She waited for him to open the door, then slipped into the seat, swinging both legs in at the same time. Her mauve skirt eased above her knees, and she quickly tucked her legs close to the seat.

Emily remembered his car well. It had been her salvation that late afternoon Nathan rescued her from the reporters. She liked its dark gray interior, the smell of new leather washed in saddle soap, the hum of the air conditioner as the car idled, waiting for the command to start moving.

As she expected, the conversation was sparse while they drove through busy streets past the capitol and on to Florida State University where the meeting was being held. She appreciated him giving her the time she needed to make a last-ditch effort to talk herself out of what she was about to do. When she realized she wasn't going to do that, she shored up her courage for what was to come.

A few minutes later Nathan stopped in a well-lighted parking area already filled with cars. Emily's stomach was in knots and her breathing choppy, but she was determined to see this through. If these people were truly working to eradicate terrorism and bring guilty parties to swift justice, she had to be a part of it.

"Do you have any questions before we go in?" he asked.

Emily snapped her head around. His face was illuminated by the shadowed light from a street lamp. He was very handsome and he cared, and that made him dangerously appealing. "No," she answered in a husky voice. "Let's just get it over with."

The room was large and crowded, which surprised Emily. She'd been under the impression this was a small organization of twenty to thirty people, not close to one hundred.

Emily felt Nathan's hand touch her back, and she let him guide her to a row of chairs at the back of the room. His touch was warm and welcome but didn't keep a small ball of fear from forming in her stomach. When they were seated, she whispered, "I didn't expect this many people. Will there be reporters?"

"Probably not. They don't usually hit civic organizations unless something newsworthy is happening or a newsworthy person is speaking."

"Thank God for small favors," she whispered as a woman walked to the front of the room and asked for their attention. The room quieted. Emily guessed her age at late thirties or early forties. Her chestnut-colored hair was swept away from her face and gathered at the back with a black bow.

"My name is Lucy Morrow. I want to thank you for joining us tonight. A few of us have been meeting for several months in my home. This is our first public meeting. Before I go any further, I want to make it clear that when this program is over I'd like for each one of you to join us in our fight against terrorism. I know the first thing you're going to say is 'I'd like to help, but—'" The audience laughed and Lucy smiled.

"Everyone can help in some way. We can use whatever you have to offer—your time, your money, your prayers. Mothers have banded together to keep drunks and alcoholics off our highways. I'm here to ask you to help us keep terrorism away from our schools, our shopping malls and our airplanes. With your help, we can make a difference. I'm going to pass out a sheet of paper that lists our objectives, so you'll know what we're all about." She picked up a stack of paper from the desk behind her and handed a portion to the first person in each row, then returned to the center of the room and stood quietly for a few moments while the papers filtered down the aisles, both Emily and Nathan taking one.

The woman cleared her throat. "We start each meeting with one of us telling of our brush with terrorism. We do this so we won't lose sight of our goals. Some of you have heard my story, but for those of you who haven't, I'll repeat it." She paused. "Even though it breaks my heart a little more, every time I tell it."

Unexpected and unwanted tears filled Emily's eyes. The woman hadn't even started, but Emily knew what she was going to say by the sad eyes that were trying very hard to be brave. A quick glance at the woman was all Emily needed to recognize the signs of despair. Her eyes were unblinking, her shoulders rigid. Her bottom lip twitched and she held clenched hands stiffly in front of her.

"One day last fall, my ten-year-old daughter was held hostage, along with twenty other classmates and a teacher, while a deranged woman took turns holding a gun to the children's heads. My greatest sorrow is that when police stormed the room, my daughter was the one with the gun to her head. She was killed. My only consolation is that no other child was physically hurt that day." Her voice broke. "This happened in America!"

Lucy's words grew fuzzy as roaring filled Emily's ears. She couldn't hold back the tears that raced down her cheeks. Her throat ached from holding back the threatening sobs that wanted to burst from her chest. The ringing in her ears increased and the woman's voice became fainter as Emily remembered the day she'd heard that Gary's plane had been hijacked to Colombia.

"No," Emily whispered softly. She wouldn't think about that right now.

But she couldn't stop the seeds of memory from growing. She was at home alone when the first report came from the nightly news. Hours later, as she watched television, they showed a body being thrown from the plane, the limp form landing carelessly onto the tarmac. Two hours later she learned the victim was Gary.

"No!" she murmured again. "I can't take this." Her legs trembling, she rose, stumbling over Nathan's feet in her hurry to get out of the room before her sobs turned to wails. She had to get away from the pain, the shock. As soon as she was out the door, she fell hard against the wall, sobbing uncontrollably.

For a long time she didn't realize she'd let Nathan pull her into his arms and hold her, comfort her. It also took her a while to realize this time she wasn't crying for her loss. She was crying for the poor woman who lost her child, for every mother who'd lost a child.

"Do you want to leave?" Nathan spoke softly into her ear when her heaving cries quieted to mere sniffles.

She shook her head and buried her face further into the warmth of his chest, the comfort of his arms.

This was the second time she'd cried on Nathan's shirt, but this time she wasn't embarrassed. Somehow it seemed right to be so distraught over a young child's untimely death, a mother's unflinching sorrow. Emily knew she could no longer run from the effects of terrorism. She had to learn to cope with it, fight it and overcome it. No, she couldn't leave this meeting. These people needed her and she needed them.

She raised her head and wiped her eyes with her hands, avoiding Nathan's eyes. "I think I just realized I'm not alone in my fears," she managed to say in a husky voice.

Nathan reached into his coat pocket and brought out a handkerchief. "Is this becoming a habit?"

She took it and looked up at him. He was smiling. She smiled, too, as she wiped her eyes, then blew her nose. "No, I think it's called a period of adjustment."

"All right, we'll call it that."

Nathan brushed a hand across her hair and Emily felt the urge to sink into his arms once again and gain strength from his comfort. She could see in his eyes that he knew how she felt. She knew he understood.

"It's just so damn unfair, Nathan." She couldn't keep bitterness out of her voice. Lucy was right. Terrorism wasn't just in foreign lands. Terrorists were gunning down children as they played at school, motorists as they traveled the expressways. Something had to be done, and she had to be a part of it.

"I know. Want to go get a cup of coffee?" he asked.

Emily took a deep breath and squared her shoulders. "No, I'm all right now. Let's go back inside."

He touched her arm and looked deeply into her eyes. "Are you sure? We can wait a while longer. No one said you had to do everything in one night."

She appreciated his concern. She didn't know how she'd been so lucky as to have Nathan rescue her from that crowd at the courthouse. "I want to go back. Really, I'm fine now."

Nathan nodded and took hold of her arm as they slipped quietly back into the meeting.

A couple of hours later, Nathan walked Emily to her front door. He was wound tight and couldn't shake a tenseness that had every muscle alert. He knew why, too. Emily Clements. When he'd pulled her into his arms, he wanted to kiss her tears away, not just stroke her back and tell her everything was going to be okay. Even now, while he was walking beside her, he wanted to stop and press her close and kiss those beautiful lips. He wanted to make love to her. And dammit, she'd probably let him, because it had been such an emotional evening for her. She'd take the comfort he offered tonight and then be sorry as hell it happened in the morning. That's not the kind of response he wanted from her. Damn, he knew he shouldn't have gotten involved with her.

He was glad it didn't take her long to find her key in the soft light above her door. If he didn't get away quickly, he might do something stupid.

"I'll wash this and get it back to you." She held up the handkerchief she'd kept in her hand throughout the rest of the meeting.

Nathan's pulse jumped. Last time she'd simply returned it. "There's no hurry. Ah—I have more." What a dumb thing to say. Was he going to stand around and stutter and stammer all over himself, or was he going to get the hell away from this woman?

"Thanks for going with me." She looked up into his eyes and smiled. "I couldn't have made it through the meeting without you. I think you must have known that."

That did it. He was hooked. "I'm glad I was there." He paused. "Ah—I have to go to a formal dinner that John's giving for a local politician next Saturday night. Would you like to go with me?"

"I can't," she answered.

He should have accepted that answer and left, but he didn't. The problem was that he didn't want her to reject him. He wanted to continue to see her. "Why?"

"Reporters will be there, and I don't think—"

"Yes, that's true," he interrupted. "But, Emily, it's a big affair. There'll be about two hundred and fifty people present. No one will notice you," he added to give credit to his statement.

"They will, if I'm with you," she answered.

Nathan's heartbeat increased. The glinting light in her green eyes filled him with a warm glow. He didn't know why, but that simple statement made him feel so damn good. Nathan moistened his lips and shoved his hands into the pockets of his slacks. How long had it been since a woman had made him feel this way?

"Not necessarily. I keep a very low profile at these things. When I talk to the press, it's usually because I've called a press conference." He paused. "Will you come?"

She sighed and looked away. "I don't know. All of this is so new to me."

"Look, Emily," he said, grasping her arms tenderly. "I don't like attending these dinners. If you'll go, I'll see to it that we sit at a table somewhere in a dark corner, with people so unnewsworthy the press will avoid it like the plague. Does that make you feel better?''

She laughed lightly. "All right, you've talked me into it. I'll come with you."

He slid his hands up her arms and gently squeezed them to give her reassurance, but realized he was the one who felt comforted. He still wanted to kiss her, to taste her, but instead he let her go and stepped back. "Good. I'll pick you up at seven. Good night, Emily." He turned and walked away.

Chapter Five

Emily sat in front of her dressing table, her skin glowing with a deep golden color enhanced by the seafoam green dress she wore. Sequins spilled over the left shoulder of her gown and down the bodice, giving a sparkling sunburst effect to the otherwise simple rayon sheath. She swept one side of her hair up and away from her ear and pinned it with a sequin-covered clasp. Out of habit, she reached for the pearl earrings she usually wore, but decided with all the shimmer and glitter, she didn't need anything else.

She couldn't remember the last time she'd been to a formal affair, or the last time she'd looked forward to an evening with such anticipation. Even shopping for the right dress to wear had filled her stomach with butterflies. Nathan was working his way into her heart and life. And without a doubt, CAT would become an important part of her life, too.

She'd spoken with Lucy Morrow on the phone and they'd agreed to have lunch together next week. Emily didn't know exactly what she could do for the group, but she was interested in finding out. If nothing else, she could encourage the membership and ask for donations.

When Nathan arrived a few minutes later, hand-somely dressed in a formal tux, he carried a bouquet of exotic-looking flowers. Emily took them and smiled up at him. "Thank you. They're so beautiful."

His eyes danced with a gleaming light, and he said, "I believe you noticed that I like to do some things the old-fashioned way."

Emily watched the way his magnetic blue gaze lingered on her face, as if he were memorizing every detail. "I have noticed, and I'm impressed."

And she was. She considered herself lucky to be attracted to a man who was a gentleman. She looked back at the flowers. "They're an unusual arrangement."

"Well, the white one is an amaryllis, the purple is a liatris, and the scaly-looking thing with the feathers on its stem is a protea."

Emily grinned. "How do you know so much about flowers?"

Nathan laughed, and followed her into the kitchen. "I don't. I made the mistake of asking the friendly neighborhood florist a question. He told me a little more than I wanted to know."

"Ah—one of those. A real talker," she said as she placed them carefully into a vase she'd filled with water. When she'd finished she turned to him and said, "I really like them, Nathan. Thanks."

"You're welcome." He looked deeply into her eyes. "I know I promised to keep the reporters away, but you're so lovely tonight every pair of eyes in the room is going to find you."

Emily felt warm all over. She didn't want to start reading anything into what he said. He was just being nice. Bringing her flowers didn't mean anything, either. To cover the awkwardness that suddenly washed over her, she looked down at her scooped neckline and wondered if it might be too revealing. "Is the dress too much?" she asked.

A slow, easy smile thinned his lips just enough to be attractive. "No, it's perfect, and so are you. We'd better go. We don't want to be late."

A short time later Nathan had them seated at a table in a dark corner of the ballroom, safely out of sight and where no one was likely to wander by. They spoke briefly to the other people sitting around the table but quickly fell into their own conversation.

"I realized something this week," Emily said, unfolding her napkin and laying it across her dress. "You know almost everything about me, but I know hardly anything about you. Tell me, is a politician's life as glamorous as we imagine it to be?"

Nathan's chuckle was more of a sigh. "That depends on the politician. Some of them love the power, the parties and the fast pace. Others are devoted family men with high ideals and abhor any of the so-called glamour that surrounds politics."

"Which category are you in?" she asked.

"I'm not a politician."

His response was abrupt and defensive, leaving Emily with the feeling he didn't want to talk about it. For a moment she wondered if he was also hiding from something. She thought about dropping the subject but decided against it. There were too many things about him she didn't know.

"I know you aren't," she finally said. "But you do work for a senator, and you do spend a lot of time in Washington. I only mentioned it because you made a reference to not enjoying this kind of function." She swept the air with her hand.

"You're right. I don't, and I don't like attending Washington's so-called gala events, either. I go because it's my job."

Emily leaned back in her chair as a waiter placed a small dish of mushrooms on the table in front of her. She picked up her fork and took a bite. Mmm—they were filled with a delicious crabmeat stuffing.

"Were you ever in politics?" she asked.

Nathan popped a whole mushroom in his mouth and chewed it before answering. "State and local only."

For some reason, Nathan didn't like the fact that his life was the subject they were discussing. That intrigued Emily. He wasn't looking at her, and his answers were short and clipped. She should let it be, but—"Have you ever been married?"

"Yes."

"Do you have any children?"

Nathan laid down his fork, and looked at her with a forced smile. "Why am I getting the third degree?"

It was the first smile he gave her that didn't reach his eyes. Although she didn't get the feeling he was angry, he didn't like her questions. "I told you. I don't know anything about you. I'd like to know you better."

"All right." He wiped his mouth, then replaced the starched napkin in his lap, taking time to stuff a corner of it under his belt. "I've been divorced for six years, and I have no children. My father lives here in the city, as does my one and only sister. Dad is retired, but still dabbles in real estate from time to time. My sister, Louise, is a fingerprint expert with the police department downtown. She has three boys she claims are driving her crazy. Now, do you want to know anything else about me before I close the book on my life?"

His voice had a slight annoyed tone to it, but his eyes held a hint of amusement, which prompted her to continue the questioning. "Yes. What made you decide to work for a politician rather than be one?"

Nathan picked up his water glass and sipped it. "It's a long story and not a pleasant one."

Emily pondered her next step while Nathan rearranged his dinner ware. It wasn't like him not to meet her gaze. This was obviously something he didn't want to talk about, and she wasn't sure she should press it. If anyone could understand the need for privacy it was Emily Clements. "Does that mean you're not going to tell me?"

He chuckled lightly and leaned back in his chair. "Do you really want to hear an unpleasant story?"

Their eyes met and Emily softened. "I know that I want to hear about you."

Nathan rubbed his chin with the back of his hand. "Not tonight. Maybe some other time." He picked up his fork and stuffed another mushroom into his mouth.

Quietly Emily returned to her food also, but somewhat more subdued. It was clear there was a part of his life he didn't want to talk about. She wasn't the only one who'd been in hiding. That made her feel better, stronger. Nathan Burke might not need a shoulder to cry on, but maybe he needed her.

The meal tasted far better than Emily expected. The mushroom caps were followed by cream of broccoli soup and a garden salad. The main course was Florida's own baked red snapper smothered in a delicate lemon sauce.

"I don't even want to look at the dessert," Emily groaned as her empty plate was removed by one of the servers.

Nathan chuckled. "I've noticed that you have a hearty appetite for such a dainty little lady."

"It comes from my Irish heritage," she said, doing a good imitation of the brogue she had learned from her grandmother.

"I'll have to remember that," he grinned. "The Irish are also known to have a bit of a temper."

Emily smiled sweetly. "That's one thing I *didn't* inherit. I wish I had."

Nathan looked at her for a long moment, then said, "Thanks for coming with me tonight. Attending formal dinners is not my favorite part of this job. You made tonight bearable."

"I'm glad you insisted I come. Sometimes it's so much easier to say no. Your determination is good for me."

"Do you think you're ready to take on a pack of reporters?" he asked with a smile.

She eyed him sideways, wondering what he had in mind. "No, not yet."

"In that case, while dessert is served, I'm going to make an appearance, so John will know I was here. Then I think we should leave, because dancing is next on the schedule and once everyone starts moving around the reporters will hit every table to see who's here."

"Sure. That sounds fine," Emily said smoothly, but inside she felt a stab of disappointment. She would have loved to dance with Nathan, to feel his arms close around her.

Emily watched Nathan walk away, a small blur by the time he reached the head table, but she kept her eyes on him. She liked the man she'd come to know tonight. But she wasn't sure that was in her best interest. Too many other things filled her life for her to have the time to become involved with a man. Not that Nathan had made any romantic overtures. Somewhere in the back of her mind she wanted him to. But she also knew it was best to keep pushing back the romantic feelings that washed over her, until she'd laid Gary to rest.

"Emily, I thought I saw you earlier. Too bad I didn't know you were coming. I would have made arrangements for all of us to sit at the same table."

Cringing, Emily slowly turned and found herself looking into Raymond Sanders's eyes. It should have crossed her mind that he might be present tonight. He enjoyed bragging about his connections in the political world. Funny though, she'd never believed him. She pasted a semi-smile on her face and said, "Hello," as her gaze drifted to the man standing slightly behind Raymond.

"Let me introduce a friend of mine, Bill Hadly. Bill, Emily Clements—or Spencer. Which is it today?" Raymond laughed and brushed at the length of his tie.

Emily didn't think Raymond's attempt at a joke was funny. It didn't appear that Bill did, either, because he didn't smile. Emily rose and reached for Bill's hand. She didn't like to greet anyone while seated. "It's nice to meet you, Bill."

"Likewise," he said and lightly squeezed her hand during the brief shake. "I know of you, but I don't think we've met before. I work for *The Daily Ledger*."

"That's nice." Even though her answer was trite, out of politeness, Emily kept a smile on her face. She suddenly had the feeling that Raymond knew exactly what he was doing in bringing over the reporter. That made her angry.

"When I pointed you out to Bill, he wanted to meet you," Raymond injected.

"That's nice," she said again and felt like a complete idiot. What was she supposed to do? She had no intention of talking to this reporter. She looked toward the head table to see if Nathan was on his way back. There was no sign of him. She'd have to get out of this by herself.

"I was hoping I could make arrangements for an interview, to talk with you about the movie that's going to be made. Maybe sometime next week? It shouldn't take more than a couple of hours of your time."

It was Bill's turn to smile. A quick glance at Raymond confirmed Emily's suspicions that Raymond had engineered the whole thing. "No, I don't think so." Her anger at Raymond gave her the confidence she needed to sound firm.

"Look, I promise to be fair, and you can approve the article before I submit it. You can't ask for better than that."

He seemed sincere. Emily appreciated that; however, she wasn't willing to talk yet. In fact, Evan had advised her not to say anything until after the hearing.

"I'm sure you'd be fair, Bill, but I still have to say no." She expected that to be the end of the conversation.

Raymond chuckled again and stepped a little closer to her. "Hey, Emily, you're making me look bad." He lowered his voice. "I told Bill we were friends and that you'd talk to him. Lighten up a little." He put an arm around her shoulder while he pulled once again at his tie with his other hand.

Furious, Emily stepped away from Raymond. She fixed him with a cold stare. "No, Raymond, we're not friends." Her eyes swept over to Bill. "And no, Bill, I won't give you an interview. With the litigation that's going on right now, I can't talk to anyone about the hearing, the movie or my husband's death. I'm sure you can understand the situation I'm in."

"Bill, it's good to see you."

At the sound of Nathan's voice, Emily realized how rigidly she had been standing. She took a deep breath while the two men shook hands. It was obvious they knew each other. Nathan probably knew most of the reporters in Tallahassee.

"I was just trying to talk Emily into giving an interview."

"Yes, I heard." Nathan picked her purse up off the table and handed it to her. "I'm sorry we don't have time to talk, but we were on our way out. Maybe later." Nathan put his hand to the small of her back, urging her forward. She didn't hesitate. "Good to see you, Bill," Nathan said over his shoulder as he hurried her away.

Once they cleared the ballroom and reached outside, Emily stopped and turned to Nathan. "Thanks for getting me out of there so quickly. I'm afraid I was a little rude."

Nathan handed the valet-parking ticket to a young man and moved Emily out of the bright lights of the hotel and into the shadows of the night. "I didn't think you were rude. I thought you handled yourself quite well. I was impressed."

"Do you mean that?"

"Absolutely. Emily, you had everything under control. I made a hasty retreat only because I promised you wouldn't be bombarded with reporters, and I wanted to keep my word."

"I thought I might have embarrassed you because you knew Bill."

Lifting her chin with the tips of his fingers, Nathan whispered in a husky voice, "You could never embarrass me. So don't ever let that thought enter your head again."

His words pleased her, his eyes held her spellbound as starlight caressed his face. He slipped his arms around her waist and tenderly pulled her close.

Gazing down into her eyes he softly whispered, "I'm going to kiss you, Emily. I know all the reasons why I shouldn't, but right now they don't mean a damn thing."

Emily felt riveted to the spot. She couldn't move, and she wasn't breathing at all. His presence held her, intoxicating her with a burning desire, as she waited for him to put his words into action. She tilted her head back and closed her eyes as his face descended toward hers.

Their lips touched and pressed lightly, savoring the sweetness that comes with a first kiss. They broke apart, smiled and kissed again, harder, deeper, sweeter. She wanted to put to memory the taste and feel of him. He whispered her name huskily, pressing closer, holding her tighter until she could feel the length of his hard body. Her long-unfed sensual hunger flamed as her arms circled his neck and her fingers curled into the back of his hair.

"You're so beautiful," he murmured.

"Nathan," she whispered passionately when his lips lightly touched her eyelid, lingering over its softness. Slowly he moved down the contours of her face to the tip of her nose. She trembled and his arms tightened around her while his lips caressed her cheek, moving ever so softly across her sun-kissed skin. Emily was lost in the sensual feel of him long before she opened her eyes and found his mouth with her own once again.

The kiss ended naturally and Nathan stepped away. He ran a hand through his hair and looked intently into her eyes. "I hope I don't have to apologize for that."

Emily's heart was hammering in her chest. "I'd be disappointed if you did."

He wrapped his arm around her shoulder. "Come on, the car's waiting."

A short time later when they entered her apartment, Emily was laughing. "I know you're kidding me."

Emily snapped on the lamp, and Nathan settled on the sofa. "I swear it's true. I drove a van painted with psychedelic designs across the country to California. My hair touched my shoulders and I wore a peace sign around my neck." He smiled. "You're a little young, but that was a time when everyone went around singing Dylan's 'Blowing in the Wind' and marching for peace."

Emily eased onto the sofa beside him, thinking he was too straitlaced to have ever done that sort of thing. "Did you do this alone?" she questioned, her eyes still filled with disbelief.

"No. There were three of us. Actually we only missed a semester of college. It didn't take us long to realize that we were too much a part of the establishment to be decent hippies."

Resting her elbow on the crest of the sofa, Emily placed her chin in the palm of her hand and looked at him. Nathan, with a peace sign around his neck? How could she imagine him as a long-haired hippie when he was so handsome in that tux? She smiled. "Do you still keep in touch with the others?"

A faraway nostalgia crept into Nathan's eyes and he stroked his chin absently. "One of them," he said thoughtfully. "The other joined the air force after graduation. He didn't make it back from Vietnam."

"I'm sorry." Her voice was low, gentle.

Their eyes met. "So was I. Enough about that. I didn't mean to change the mood of the evening. We were laughing, remember?" His eyes rested on her face and he placed a finger under her chin. She lifted her lashes to stare into his eyes, smelling the scent of lemon on his hand.

"Yes, and it feels good to laugh. It's been a long time since I've enjoyed myself as much as I have tonight. Thanks. I was feeling a little down because the hearing date has been moved up to next Friday."

"About the movie?" he asked, as he gently slid his hand to the back of her neck and massaged her nape.

She nodded.

"I'll go with you, if you like," he offered.

Slowly Emily shook her head, pleased he'd offered, but knowing she couldn't let him go. "No. I have to go alone. The judge will have read all the facts. Dreamstar has asked for a summary judgment, so it will only be a matter of hearing the decision. I won't even be allowed to speak."

"It's still going to be difficult for you. Can't your lawyer take care of it? Do you have to be there?"

His concern warmed her. She waited a long time before she replied. "Not by law, no. But I need to be there."

He spoke only with his eyes as they swept over her face. With the backs of his fingers he traced the length of her throat. Their breaths mingled in the silence. Their shadows shimmered on the snow-white walls behind the couch.

"All right," he consented. "I'll let you go alone, but I want to see you afterward. I'll stop by after dinner. I won't stay long. Just a few minutes."

"Thanks. I think I'd like that."

Suddenly, from the corner of her eye, she caught sight of the tall purple flower he had called the liatris and pulled it from the bouquet. She turned back to Nathan and asked, "Why such exotic flowers? Why not daisies?"

He chuckled and stretched his legs out in front of him. "The florist talked me out of them. But I like the daisy. It reminds me of innocence, freshness and beauty—the same things I see in your face."

His words were a sincere, glowing compliment and Emily's pulse quickened. His voice had been soft, seductive, and she moved her lips closer to his, wanting to feel his breath fan her face, wanting to feel his lips pressed against hers once again. Emily hardly dared to breathe for fear the moment would be lost. The sensual intimacy of his caressing words was building a fire inside her that wouldn't be easily put out.

A deep, sighing breath broke from his lips and he said, "This has been a special evening, but I have to leave before I do something crazy."

"Like what? Kiss me?" she asked, even though she was sure she knew the answer.

Nathan shook his head. "No. It's not kisses I'm worried about." He carried her hand to his lips and kissed the open palm tenderly with soft, moist pressure. From there his lips touched hers with gossamer lightness, before whispering huskily, "No. I want more than kisses, and I don't think you're ready for that. Good night, Emily." He rubbed his thumb over her lips and kissed the tip of her nose before he rose and walked out the door.

EMILY REACHED UP AND HUGGED her friend. "Janice, come in. I want to hear all about your vacation, and I've so many things to tell you."

The two friends walked arm in arm into the kitchen, and Janice sat down at the glass-topped table that stood in front of a bay window. Morning sun streamed in through the vaulted ceiling's skylights and the open miniblinds that covered the window.

"Your tan is gorgeous. I'm jealous," Emily exclaimed while pouring coffee into black ceramic cups.

"You know what they say, there are no words to describe heaven. Two weeks on the beach is paradise."

Emily watched her friend push her long, straight hair behind her ears, uncovering dainty gold earrings fashioned in the shape of sand dollars. "You're an English teacher. Find some words." Emily set the cups on the table and took the white padded chair opposite Janice.

"Okay, you talked me into it." Janice smiled dreamily. "It was wonderful. Early every morning we went jogging on the beach. We soaked up the sunshine in the late afternoon when the worst of the heat was over. Walter was so loving and romantic. We walked along the beach at sunset and took midnight strolls along the water's edge with the waves licking at our ankles. It was heaven, Emily, a second honeymoon for us."

Emily sat quietly and listened to her friend. She was glad Janice and Walter had had such a marvelous time on their vacation. Janice's vivid description reminded Emily of how lonely her own life had been. Nathan's kisses had already made her aware of the fact that she was ready for romance.

"How could you bear to leave a place that sounds so perfect?" Emily closed her eyes and was certain she smelled salt air.

"Reality," Janice admitted, puckering her lips and lifting her thick eyebrows. "Walter had to get back for an important meeting, and I have five kids to tutor during the next six weeks. But that's enough about me. How've you been doing? How are things going with Dreamstar?"

Emily took a deep breath and ran her fingers through her short cropped hair. "A lot has happened in the two weeks you've been away. Naturally the press found out I'm living here, but it hasn't been as bad as I expected. At least not since that first day at the courthouse. That was a difficult time. Either the reporters are not as demanding here as they were in Birmingham, or they've finally decided this story doesn't deserve all the coverage they've given it in the past."

"Oh, I think a lot of it has to do with the fact that this isn't Gary's hometown."

"I hope you're right," Emily said. "Of course, Mr. Stobey wasn't pleased I hadn't told him I was Gary Spencer's widow. He didn't give me too hard a time about it. He said for me to do what I have to, as long as it doesn't affect my work or reflect badly on the office."

"That was nice of him."

Emily laughed. "It didn't last long. Three hours after our discussion two reporters invaded the office looking for me and Mr. Stobey got a little hot under the collar."

Janice laughed, too. "So I guess it's sit back and wait." Janice added cream and sugar to her coffee, sipped it, then added another spoonful of sugar.

"The wait is shorter than I thought. It seems Mr. Aubrey wasn't happy about the August deadline. He asked the court for a summary judgment, which he was granted. The hearing on that is set for Friday." Emily rose and rubbed the back of her neck, a habit she'd recently started. She looked into Janice's dark brown eyes. "Actually I'm glad it's been moved up. Waiting around for answers is no picnic."

Janice pushed her chair back and crossed her long legs at the ankles. "What's wrong, Emily? You seem restless—like you have an I-don't-care attitude, all of a sudden. What's happened that you're not telling me."

"It's been so long, Janice," she murmured. "Just when I think I'm getting over the pain something comes along to bring it all back again. Gary's gone, but I won't be free to go on with my life until he's put to rest for good."

Janice stood up and laid a gentle hand on Emily's shoulder. "That's not all that happened. Tell me the rest," she prompted.

Emily sank her teeth into her bottom lip and looked out the window. "I've met a man."

"Go on," Janice encouraged her.

"I know he could make me forget about Gary. When he kissed me, I—Well, it was very nice."

Janice smiled, with a knowing look on her face, and sat back down. "Nice, Emily? Are you sure his kisses were nice?"

"All right." Emily smiled. "They were wonderful. Something was there between us. I could feel it."

"Do you think he felt it, too?"

"Yes, I think so. I mean—" She stopped, not sure how much she wanted to tell Janice.

"Emily, isn't this the first real kiss you've had since Gary's death?"

Emily's skin prickled. "Yes, but that doesn't have anything to do with the way he made me feel."

"Are you sure? Maybe you're just lonely." Janice held up her hand to keep Emily from speaking. "Look, I'm not saying there's anything wrong with it. You were bound to become interested in another man sooner or later. I don't think Gary would've wanted you to be alone for this long."

Emily rubbed the back of her neck and walked over and picked up her coffee and sipped it. "Oh, I don't know, Janice. Is it wrong to be interested in another man, when I have so much to do for Gary?''

"Emily, I know you keep saying you're trying to stop this movie for Gary, but the truth is you're doing it for you.''

"No, that's not true!" Emily turned angry eyes on her friend. "Gary wouldn't have wanted his last few hours of life shown on national television. You know how I felt when they kept showing his body being dumped on the runway.''

Janice grabbed Emily's shoulders. "Shh—all right, don't get upset. I'm sorry I mentioned it. We won't say any more about that, okay?''

Emily moved away from Janice and rubbed her arms as if she were chilled. "I'm doing this for Gary," she whispered desperately.

"I know. I believe you." Janice tried to soothe her. "Now come back, sit down and tell me all about this new man in your life. I've wanted you to get active socially again for a long time. I hope this is the man.''

HOT WATER STUNG Emily's back, but she stood in the shower beneath the pelting droplets without flinching. Seconds passed before she stepped aside and adjusted the water to a cooler temperature, realizing how foolish she'd been to punish herself.

Several minutes later, she wrapped a green cotton robe around her damp body and made her way to the kitchen for a cup of the coffee she had made earlier.

After the hearing, she'd waited a long time before returning home. Home was the last place she wanted to be. Her need to get away prompted her to stop by a travel agency and make arrangements to fly to Fort Lauderdale to spend a few days with her parents. She'd then called Janice and told her the outcome of the hearing. Everyone else would hear on the six o'clock news. Janice asked Emily to stay the night with her, but Emily refused, wanting to be alone.

Emily stood in the middle of the winter white kitchen, pushing her wet hair away from her face, wondering if she had done everything humanly possible to stop the movie. Was there something else she could have done? The appeals court was the only recourse left. Evan had advised they file immediately, and she had agreed.

The doorbell rang as Emily poured coffee into a cup, and she padded barefoot to the front door. She wasn't surprised to see Nathan on the other side. However, she *was* surprised to see him clutching a bunch of yellow daisies. She remembered him saying something about the daisy a few days ago, but her thoughts were too cloudy to remember clearly.

"May I come in?" Nathan asked. She looked better than he'd hoped. Her drying hair was curling about her face. There was no redness or swelling in her eyes as there would have been if she'd spent the afternoon crying. He didn't even know why he was here. He was getting in too deep, finding her too appealing. Every time he told himself he wouldn't see her again, he found himself standing on her doorstep. It didn't seem to matter that he didn't need her or her troubles.

"Sure," she answered, stepping aside.

"I'll put these in water for you," he offered when she didn't take the flowers. He had no idea where she kept things, but had a stroke of luck when the first cabinet he opened in the kitchen revealed several tall iced-tea glasses. He filled one with water and stuffed the daisies in it, then placed them on the bar.

"The decision was in Dreamstar's favor," she said, sitting on one of the rattan stools in front of the bar.

Nathan looked closely at Emily and his chest tightened. He should have found anger, not passivity, in her eyes. Dammit, she was acting just like Michelle that night he lost the election. Only he hadn't known how to help her at the time.

"I know," he answered quietly, wanting to take her in his arms, but knowing from experience that was the worst thing he could do. He leaned against the counter, so he could be closer without touching her. He took a deep breath, trying to prepare himself for what he had to do. "I'm sorry. There's no way I can make it better."

She laced her fingers together and placed her hands in front of her. If she heard him she didn't respond. When she looked at him, he didn't think she really saw him.

For a moment Nathan wondered if he should just leave her alone to get over this the best way she could. So he'd kissed her and it was good. That didn't give him the right to barge in and take over her life. But he couldn't let her go. Like it or not, he'd become involved with her that day at the courthouse. What happened to her mattered to him.

"It's over, Emily. You've got to accept the fact that you did the best you could. It's time to forget this and get on with your life."

She lifted her lashes as if they were weighted and looked at him. "I don't understand, Nathan. Why won't they let Gary die? Why do they want to keep his story alive? He was just an ordinary man, doing what he thought was right. Why do they want to make a movie about him?"

Nathan watched her intently. She was asking all the right questions, but with no passion in her voice. She was too calm, too quiet. He knew there was pain inside her, but she wasn't letting it show on her features. She kept it bottled up inside.

He longed to take her in his arms, to hold her. He wanted to give her comfort, but he knew that wasn't what she needed to get her through the night. He felt so inadequate, remembering the time he'd tried to help Michelle and failed miserably. If Emily ended up in a deep depression, he'd never forgive himself. Closing her anger inside wasn't the answer. She had to get it out, and he didn't like the idea of being the one who would force her to do it.

"Emily." He said her name softly, unable to be harsh. "You haven't come to terms with some things yet. Once you do, I think you'll understand all of this a little better." He took a deep breath. This wasn't going to be easy. He didn't want to do it, but it had to be done.

"They're making a big deal out of this because Gary wasn't an ordinary man. Me—I'm an ordinary man." He struck his chest with his thumb and moved closer to her. "Look at *me*, Emily. I'm an ordinary, run-of-the-mill type of guy. Gary was a hero! That's what makes his life worth writing about. That's what makes his story worth telling to millions of people."

He had hoped his last remark would get a rise out of her. It didn't. She blinked a couple of times, but her placid expression didn't change. His throat constricted as he roughened his tone of voice and edged it with meanness. "What was your real reason for fighting Dreamstar?"

Her head snapped up. "What?"

"You heard me," he remarked callously. He walked around the counter and stood before her. "Answer my question, Emily. *You,* of all people, should want Gary's story told. What are you hiding?''

She pushed damp hair away from her cheek and lifted her chin. ''I'm not hiding anything. What are you getting at?'' Her voice was stronger.

''Why are *you* the only one who's not singing Gary's praises? Dammit, he was your husband! Why is Gary a hero in everyone's eyes but yours? Was he into something illegal?''

''No, of course not. That's a horrible thing to say!'' She moved away from the bar stool, putting distance between them.

Nathan grabbed her upper arms and swung her around, forcing her to face him. A spark of anger showed in her eyes, her cheeks reddened. He had to be relentless in his pursuit, no matter how much he hated it.

''Is it? The truth, Emily? It's time to tell the truth. What was your husband really like? Why wasn't he a hero?''

She glared at him and tried to pull free of his grasp, but he held tighter. ''I don't know what you're talking about. And I'm not going to listen to you. You're being mean!'' She continued her struggle, but not with any real strength.

''Tell me why you don't want Dreamstar to make this movie!'' he insisted harshly.

''Because they'll make a circus out of his death. He doesn't deserve that!'' She wrenched free of his grip and hit at him.

Nathan caught her wrists and pulled her against him. ''No, there's more to it than that.'' His voice was low and menacing, his gaze raked across her face. ''Maybe Gary was involved in something illegal and you're afraid someone will find out? Is that why he was in South

America? Was he down there to do a drug or weapons deal? Maybe he was into smuggling artifacts? What are you hiding? Tell the damn truth, Emily!''

"Nothing!" she screamed, struggling against his strength. "You don't—know what you're s-saying. Get out of here!" Her words were slurred with passion.

"What are you hiding?" he demanded yet again.

"Nothing! Nothing, dammit!" She jerked away from him and with one swipe of her hand sent the glass of daisies crashing to the kitchen floor. "Get out of here, I never want to see you again."

She shook all over, her eyes glazed with wildness, with rage. Her hair drooped in her face, and her robe fell off one shoulder. God help him. She'd never looked more beautiful. Silence followed, as both of them looked at each other and then the broken glass and scattered flowers.

Nathan breathed a sigh of relief. She had finally gotten angry enough to strike out at something. He closed his eyes for a moment, remembering Michelle again. He couldn't help but wonder if things would have turned out differently if he'd known how to handle her that night.

When Emily looked at him again he took a step toward her, but she backed away. A knot formed in his chest. The sting of rejection cut deep. He watched her wipe her hand down the front of her green robe and knew she must have bruised it when she knocked the glass off the counter. He wanted to hold her.

Her shoulders slumped, tears gathered in her eyes. "Gary was the most honorable man I've ever known." Her lips quivered and her voice shook, but she continued. "He was not doing anything illegal. He wasn't in any kind of trouble." Her voice grew stronger. She took a deep breath. "He was not the frightened, irrational man Jeremy Smith portrayed in his book. I only wanted to stop the movie to preserve Gary's dignity, his right to privacy, and to spare myself the heartache of reliving his death once again."

"I know," he whispered huskily. Now wasn't the time to tell her he was sorry for hurting her. It wasn't the time to explain. After the things he had said, she might never give him the opportunity.

She pulled her robe together and tightened the belt. "Go away. I want to be alone." Her soft voice expressed the tiredness he saw in her face, in her lovely green eyes.

Nathan's stomach contracted in a spasm of guilt. "I don't want to leave you." He wasn't sure she was ready to be left alone.

"I need to be by myself."

"Emily." He took another step toward her and she backed away again.

With cold eyes she said, "Can't you see I don't want you here? You've said enough."

He deserved that. He even understood—still his arms ached to hold and comfort her.

"Emily, it had to be said." It was a feeble excuse. At this point he couldn't say anything that would make her feel better, or himself.

"Please leave." She refused to look at him, but spoke with an earnestness he couldn't ignore.

Looking at her, Nathan realized she did need to be alone. Although it was like a knife in his stomach, he turned and walked away.

Outside her front door Nathan waited, hoping she might call him back. He wanted to be there if she needed him. When several minutes passed and the door didn't open, he went home.

THE RINGING OF THE telephone disturbed Emily's slumber. She turned her head only to find that she had a painful crick in her neck. She opened her eyes to find she lay on the sofa with her robe hanging loosely on her sprawled figure. When she raised her head, it throbbed with a dull ache. The telephone rang shrilly a second time, and Emily stumbled her way to the kitchen to answer it. She jumped back as if she'd been struck, when she saw the broken glass and wilting daisies strewn across the floor. The phone pierced the air for the third time before Emily grabbed it.

"Hello," she said breathlessly, trying to rub the crick out of her neck, the sleep out of her eyes.

"Emily, thank God you answered. I was about to hang up and come over."

"I was asleep, Janice. It took me a while to get to the phone." Not only did her neck hurt but her back and shoulders, as well. She didn't remember falling asleep on the sofa, but she did remember Nathan's visit. The dead flowers brought a vivid recollection of what had happened the previous night. Emily leaned heavily on the bar and let her forehead drop into her hand.

"It's a good thing I called. Doesn't your plane leave in a couple of hours?"

Emily looked at the clock. Janice was right. She rubbed her neck again, then let her hand move over to smooth her hair away from her eyes. She had to get busy.

"I was hoping to come over for a few minutes before you left."

"Janice, you're so sweet, but I don't think so. I have a lot of things to do here, and I need to stop by the office. I'll call you from Fort Lauderdale, and we'll talk."

"Are you sure you're all right?" her friend asked in a worried tone.

"Yes, but I won't be if I miss that plane. Don't worry about me. I'm fine. I promise to call later. Give my best to Walter."

Emily hung up the phone and went to work. She straightened her robe while she rushed to get her bedroom shoes. After sweeping up the mess in the kitchen she put on a pot of coffee. She needed to do one more thing before she packed. With trembling fingers, she quickly dialed Nathan's number.

"Nathan, it's—"

"Emily," he broke in. "I'm glad you called. I've been worried about you. How are you this morning?"

She heard concern and relief in his voice and appreciated it. From the first time she'd met him she'd known he was a nice man. "I wanted to tell you that I'm going to Fort Lauderdale for a few days."

"When did you decide this?" he asked.

"Yesterday. I made plans before I came home. I haven't seen my parents in a while, and they want me to come."

"When are you leaving? I'd like to see you before you go."

"Actually my plane leaves in a couple of hours, and I have a lot to do. I need to go."

"Emily, wait. I want to explain about last night." His voice had an anxious quality.

She rubbed the back of her neck, the crick still bothering her, and swallowed the lump in her throat. "No. There's nothing to explain."

"Yes, Emily. I need to talk to you. When can I see you?" he asked.

She gripped the telephone receiver tighter and squeezed her eyes shut. He cared, and that made her feel wonderful, but this was something she had to do. "I'll call you when I get back."

"Don't go, Emily. Let's meet for coffee and talk. Don't run away and hide again," he said urgently.

"I'm not hiding this time," she answered confidently. "I need some time with my family." She inhaled deeply. "I'll be back in a few days." There was a long silence on the other end of the line, and Emily wondered what Nathan was thinking.

"Are you sure there's nothing I can say to make you change your mind?" he asked.

"I'm sure. I need some time to think things through."

"All right," he agreed. Give me a call when you return."

"I will. Goodbye, Nathan."

A wave of expectancy washed over Emily when she hung up the phone. She ran both hands through her hair, then massaged her temples. Nathan was wrong. She wasn't running or hiding anymore. She was gaining strength.

Chapter Six

Five days was a long time for Emily to be away from home and work, but she felt better for it. She came back to Tallahassee feeling good about herself. She was also sporting a rich, golden tan, and her hair was a couple of shades lighter.

Her mother had played a large role in helping Emily overcome her disappointment in the court's decision. Lacy Clements had reminded her daughter of a line in an old poem, "Accept the things you cannot change." That was exactly what Emily had decided to do.

Not wanting to wait until she unpacked, Emily checked the fish to make sure Janice had taken proper care of them. It didn't look as if there had been any casualties.

The next thing on her list was to call Nathan, which she did with disappointing results. Nathan's secretary informed her that he would be in Washington for the rest of the week. It had taken her some time to sort out her feelings about Gary, the movie and Nathan, and what he was trying to do the last time she'd seen him. She now realized he had forced her to break out of the stupor she'd fallen into and had given her a reason to fight.

Later that evening when she returned to her condo the phone was ringing, and she hurried a breathless hello into the receiver.

"Emily," Nathan said, "I've been calling every thirty minutes for the past three hours. I was beginning to think my secretary made a mistake and you had called me from Fort Lauderdale."

Emily smiled. It was good to hear his voice. She closed her eyes and smelled his lemon scent. "I got back late this afternoon and had an early dinner with Janice and Walter."

"Welcome home. How are you feeling?"

"I feel good, rested," she answered.

"I'm glad you called. I didn't know whether or not you would." His voice was hesitant.

"When are you due back in town?" she asked, not knowing what she expected or wanted from him at this point. She only knew she wanted to see him.

"Friday at the earliest." He paused. "Would you like to have dinner?"

She breathed a sigh of relief. "Yes, I'd like that."

"Good. I'll get back to you on the time when I've checked my flight schedule."

A couple of minutes later Emily hung up the phone and headed for bed. It surprised her how much she missed Nathan, how much she wanted to see him.

"IT'S GOOD TO HAVE YOU back," Melody said, when Emily walked into the office the next morning, a cheerful expression on her face. "You look wonderful."

"Thanks. I'm feeling terrific. In fact, better than I've felt in a long time. A mini-vacation was just what I needed. Want to come over for a game tonight and maybe a swim later?"

Melody laughed and blond hair caressed her shoulders. "Are you kidding? You've beaten me so badly the last two times we've played I'm losing my confidence."

Emily joined her laughter. "Now's the time to redeem yourself. It should be easy for you. I'll be the one with a new racket this time. I picked it up in Fort Lauderdale."

"I hate to pass on a grand opportunity, but can I take a rain check for later in the week? I've already made plans for this evening."

Hearing disappointment in Melody's voice, Emily quickly said, "You bet. I'm free every night except Friday, so how about Thursday? Does that sound okay?"

"Great. I'd love to." She handed Emily a large stack of yellow memos. "You had a lot of calls while you were away. I don't think they were all business, if you know what I mean." Melody lifted one eyebrow to make her point.

"Ah—yes, I know what you mean," Emily said, briefly looking over the papers. She recognized some of the names as reporters, including Raymond's friend, Bill Hadly. Nathan's name was among them and Lucy Morrow's, too. Emily decided she'd call her first and set up a time they could get together.

"Oh, before I forget," Melody said. "Remember the Saxtons? You did a market analysis for them just before you left."

"Yes. They were undecided about selling."

"Well, they decided to put their house on the market. Raymond was on duty when they called so he worked up the listing for you. It should be in Friday's multiple-listing book."

Emily cringed inside. What luck. With six other agents in the office, why did Raymond have to be on duty when one of her clients called? Because of office policy, she would be forced to work with him on this.

"When you have a moment, could you get the Saxtons' file for me? I'd like to look over it."

By the look in her friend's eyes, Emily knew that Melody sympathized with her. They had talked about Raymond many times.

"Sure. I'll get it now."

A few minutes later Emily gasped in outrage as she looked at the listing sheet Raymond had prepared. He had listed the house twenty thousand dollars higher than she had suggested to the Saxtons. The nerve of him! The other agents often joked about Raymond's penchant for overpricing houses, but it was no laughing matter when it was one of her clients.

Maybe it was lucky for Raymond that it was almost an hour before he came into the office. Emily had cooled down some but not enough to keep from approaching him the minute he walked through the door.

She met him in the middle of the office with the listing sheet in her hands. Deciding to give him the benefit of the doubt, she kept her voice low when she asked, "Why is the price of the Saxtons' house twenty thousand dollars higher than the amount I quoted them two weeks ago?"

Although it didn't happen often, some clients wouldn't take their Realtor's advice when it came to pricing their house.

"Welcome back," Raymond said sarcastically, then grinned while he shoved the tail of his jacket aside and slid his hands into the pockets of his pants. "We missed your cheerfulness while you were gone."

Emily wasn't in the mood to play games. "Where did this price come from?" she asked again, trying to keep her voice normal and her anger under control.

Raymond took the sheet from her hands and looked over it as if he was seeing the document for the first time. "Oh, yes, that house." He smiled. "Nice couple." He gave the listing back to Emily and started to walk away.

Emily wasn't going to let him get off so easily. "I'm not through, Raymond." Her commanding voice stopped him. "Where did this price come from?" She couldn't help but notice that Melody and some of the other people in the office had stopped to stare at them, but she wasn't backing down.

"The price came from the owners. You did notice their signature on the dotted line, didn't you?" he remarked snidely.

His innocent act only made her madder. She stepped closer and lowered her voice, not wanting to make a spectacle of their conversation. "I did a detailed market analysis, then added six percent to cover the commission. The price was more than fair market value, and when I left the Saxtons they were completely happy with the figure I gave them. How did you talk them into changing the price?" Anger burned on her tongue and in her eyes.

Raymond pushed his European jacket aside and slid his hands into the pockets of his summer wool slacks. "It's no big deal, Emily. If the house doesn't sell in a couple of months, we'll lower the price."

"It's a big deal to me," she said, holding her teeth together, hoping her voice wouldn't carry across the office. "I don't work that way. Furthermore, I resent your taking it upon yourself to advise my clients without first consulting me."

Silent rage made his cheeks and nose turn red. "You know the office rules. Whenever an agent is out of town, the agent on floor duty takes care of any client that calls.

If you don't like the way this office works, talk with Mr. Stobey. I don't have time to listen to you right now." His eyes glared into hers and an overconfident expression softened his angry features.

Raymond was right about the office rules. Most firms allowed each agent to pick someone of his or her own choosing to handle clients while away, but at Stobey and Ackerman things were different. At the time she joined the staff, she didn't know Raymond.

"I intend to speak with Mr. Stobey and the Saxtons, to see if I can have that price changed before it hits the multiple-listings book." She took a deep breath and defiantly shoved the paper back into its folder. Other agents might be content with saying, "Oh, that's Raymond for you." Well, Emily wasn't going to settle for that old line anymore.

Looking Raymond in the eyes, she said, "Don't contradict me with my clients again." She turned away from him and walked back to her desk.

Naturally, as she suspected, he wasn't going to let her have the last word. He followed her and leaned over her desk as she took her seat.

"You don't scare me, Emily Clements Spencer Clements." He grinned diabolically. "You make me more determined."

Emily watched him saunter over to his own desk and sit down. She contemplated the idea of changing her licenses to another office. The only problem with that was she was through with running, from anyone or anything.

Because Emily spent the entire day showing houses to out-of-town clients, she had to rush to get ready for Nathan. She showered quickly and rubbed her skin with a rich mink-oil lotion. The tan she had gotten beside her parents' pool was as fresh as when she first arrived home. Emily changed into a bright print sundress she had bought in Fort Lauderdale, then clasped a thin gold chain around her neck.

The doorbell rang as she was combing her hair, so she threw the brush down and picked up her cologne and sprayed her wrists. Of all the times for Nathan to be early, did it have to be when she was running late?

Her eyes sparkling, Emily opened the door intending to give him a big smile. Instead she was brought up short by the man who stood in front of her. Momentarily frozen, she stared wide-eyed at a darkly tanned, handsome man. Black thick hair swept attractively away from his face. His eyes were deep brown. He was stylishly dressed in a white shirt and slacks and a blue sports coat with the sleeves pushed up to his elbows. All at once it hit her. The president of Dreamstar Productions had invaded her home.

As it dawned on her who he was, she moved quickly to close the door. It wouldn't shut. She looked down and saw that his foot blocked the door and held it open. "What are *you* doing here? What do you want?" she gasped. She felt the blood drain from her head and her cheeks pale. Her heartbeat quickened and her breathing became choppy.

"Mrs. Spencer, please don't close the door," he said in a European accent. "I want to talk to you. For just a minute. I promise I won't take up much of your time."

She kicked at the white deck shoe that held the door open. Leaning all her weight against the door she pushed again. "Go away. I don't want to talk to you."

"Please, just let me have a few words with you," he pleaded. His strength overpowered her, and he wedged his body between the door and the frame while Emily continued to push one way and he the other.

"What could we—possibly have to say to each other?" Her words were broken, her breath mere gasps as fear continued to pound in her chest.

"Let me come in, and I'll explain. I want to talk about your husband."

Their eyes met. She calmed down. The struggling ceased. Her body ached, her hands trembled. The man was crazy—or was she? Maybe it was curiosity. It could have been the mention of her husband, or the sensitivity she saw in his eyes. She wasn't sure, but slowly stepping aside, she allowed Tad Aubrey to enter her home.

They walked silently, side by side, into her living room and stood under the skylight. Late-afternoon sun cast their shadows around the room. For a brief time, the only thing that could be heard as the two stared at one another was the bubbling of the filter system on the fish tank.

Emily felt exposed. Her mouth was filled with a metallic taste. Taking a deep breath and peering deeply into this stranger's eyes, she spoke first. "Now, tell me why you're here."

"You look frightened." He smiled warmly, his voice soothing. "Don't be. I'm not going to hurt you. I only want to talk. May I sit down?" he asked.

She stared at the dark, questioning eyes. The large lump that had formed in her throat was diminishing as she recovered from the shock of seeing him. He was right, though. She was frightened of him, but not physically. It was what he could do to her emotionally that worried her. She had put her fight with Dreamstar Productions behind her, content to let the appeals take their course, and now Tad Aubrey was living and breathing right beside her.

Reluctantly she gave him the nod to sit down. She watched him closely as he eased onto the white leather sofa.

After he had made himself comfortable, Tad glued his gaze on her face and said, "I need your help. I'm asking you to come in and work as a consultant to me on the movie about your husband."

"What?" she exclaimed. Emily hadn't planned on sitting down, but his words took all the strength from her legs. She sank into the sofa beside him, feeling as limp as a rag doll. "You're crazy!" she whispered.

Tad moved to the edge of the sofa. "I know your initial reaction is that I'm being cruel to even suggest such a thing, but if I could have a few moments to explain, I think you'll feel differently."

He had the moments, whether or not Emily wanted him to, because she couldn't move to stop him. His words had taken the very breath from her body and left her speechless.

"I know I'm a stranger, but I didn't want anyone else to speak to you. I had to do it myself, so I could make you see the importance of this matter. I know we've been on opposite sides in the past, and you're a formidable opponent. This time I'm hoping we can be on the same side. In my opinion, Jeremy Smith didn't quite capture your husband's . . ." His hand came up in frustration as he searched for the right word. "For now, let's say integrity. Smith didn't come up with all the little things that made your husband the only one of two hundred and fifty people willing to risk his life in order to gain freedom for all. Only Gary Spencer was willing to do that. I need you to help me bring out all the facts about Gary's truly noble character.''

''No,'' she said in an anguished whisper, shaking her head. ''No,'' she said again, staring at him, unable to take her gaze from his face.

''I expected this to be your first reaction, but I want you to think about it. With your help, I can make this a movie you'll be proud of, not one you'll want to hide from.'' He paused. ''Our fight is over. It's time for us to work together.''

''You have no right to ask such a thing of me. You have no right to be here. I can't believe you would be so crass.''

''I'm sorry that my coming here has upset you. I apologize for that, but I couldn't let lawyers handle so delicate a matter. I can appreciate that you didn't want this movie to be made. But like it or not—it will be. I don't intend to give up. Stop fighting and join me. With your help I can accurately portray Gary the way he truly was. I'm asking you to drop the appeal and give me what I need to make this movie the best it can be for your husband's memory.''

His last words tugged at her heart. She did want the true side of Gary to be shown, but could she help with it? Would she be doing Gary's memory an injustice if she worked on the movie?

The doorbell rang and Tad rose. ''I'll go now. I know you need time to think about what I said.'' His eyes held hers for a brief moment. ''I'll be in touch.''

On shaky legs Emily followed Tad to the door and watched silently as he hurried past a stunned Nathan who held his gaze on Emily's face. She wanted to sink into Nathan's arms and tell him what Tad had suggested, but she couldn't move.

With Tad gone, Nathan stepped inside and closed the door. His eyebrows raised in question. "Who was that?"

Nathan's remark brought her back to reality. "Tad Aubrey, president of Dreamstar Productions."

"Hey, you're not kidding, are you? What the hell was he doing here?"

Emily swallowed the lump that had been in her throat for the past ten minutes. "I—I'm not sure," she managed to say.

"Well, it's obvious he's upset you. Come on, we'll talk about this guy over dinner."

Nathan took hold of her hand, and his warmth relieved some of the tension from her back and shoulders. She reminded herself how dangerous it was to become dependent on him as they walked out the door to the car.

Nathan selected a quiet restaurant not far from Emily's home and the hostess showed them to a table by a large window. Emily smiled with pleasure when she looked out the open window and saw that a large gardenia bush was in full bloom. The sweet scent of the flowers drifted through the air and lingered around their table. A faint light prevailed in the western sky. Purple ridges edged the horizon.

"That tan looks beautiful on you," Nathan said after the waiter had taken their order. "Actually you look wonderful. Do your parents live close to the beach?"

"Thanks," she said, letting her eyes linger on his face. "And yes, my parents do live on the beach. Dad retired from the post office a couple of years ago and they were lucky enough to buy a house they had rented for several summers."

"The vacation seems to have done you a lot of good. You look rested, and lovelier than I remembered." His eyes glowed with appreciation.

"Thank you again. *And* I do feel good. My parents are great people. But how about you? What are your vacation plans for the summer?" They were doing a good job keeping the conversation light. At the back of Emily's mind she knew talk of Tad Aubrey was only a few words away.

"I usually take a winter vacation out to Vail and ski for a couple of weeks."

"That sounds like fun. I love to water-ski, but I've never been snow skiing. I always thought I'd like to someday," she said as the waiter approached and placed their drinks on the table.

"Emily, before we talk about anything else, there's something I want to say about the last time I saw you. Before you went to your parents."

"No, don't." She tensed. "I'd rather you didn't. That night is behind us. I don't want to think about it."

He took a sip of his wine. "I can't let it go that easily. I'd feel better if we talked about it. I said some pretty rotten things to you, and it's important to me that you know what I was trying to do that night."

Emily knew he was right. They needed to talk about it. "All right," she said. She picked up her water glass and took a sip. "I remember I was an emotional basket case." She leaned on the table, placing her hands in front of her for support. A knot formed in her chest as she looked into his eyes. "What you said was cruel, mean and totally off base. Gary was on his way to Atlanta when his plane was hijacked. He wasn't on his way to South America, and he certainly wasn't into anything like drugs or weapons."

"I know. I was only trying to make you angry. I knew if you continued to hold in your hurt and anger you would end up in a depression, and I didn't want to see that happen to you."

"You certainly succeeded in making me angry." Emily remembered the broken glass and scattered flowers. "Gary was a man of principle and honor, and he hated injustice of any kind. I know that's why he took it upon himself to try to overthrow the hijackers."

"I'm sure that's true," he said, his gaze sweeping across her face.

She looked deeply into his eyes. "Nathan, I need to know whether or not you believe any of the things you said about Gary."

"No," he assured her without hesitation. "I had only one reason for saying those things about him. I was trying to make you angry enough to fight. You were holding all your feelings inside, and it was the only way I knew to force you to strike back."

Emily sighed relief. It was true that Nathan's words had hurt her terribly that night, but as he intended, they had also made her act. "The things you said couldn't have been further from the truth. He wasn't the kind of man Smith portrayed in his book, either. I'm sure Gary knew exactly what he was doing. He must have thought he had a good chance of freeing those people or he never would have attacked that hijacker."

"I know. Gary simply put into action what most people on that airplane were only thinking about doing. I'm sure that every man who's ever been in that situation wished he had the courage of Gary Spencer." He took another drink from his glass. "That's why he deserves to have his story told, and that's why I'm jealous as hell that you loved him."

Emily gasped at his admission. Admitting that took a lot of courage, and it warmed her heart. "You don't have any reason to be jealous of Gary." She smiled, trying to let him know just how much his words meant to her.

His eyes met hers. "Maybe not, but I am."

She swallowed hard. "I won't deny that I loved my husband."

"I don't expect you to."

Nathan took another sip of his drink. He wasn't playing it cool. It hadn't been very smart of him to tell Emily that Gary was a hero, and then admit his jealousy of him. But dammit, he *was* jealous. It was apparent that Emily was very proud of her husband's heroic action. Here he was wanting to be the only man in her life and what was he doing? Telling her that every man wished he had Gary's courage. And it might make him an unfeeling cad, but he wanted to make her forget about her Gary Spencer.

He'd tried to keep her out of his thoughts, his mind, but it wasn't working. He didn't want to be involved with a woman who had Emily's kind of problems. But he could no longer pretend he was only interested in her for what she could do for CAT and John's political campaign.

Rubbing his forehead, Nathan decided a change of subject was in order. He wasn't going to win any brownie points by extolling someone else's virtue, especially a man she'd loved.

"So do you want to talk about this guy named Tad?" Nathan asked the question politely, but inside he was dying to know why the president of Dreamstar had come to see her.

Emily refolded the starched napkin that lay in her lap. "Yes, if you don't mind."

He smiled. "You know I don't. I'm interested in anything that concerns you." Nathan wanted to hold Emily, to have her next to him. All this talk of her husband had left him feeling insecure, and he didn't like that feeling. He wanted to reach over and touch her hand, to remind himself and her that something special was growing and developing between them.

The softly lit room enhanced Emily's beauty; her beautiful green eyes, cheeks a light shade of pale peach, lips a tinge of rosy pink. As he looked at her an ache started in the pit of his stomach. He realized he wanted so much more from her than she was ready to give.

She started by taking a deep breath. "When the doorbell rang I thought it was you, so naturally I answered it. I couldn't believe Tad Aubrey had actually come to my door unannounced, but I think he knew I'd never agree to see him if he'd telephoned. Anyway, as soon as I recognized him I tried to close the door, but he put his foot in the way." She picked up her white wine and nervously took a small sip.

"Sounds like he wanted to talk to you about something important. I'm not surprised he had the audacity to show up at your door, but I am surprised he forced his way inside. That doesn't sound like a smart move on his part. Did you call the police?"

She shook her head. "When he promised to stay only a minute, I agreed he could come in. I guess I was a little curious as to why he'd come. At least he kept his word and didn't stay long. It was what he wanted that really concerns me."

Nathan's throat tightened. "What's that?"

Emily pushed the wine aside. Refusing to meet his eyes, she said, "He wants me to drop the appeal and be a consultant on the movie. He wants me to help him bring out Gary's true character."

Damn Tad Aubrey! He didn't want her to do it. He'd just been trying to figure out a way to make her forget about her husband and now this jerk wanted her to work on the movie with him. He remembered what Emily said that day in the diner. "They won't let my husband die." He now knew what she meant. Gary Spencer was dead. But he was still very much a part of her life.

Swallowing wasn't easy for him. He had to mask his true feelings and say what Emily needed to hear. "How do you feel about that?" It was difficult to keep his voice under control.

"My first reaction was to hit him, scratch his eyes out or something like that." She gave a nervous laugh, before looking at him. "But then I started listening to what he had to say, and it seemed to make sense. He said he didn't believe that Smith had captured Gary's true character in his writing. He said almost the same things you did. Gary *was* different. He had a sense of morality that made him different from everyone else on that plane. Tad Aubrey wants me to help him bring that out on the screen."

Nathan carefully watched Emily as she talked. God, he wished he could hold her. "You sound as if you're considering his suggestion."

"Considering it?" Emily slowly shook her head. "I don't know."

"Why not?" he asked. There was no way in hell he wanted her to be Aubrey's consultant, but he was a realist and knew it would be the best thing for her.

Her eyes locked with his. "Nathan, I just tried to stop production of this movie because I wanted to put all this behind me and get on with my life. I don't want Gary's death shown on television. I saw it once and it's not pretty." Her eyes clouded with tears.

Nathan felt like a complete fool. She was sure to have seen her husband's body thrown from the airplane as it sat on the runway.

"Emily—"

"No, don't feel sorry for me, Nathan," she cut in. "I've had too much of that the past couple of years. The plain and simple truth is that I don't know if I can cope with working on the movie. All I ever wanted them to do was leave Gary's memory alone."

Nathan thought for a moment. If Emily didn't want comfort or sympathy, he'd give her facts. "But now you know that's not going to happen and you have to go from here. You could very well lose at the appeals level, Emily, and the movie would still be made."

"I know that." Her voice held certainty. "What I don't know is whether or not I can help with it."

"It'll be a hard decision to make. You *can* do it, Emily. I know you can. You're stronger than you think you are." Was he really trying to talk her into doing this? He would kick himself when he got home.

"I agree that I have more confidence in myself than when we first met. I've told Lucy Morrows I'll join CAT and that will open me to more exposure and publicity. But the idea of working on this movie is too new. I'm not sure what my feelings are."

Nathan picked up his wine and sipped it. Tad Aubrey sure knew how to get at the heart of the matter. He wasn't happy about encouraging her to do something that would take so much of her time, something that would be a constant reminder of her love for her husband and the pain of his death, but he knew that she needed to work on that movie.

He drank from his wine again and noticed the glass was almost empty. He didn't usually drink so fast or so much. "I have to be honest with you, Emily. I don't want you to do it." His eyes searched her face for a reaction that didn't come. "On the other hand, I think it's the best thing you could do for yourself. I think it will help you to understand this whole business with Gary a lot better." He reached for her hand, but she snatched it away.

"I don't think you're being honest with me." She held herself rigid. "I think you want me to work on this movie so CAT can get the publicity, and somehow that is going to help the senator. If that's what you want, why don't you just come out and say it. Don't stop being honest with me now."

"Wait a minute, Emily," he answered, suddenly angry that she'd accuse him of something that hadn't crossed his mind—this time, angry that she wouldn't let him touch her when he desperately needed to. "Neither CAT nor John enters into this. I was thinking about you, and how you might finally get your husband out of your system if you worked to get the damn movie made."

Her eyes filled with fire. "What do you care whether or not I get my husband out of my—system, as you called it. Why should I? I loved him."

"He's dead, Emily."

A sigh escaped her lips and pain filled her eyes. Nathan groaned. He didn't mean to say that. It was heartless and uncalled for. He didn't want to hurt her. Suddenly he was saying and doing all the wrong things. "I'm sorry. I'm speaking out of turn."

Her clear emerald eyes met his unwaveringly. "Yes, you are. It's my decision to make," she reminded him.

"I know," he answered, as the waiter approached them with menus.

Chapter Seven

A warm breeze blew a wisp of hair in Emily's face as they walked to her door later that night. The tone of the evening had turned somber, because neither of them wanted to risk talking about anything relevant or important to their relationship. It seemed that both of them had decided to play it safe and stick to small talk.

Emily berated herself. How had she allowed the evening to drift along on small talk when she had some major decisions to make about the movie and working with CAT? And Nathan? What to do about Nathan was probably the hardest decision to make. The time had come for her to either go forward with him in the direction her attraction was taking her or cut the ties completely. And if she did that, it needed to be tonight. She was smart enough to know where her feelings for Nathan were leading, and she wasn't sure she was emotionally ready for that kind of relationship with any man.

She looked over at him walking beside her. He was always so handsome in his dark blue suits, clean, crisp shirts and conservative striped ties. She loved the way he dressed.

He'd only kissed her once, but it had been very heady. Could Janice have been right when she suggested it was loneliness that had made the kiss so special? Maybe? But if that was the case, why hadn't she wanted to kiss any other man? Why had she been willing to spend time with this man when she'd successfully, easily passed on every other man who'd shown an interest in her? Emily knew the answer. Nathan was different, special. She'd liked him from the beginning.

When they reached the door, Emily turned to him and asked, "Would you like to come in?"

Nathan looked down at her, folded his arms across his chest and chuckled. "I don't think so. The evening's been over for a long time."

His words surprised her. They stung like little needles, too. If she didn't have really strong feelings for him, this rejection wouldn't have hurt. Emily lowered her eyes. "That's my fault, and I'm sorry."

"It's not anyone's fault, Emily. I—" He paused. "But I'm sorry, too. I was hoping for something more from us."

She looked up and met his eyes. Yes, she was also hoping for more. Why did it have to be over between them? She didn't want to give up Nathan. This was one thing she could control, and she intended to do it.

"You know the problem is that I spent most of the evening feeling sorry for myself, and you let me." She stepped back from underneath the glare of the porch light so she could see his face clearly.

"Oh, so now it's my fault?" he asked quietly.

"Yes," she answered breathlessly.

"I'm the one who ruined our evening together?" he asked, and took a step toward her.

"Yes."

His voice was soft but seductively husky. His dark blue eyes were gazing down into hers, sending a warm glow to surround her. With the back of his fingers he caressed her cheek, sending ripples of longing through her. He moved closer.

"That means it's up to me to make the evening right?"

"Yes," she answered, and tilted her head back farther to reach and meet his lips as they touched hers.

The kiss was gentle at first, and so good that Emily pressed her body against his. Their breath mingled hot and moist, lighting a flame inside her. As his lips explored hers, his hard chest pressed her soft breasts, leaving her breathless in the wake of the thrill.

When he lifted his head and looked into her eyes, he whispered through gusty breaths, "You're beautiful. I'm glad you're not ready to give up on us."

Nathan covered her lips with his once again and Emily melted against him, wanting the kiss to last forever. She tried to suppress the gnawing in her stomach, the tightening of her abdomen, the ache in her breasts. It wouldn't go away. Emily knew what she wanted.

She pushed him away and mumbled. "I—I think we should go inside. It's not very private out here." She looked down and fumbled in her purse for her keys. That kiss had left her shaken. She hadn't expected it to be so potent. She hadn't expected it to make her want more.

"Let me do that," Nathan said, when it was obvious she couldn't find the keyhole.

When the door swung open, Emily walked inside and threw her purse on the foyer table. This was the hard part. Where did they go from here? "Would you like something to drink?" she asked as he followed her into the living room.

"No." He shook his head as he answered.

"Why don't we go and sit on the patio? It's nice out tonight, not too humid or hot." She was nervous, and it was ridiculous. It was just a kiss. He hadn't asked anything of her. She was being silly.

Not waiting for him to answer, she spun around and hurried over to the glass door, slid it open and stepped out. Her small cement patio was enclosed by a seven-foot cedar fence and lined with potted geraniums. Emily folded her arms across her chest and held herself tightly, glad she hadn't turned on any lights. The twinkling stars gave enough brightness to the black night. The darkness covered her, and she liked that. She felt as if she was hiding again, but she didn't know why.

"Maybe I should go," Nathan suggested as he stood behind her.

She spun around. "No, don't. I'm not ready for the evening to end. Come on, sit down." She took one of the lounge chairs and pointed to the other for him. Emily stretched out, pulling the hem of her red skirt over her knees. She was acting like an idiot. It was true she wasn't ready for the night to end, but she wasn't ready to admit that she wanted more than kisses from Nathan. She wasn't ready to admit that she wanted to make love.

Instead of taking the other chair, Nathan walked over and sat on the edge of her chair. "How long has it been since you've done any stargazing?" he asked in a raspy voice.

Emily's heartbeat increased. She searched his eyes in the shadowed light, puzzled. "Stargazing? What are you talking about?"

Nathan pulled out the knot in his tie, then slipped it from around his neck and stuffed it in his pocket. "You mean to tell me you've never stargazed?"

Emily's breathing was ragged, as if she'd been running. "No," she answered innocently, as her heart continued to drum loudly in her chest. She moistened her lips and asked, "Do you have a telescope?"

Nathan opened the first three buttons of his shirt, and Emily's stomach knotted with anticipation. The tension he was building excited her.

"We don't need one for what I'm talking about." Keeping his eyes on her face, he bent closer and said, "First we take a long drive in a convertible and let the wind blow through our hair and turn our cheeks pink. Then we park on a dark country road. While I pop the cork on a bottle of wine you unwrap the strawberries."

"Strawberries?" she asked, immediately caught up in the picture he was painting.

"Yes," he answered, and moved his face still closer. "I'm trying to find just the right kind of music on the radio. You know, something soft and romantic. Meanwhile, you're taking small bites out of a plump, juicy strawberry. It's good, so you give me a bite. I take it all."

Emily couldn't breathe properly, and her stomach was tied in knots of desire. She could have sworn that she smelled the faint scent of strawberries in the air.

"What's next?" she asked, caught under his spell, lulled by his sensuous words. Moonlight danced off his rumpled hair and landed on her face. She welcomed it, letting it bathe her, fill her.

"After you've had a sip of the sweet wine, we put it away and lay the seats back. Now it's time for me to move over to your seat, just like this."

She scooted over, giving him more room on the lounge chair, allowing him to lean back and stretch his legs out beside hers, fit his body along her length. "Then I'll give you a couple of kisses like this." His tone was seductive as he cupped her face and kissed her lips softly, briefly, moving agonizingly slow to make sure his lips touched all of her face.

"And like this," he murmured against her ear before his kisses burned a hot trail of moisture from her cheeks and down the slender column of her neck.

Filled with the sweet rush of desire, Emily groaned aloud. She ached from wanting more of what his kisses promised. With skill, he had brought her to the edge of loving and she was ready to go wherever he led. Emily reached up and kissed the hollow between his throat and shoulders, tasting his tangy cologne-scented skin. Nathan moaned his approval.

"A few caresses like this," he whispered huskily. His hand waved down her hair, across her cheek, slipped to the base of her throat and paused before moving to caress her breast with the slightest pressure. The red silk dress she wore heightened his touch rather than impeded it.

Emily held her breath. She didn't want to ever breathe again, if it meant breaking this magical moment with him.

With his dark eyes staring into hers, he whispered, "You are the most desirable woman I've ever met. You're beautiful and sexy."

His lips found hers in the semidarkness. The kiss was passionate, seeking, finding and delivering. In a rush of hunger his lips left her mouth to graze her cheek, her jaw, her throat, while she whispered his name. His hand tightened possessively around her breast before his lips met hers once again. The need, the desire, the intensity rocked her senses.

Emily fed on his passion, encouraged his caresses. She tried to arch against him, but she was wedged too tight in the chair. She couldn't deny her wanting. His hand slid up and down her stocking-covered leg while she pulled his shirt free of his slacks and slipped her hands up his damp muscled back. A light film of moisture beaded his skin and it felt wonderful, exciting. He had created a need inside her, and she knew he could fill it.

The heat of his hands easily penetrated the thin material of her dress, as he caressed her hips with slow gentle movements that outlined every curve from her waist to the back of her thighs. His erotic exploration of her body, the feel of his arousal pulsating against her abdomen sent the desire for more than kisses spiraling through her. They kissed with passion, seduction and fervor, their hands explored, caressed, sought and satisfied.

"I want you, Emily," he whispered as his hot breath fanned her ear, increased her desire. "Let's go inside."

"Yes," she murmured, hot with desire for him.

Nathan scrambled off the chair and grabbed Emily's hands to help her stand. When her feet hit the ground, reality returned. He wanted to make love to her. She wanted him to. What was she doing? She'd only known him a month! She pulled away and turned her back on him. Darkness was the only thing she saw, and once again, she suddenly wanted to be hidden by it. Maybe if she hid in the black night no one would know she wanted to make love to Nathan.

Her body was still taut, her chest heaved with deep breaths. She didn't know why, but when she admitted she wanted to make love to Nathan it frightened her. Her skin was burning, yet she shivered. She gulped the humid air into her aching lungs.

She heard Nathan's deep intake of breath as he came up behind her and gently laid his hands on her shoulders. Comfort issued from him, and she leaned against his sturdy chest. He rested his chin on the top of her head.

It was time to make a choice. Would she try to hide behind some flimsy excuse or tell the truth? The truth, she answered to herself. "I know this is going to sound strange, considering the way I just responded to you, but I'm not ready to go that far. Are you angry?"

"Angry? Of course not. It's okay. That's not the sort of thing you rush." He squeezed her arms lightly.

She turned in his arms and sought his eyes in the twinkling starlight. "It's not that I didn't want to. I guess that was obvious."

He smiled and chuckled lightly. "Yes, Emily, it was. I hope it was just as obvious how much I wanted to make love to you."

His breath fanned her hair, sending ripples of pleasure throughout her. She cleared her throat and moistened her lips. "I've never been with anyone except Gary. I've never wanted to before tonight."

Nathan pulled her close and wrapped his arms around her waist. "I'd say that makes me one damn lucky man."

Emily smiled and rested her head on his chest. His arms hugged her tightly, and she sighed achingly as she breathed in the clean, fresh-washed scent of his shirt.

She wished the fantasy he'd spun was real. Maybe it was silly or juvenile, but she wanted to feel the wind in her hair and the flush on her cheeks. She wanted to eat strawberries, drink wine and do some stargazing.

"What are you thinking?" he asked. "Emily, don't shut me out. Talk to me. Tell me what you're thinking."

Slowly Emily let her head roll from one side of his chest to the other. She loved the feel of his firmness, she loved the smell of him. "I wish you had a convertible," she finally said.

"What?" He lifted her chin and looked into her eyes. "What did you say?"

A warm breeze flitted across her face and moonbeams lighted her eyes. Her voice soft, she said slowly, "How can you take me stargazing when you don't have a convertible?"

The moonlight made his face glow. "That just shows how much you still don't know about me." He laughed as he hugged her to him once again. "I do have a convertible. I have a 1964 Mustang convertible."

She raised her head from his chest. "Are you serious?" she asked.

"Of course I am. What do you say about taking the old convertible out on Saturday? We'll make a day of it. We'll drive along the coast, spend a little time on the beach and maybe catch a few stars on the way home."

Emily's eyes brightened and she smiled. "What time should I be ready?" she asked quickly.

"Seven sharp," he answered, then kissed her sweetly, briefly, whispering her name softly before he withdrew from the kiss and stepped away. "I'd better go," he said, sticking the tail of his shirt back in his pants.

"Are you disappointed that you're not staying the night?" she asked, although she wasn't sure why she wanted that reassurance.

"Hell, yes," he answered with a grin. "Frustrated, too. But I can live with it." He reached over and touched her cheek. "See you Saturday."

"JANICE, I'M SO GLAD you could come for lunch," Emily said to her friend, as they sat down at the glass-topped kitchen table. Noonday sun filtered through the mini-blinds and made a pattern of slatted shadows across the table.

"How could I resist, when you told me you'd made chicken salad? You know how much I love it." Janice peered over the rim of her tinted glasses. "Besides, you asked me on a day when I'm really hungry." She served herself a generous portion of salad and placed a bran muffin on her plate.

Emily sipped her iced tea and wondered how Janice was going to take the news. Her friend had advised her against working on the movie. Janice had a lot of good arguments, but none of them had convinced her she shouldn't agree to Tad's offer and be a consultant.

"So tell me what gives. I know you asked me over for a particular reason." Janice spread creamy butter on her muffin, taking her time as if she were doing a work of art.

Emily smiled. She'd never been able to hide anything from Janice. That was one of the reasons she was such a special friend. She could always turn to Janice when she needed a practical opinion.

"Tad Aubrey is coming over this afternoon, and he expects me to have an answer for him."

"And what's it going to be?" Janice asked.

Taking a deep breath, Emily looked up. "I'm going to do it. I'm going to work with him on the movie." Emily watched Janice patiently, waiting for her reaction.

"I think you're making a big mistake," Janice replied as she wiped her mouth on a black-and-white checked napkin.

"Why?" Emily pushed her salad around on her plate, not ready to take a bite.

"One reason is the fact that he just asked you to do it a few days ago and you haven't had the time to give it a lot of thought. Emily, you've been running away from Gary's death for two years because you said you couldn't deal with all the publicity. Now you're ready to jump in headfirst. What makes you think you can handle all this?" Janice bit into her overbuttered muffin.

"I'm going to make myself do it. I have to. I didn't need to take too much time to think about it. It just feels right, somehow." Emily leaned across the table to give emphasis to her words. "Besides, I haven't been running or hiding since I decided to stop Dreamstar. I knew the reporters would be after me when I filed those papers, but I had to do it—just as I have to do this. I can't hide from the press or life anymore."

Janice pushed her long, straight hair behind her ears, then pulled at the neckline of her blue blouse. "Speaking of that, what happened to the woman who took this guy to court?" For the first time, Janice's voice rose a fraction in pitch. "Emily, just a few weeks ago you were trying to stop production of this movie. You even had Evan file an immediate appeal. Now, all of a sudden, this producer has offered you a job working with him and you're all for it. Doesn't that strike you as a little odd?"

"No! Yes! In a way." Emily pushed her plate aside. Janice knew how to get to the heart of the matter. "I'd still rather the movie not be made. Janice, I talked with Evan about this. He doesn't think I'd have a chance in an appeals court, the only thing I'd do is keep Dreamstar tied up in court for a couple of years, if we can obtain an injunction to keep them from going ahead with filming. I've thought this through. I don't want to still be worrying about this movie two years from now. I want it over with. I did everything I could to stop it. If there was anything else I could do, you know I'd do it."

Janice continued to eat her salad. "One of the things that worries me the most is your motivation for agreeing to be a consultant for this man."

Emily felt a prickle of defensiveness. "I think my motives are clear. I'll see to it that Dreamstar and Tad Aubrey don't make a circus out of Gary's death."

"Is that all? And if it is, will it be worth all you'll have to sacrifice?" Janice laid down her fork and held her hand to silence Emily. "Let me finish. Every day that you work on that movie you will relive Gary's death. Have you thought about that?"

"Yes," Emily answered firmly.

"And you're willing to go through with it?"

"Yes."

"The press will hound you for interviews until you're ready to scream." Janice tried a different approach.

"I know."

Janice pursed her lips and stared at Emily, not ready to give up. "What about this new relationship with Nathan? Are you willing to jeopardize that?"

Janice's mention of Nathan brought him vividly to her mind's eye. Emily rubbed the condensation on her tea glass, letting her finger slide up and down in a lazy motion. "As for Nathan, there's no problem there. He wants me to work on the movie. Although he hasn't exactly said it in so many words, I think he believes doing this will act as some sort of therapy for me."

Pushing thoughts of Nathan aside for the moment, she continued. "You're right, I'll have to live with Gary's death. I don't for a moment think that will be easy." Her voice quivered suddenly, but she knew she had to tell her friend the truth. "Janice, I've been doing that for two years anyway. It may sound cruel to say it, but his memory fades a little each day." She looked up to see if Janice was outraged at her statement. She wasn't.

"How do you feel about that?"

"Saddened," she answered, knowing she would always remember the love she felt for Gary, but also knowing it was time to let him go.

"What made you decide to compromise your ideals?"

Emily rubbed the back of her neck. As she suspected, Janice was giving her a hard time, forcing her to talk it out and get everything straight in her mind. Janice was right, too. In a way she was capitulating. She'd put up a good fight, but she had to know when to quit. Tad Aubrey was right. It was time for them to work together.

She met her friend's steady gaze. "I have to," she said earnestly. "I've never acknowledged to the world that Gary was a hero. I never understood why Jeremy Smith wanted to write a book about him, or why Tad wanted to make a movie. He was just an ordinary man who hated injustice and thought he was doing the right thing. I couldn't figure out why some people were treating him as if he were a famous victim. It's taken me two years to get to where I am today. I don't know that I fully understand all of it, but in his own right Gary is important because he touched people's lives. He was willing to die for what he believed in and that makes him a hero, a man with a story worth telling," she finished softly. Emily took a deep breath. It was the first time she'd admitted out loud that Gary's story should be told. It felt good, right.

"Realizing Gary is a hero is one thing, but working with Dreamstar on the movie is entirely different. That's the same thing as giving your stamp of approval."

Emily grabbed her friend's hand and held it tightly. "Don't confuse me, Janice. If I had my choice, I'd prefer the movie not be made. But since the movie will be made with or without me, I'm going to work to see that it's done right."

"So what you're saying is that you're now ready to meet whatever comes up, head on."

"Yes. Not because I want to, but because I have to." She rose from her chair and pushed her hair away from her face. "I don't want Gary to come out of this movie looking like some hothead who didn't know what he was doing. I don't want anyone thinking he grabbed that— terrorist because he went berserk. Gary would have looked at all the angles, thought everything through carefully, before he made a move. He would have decided he had a very good chance of freeing those people." Her eyes glistened and her voice had drifted to a hushed whisper. "I didn't ask to be a part of this. I didn't even want the movie to be made." She paused. "But now I can't turn away from it."

Janice stood and wrapped a friendly arm around Emily's shoulder. "All right, you've convinced me. Sounds to me like you know what you're doing and why. I just hope you're right. Now sit back down and finish your salad. We'll talk about something else."

LATER THAT AFTERNOON, Emily opened the door for Tad Aubrey. He wore white slacks and a matching white sports coat that partially hid his blue T-shirt. There was an undeniably chic look to his style of dress. A bit of arrogance showed in the way he carried himself, proudly with his chin always slightly lifted. His cologne had an expensive musky smell that seemed to fit him well.

When they were settled on the couch, he said, "I'm glad you agreed to see me again, Emily."

"Believe me, I gave it a lot of thought before I decided to talk with you." She cleared her throat and brushed at her brown slacks. "I'd like to hear more about what you had in mind when you asked if I'd work with you on this movie.''

"Certainly," he said, crossing one leg over the other, showing a pair of white Docksiders. She couldn't help but notice he wore no socks. And she also noticed that he had very hairy legs. His ankles were as dark as his face. His sunny California tan rivaled her golden Floridian coloring.

"Let me start at the beginning. I've just spent the past few days in Birmingham, where you lived with your husband."

Emily's eyes widened with surprise. Tightness gripped her throat. "Why did you do that?"

"Background. I wanted to get a feel of the area where Gary came from. I wanted to know what his friends and co-workers thought about him. I'll also have to know what your feelings were at the time of his death."

A chill ran through her. "I don't understand. What has all of that got to do with what happened on that plane?"

"A lot goes into the production of a movie, Emily. I did mention to you that one of the things I want is accuracy. Visiting Gary's hometown is part of that. I have to know everything about him, and what shaped his character is very important. Every time the actor speaks, the viewer has to be aware of the fact that this man is different from all the others on that airplane. But we can talk about these little things later."

"You sound as if you've already started on the movie." She couldn't keep the coolness out of her voice.

He smiled. "Oh, no, not production. But I do plan to have everything in line and ready to go." He turned serious. "You can keep me in appeals, but you can't win. The only way you are going to win is to work with me."

"I'm beginning to believe that."

"I will tell you up front, Emily, that if you decide to do this I will ask you many questions—personal questions you may not want to answer. In order to make this movie work, to make it the best I possibly can, I have to know everything about Gary."

Tad stopped and waited for her to reply, but she couldn't. Agreeing that she, too, wanted the movie to be the best, she didn't know if she could supply all the answers to make it that way.

He sat back on the couch and placed his arm across the top. "If I'm going to portray Gary as the gallant hero he was, I have to know what made him tick. I have to know what made him different. I didn't get a feel for his character from Smith's book. That's what I want from you. I'll only have two hours to show why Gary Spencer had the courage to attack a terrorist who held a gun when at least fifty other men on that plane had the same opportunity and didn't take it, or rush to help him."

Emily's stomach knotted. When he went into action, he didn't mince words. Was she really going to do this? Could she answer this man's intimate questions? His probing questions? She knew she must, for Gary's sake. She couldn't let this movie turn out like Smith's book. She had to make sure Gary was portrayed as a mature, levelheaded man who had taken a calculated risk, and—she closed her eyes briefly—lost.

She straightened her shoulders and took a deep breath. When she looked at him, his dark brown eyes seemed to be peering into hers. Suddenly she had the feeling that Tad also wanted to know what made her tick. "I understand. Go on."

"The first thing you'll need to do is read the script. I brought a copy with me, in the event you decided to accept my offer." He reached into his briefcase and extracted a copy of the bound pages. He held it out to her.

For a moment, Emily just looked at the script. She felt as if a weight was pressing against her chest, constricting her breathing. She watched her hand as it slowly moved toward his offering. Taking those pages meant she couldn't look back.

She took it. The book was heavy in her hands, the paper seemed to burn her skin, but she felt cold as she looked at it. She laid the script aside and ran her hand down her skirt. Did she have the strength to participate in the re-creation of her husband's death?

"As you read the script, you can make notes on the things that are characteristic of Gary and those that aren't. There's something I want to point out before we go any further—if we should disagree on anything, even something you may feel strongly about, I have final say."

Emily listened intently and didn't doubt his words for a moment, but she couldn't acquiesce so easily. "What if you want to do something that is completely alien to what Gary would say or do?"

"Still, the final word will be mine." He smiled. "However, you will be at liberty to attempt to convince me otherwise."

His smile was rather reserved, not at all as dazzling as she'd expected it to be. She watched as he pushed up the sleeves of his coat, exposing his arms. A thick gold bracelet circled his wrist, but he wore no other jewelry.

The day they'd first met she had thought him pretentious, with his pastel clothing and his pronounced European accent, but now she realized he wasn't putting on an act. He was simply a man of rare sophistication. If they had met under different circumstances she might have been impressed.

"You've been very honest. I appreciate that and feel I have to be the same. If I thought there was still a good chance that I could keep this movie from being made, I would." Her tone of voice had a firm edge. "I don't want this fight with you to drag on any longer. It's time to settle." She took a deep breath to calm her quavering stomach. "At first, the very idea of working with you was unthinkable, totally unacceptable. Then I realized I agreed with something you had said about Smith's book not doing justice to Gary's character. Because of this, I have decided to work with you. If the movie has to be made, I want to be there to see it's done right."

"My sentiment's exactly, Emily." His tone was direct, eyes bright with satisfaction. "Now, let's get to work on the details. The casting is most important."

"There's one other thing I'd like a commitment on first."

"And what's that?"

She held her breath for a moment. It was imperative that her voice not tremble when she spoke to him. "I would like to be paid one hundred thousand dollars."

Relief flooded her. She'd sounded quite confident. His shock was so visible that Emily couldn't suppress a smile. There was a certain satisfaction in seeing him uncomfortable, a small amount of justice. She felt a little better.

While Tad was still speechless, and she had the upper hand, she continued. "Of course, I'll be signing the money over to a charitable organization, which I will specify at a later time."

"This is unexpected," he said, watching her closely. "All I anticipated paying was your expenses."

"That won't be necessary. I'll take care of the expenses, and you take care of the one hundred thousand. If you agree to that, we have a deal."

He didn't answer immediately. A frown creased his forehead and his eyes were shaded by his dark lashes. Finally he said, "Why do I have the feeling your reasons behind this are punitive?"

Emily decided it was best to ignore his question and drive home her point before they drifted into an argument. "Do we have a deal?"

Tad sat back in the sofa, folding his arms across his chest. "Since you would be donating the money to charity, I'd look like Scrooge if I said no." His dark eyes narrowed and his lips pursed for a moment. "We've got a deal."

Chapter Eight

Underneath her brightly printed shorts and matching T-shirt, Emily wore a black one-piece swimsuit. She'd bought a new one earlier in the week, but when she put it on that morning she decided she couldn't wear a swimsuit that was cut to her waist in one direction and above her pelvic bone in the other. It might be the latest style, but it definitely wasn't her. She'd stay with her black swimsuit. With its simple styling, it flattered her petite figure.

While she was trying to decide between sandals and sneakers, the doorbell rang. The short nap of the soft carpet tickled the bottom of her feet as she padded to the door.

Nathan greeted her with a smile and said, "We couldn't have picked a better day. The gods have blessed us. Clear blue skies, sunshine and a mild eighty-five degrees. Not bad for an early August day."

Emily looked into his eyes and smiled. She loved that shade of blue. "I'll get my shoes and bag and be right out." She hurried back to the bedroom, slipped her feet into the sandals and threw her sneakers into the bag. She'd take both. If they did any walking on the beach, she'd want the sneakers.

Outside Emily oohed and aahed over the shining red convertible with white interior. "I've seen a few of these cars around," she said as they stashed her gear in the trunk.

"There was a resurgence in their popularity a few years ago, but it's settled down again now. I spend so much time in Washington, I don't drive this one as much as I should." He shut the trunk with a bang.

"You've taken good care of it," she complimented. He opened the door for her, and she sat on a seat warm from the sun.

Nathan chuckled as he slid behind the wheel. "You should have seen the car before I had it restored. I bought it from a salvage company. It was in rough shape."

Emily reached across the bucket seat and touched Nathan's shoulder. She loved the feel of him. "I'm glad you're taking me for a ride in your car."

"So am I." He reached into the backseat and brought out a wide-brimmed straw hat. "Here, you'll need this a little later when the sun gets hotter. And don't forget to buckle your seat belt."

She took the hat from him and watched as he put on a New York Mets baseball cap. "I'm surprised you don't have a cap with Miami Dolphins written on it."

Nathan laughed heartily. "I would, if I were wearing a football helmet. This is a baseball cap."

"I know that."

"Yeah, sure. I can tell you know a lot about sports." His grin and tone of voice let her know he didn't believe her.

"No. I really do know a lot about football," she insisted, as he backed out of the parking space.

"Uh-huh," he mumbled.

"Okay, ask me any question." And so the conversation went as they headed for the coast.

After they had been driving for a couple of hours, Nathan suggested they stop and spend a little time on the beach. He parked the car along the side of the road, and they walked down to the sandy white beach, which was littered with broken seashells.

"It's so beautiful here. Look how blue the water is today," she exclaimed as they spread the terry-cloth blanket. "I wish I had a house on the beach."

But Nathan didn't want to look at the water. How could he take his eyes off Emily when she was so lovely? She looked the way he imagined she would after a night of intense lovemaking. Her hair rumpled, her cheeks flushed and her lips so damn tempting he wanted to ease her down on the warm sand and— No, he had to keep those kinds of thoughts out of his mind. She'd made it clear she needed time, and he was determined to give it to her.

"Would you settle for a condo?" he asked, as he positioned the cooler in the middle of the blanket.

"I'd settle for a grass hut," she teased.

Nathan watched Emily smooth the wrinkles out of the blanket before she sat down and stretched her legs out in front of her. He'd always thought she had nice legs. The shades she wore hid her eyes, but he knew they were beautiful and sparkling—the same way sunlight sparkled on her hair. He'd had one helluva time trying to get any work done the past week. All he could think about was those few minutes he'd spent with her on that lounge chair and how much he wanted to taste her once again.

"Have you thought any more about whether or not you're going to work on that movie?" he asked, trying to get his mind off that starry night.

"Yes, I've decided to do it. I spoke with Tad yesterday. I was going to tell you later."

She looked at him, but between her shades and his he couldn't tell what was written in her eyes. "I think you've done the right thing. You wouldn't have been happy with any other decision."

"I think you're right. I must have known from the moment he suggested it. I've always regretted not giving Jeremy Smith an interview before he wrote his book. I couldn't let a mistake like that happen again."

Nathan looked out over the water. Somewhere in the back of his mind he had been hoping she wouldn't do it. "I have to admit I'm not happy about the idea of your spending a lot of time in L.A. I assume that's where the movie will be made."

"Actually it will be in Hollywood. Apparently Tad has a contract with Paramount Pictures for the movie to be shot at their studios."

"Sounds like you have a lot to look forward to." Nathan could have bit his tongue out. How could she be looking forward to making a movie about her husband's death? He usually had a little more tact. "Not many people get the chance to work on a movie studio in Hollywood, California," he added quickly.

She smiled. "I knew what you meant."

Nathan took his shades off and rubbed his eyes. He might as well go ahead and ask all the questions he didn't really want the answers to. He'd encouraged her to work on this movie, and he'd look like a fool if he didn't show an interest in it. "When will you be going?" He settled the glasses over his eyes once again.

"I leave on Monday."

"Monday! That's too soon. I mean—" He looked at her and he wanted to rip those damn glasses off so he could see what was in her eyes. He didn't want her to go, but he didn't have the right to ask her not to. That was the real problem. He had no rights where she was concerned. He knew better than most that she needed to work on this movie. He just had to figure out a way to keep her from forgetting about him while she was gone.

"How long will you be gone?"

"Probably a week, the first time. I'm going to fly out for the casting next week, then come back here to make arrangements with my office, and I'd promised Lucy Morrow I'd help with CAT so I'll have to speak to her. Tad doesn't expect the filming to take more than three to four months."

"So we're looking at Christmas before it's finished?" he asked, thinking that Christmas seemed like it was three light-years away.

"If all goes well with the production," she answered. "But we don't need to talk about that right now. Do you mind if we talk about something else?"

"No," he said. In fact, I'd prefer it, he thought to himself. "Why don't we go for a swim?"

"Sounds good to me."

Nathan watched as Emily pulled her blouse over her head, taking time to fold it before laying it on the blanket. The round neckline of her black swimsuit revealed just enough of her breasts to make him wish it showed a little more. He loved the golden color of her skin. Her arms were well-toned, and her shoulders were beautifully rounded and sexy.

"You're going to get a farmer's tan if you don't take your shirt off," she told him.

"Well, I can't have that," he said as he unbuttoned his white shirt, which had little blue anchors sprinkled on it.

As soon as his shirt was off he wanted to take Emily in his arms and feel her against his naked chest. Her sun-kissed skin glowed invitingly in the sunlight. He watched as she stripped off her shorts where she sat, revealing golden tanned legs. He wanted to run his hand up her thigh and feel the silky smoothness of her skin.

Emily didn't make it easy for him. She quietly watched as he unzipped his shorts and stepped out of them. Suddenly his swimsuit felt like a second skin. He wanted to make love to her and sometimes it was difficult to hide it.

He understood that Emily wasn't ready for that kind of commitment. He was willing to wait until she was ready to come to him freely, without any hang-ups from the past or from what their relationship would be like in the future.

"I think it's time for a swim to cool off," he said, and knew his heat had nothing to do with the giant fireball hanging high in the eastern sky.

Looking down at her, he asked, "Are you coming in, or are you going to stand there watching me?" He threw his sunglasses on the blanket beside her.

Emily stood in a single graceful motion, brushing back a lock of shiny brown hair. "I'll be right behind you," she told him.

Nathan didn't wait. Watching her watch him made his blood boil with desire. Any more and he'd be over the edge. He waded into the lukewarm water of the gulf until he was chest deep, then dove into an oncoming wave.

The water was mild and Nathan stayed under for as long as he could before surfacing. As his head popped out of the water, he saw Emily walking toward him. The one-piece swimsuit perfectly outlined all of her curves and sent his blood to racing once again. She might as well have been naked for what it did to his manhood.

Surely she knew what she was doing to him as she continued to walk deeper into the water, closer to him. Surely she knew he was fighting with the devil himself. He didn't want to rush her.

When she reached him, their eyes met and she wrapped her arms around his neck and pressed her body against his. He saw desire in her eyes, he felt it inside her. He remembered the way she responded the previous time he'd held her in his arms.

Nathan groaned desperately when she offered her lips to him. She must have known what he was thinking. She must have known this was what he wanted. Emily pressed closer to him and cautiously slipped her tongue into his mouth. Nathan sucked it in deeply and held her tightly.

"You feel wonderful," he said between wet, salty kisses.

Waves crashed against him from behind, almost knocking him over, but he held on to Emily. Her lips burned on his. They were soft, yielding more pleasure than he ever dreamed possible. His wet hands caressed her sun-hot back and shoulders, then slipped below the water to span the width of her waist and press her closer. His hand slid back up to her breast, the wet swimsuit adding to the pleasure that swelled him. All too soon she broke away from the kiss.

He heard her intake of breath and knew she didn't want the embrace to end, either. Although they were alone on this area of the beach, several people could be seen a good distance from them. This wasn't exactly the best place to be making love.

Nathan raked both hands through his wet hair. The water lapped at his chest. Looking up he found Emily's bright green eyes staring back at him, her soft lips were reddish pink and just as desirable as when he'd kissed them.

Nathan surveyed his surroundings as he tried to come down from the high he had reached just moments ago. The waves crashed against his back, threatening his balance, and the sand shifted beneath his feet. He cupped the salty water in his hands and splashed it on his burning face. "Emily, I can't kiss you without wanting to take it all the way and make love to you."

"I feel the same way," she said quietly.

Refusing to let his eyes leave hers, he wiped at water running down his cheek. The hot sun beat on the top of his head, the waves continued to lap his back. He took a deep breath and a grim smile touched his lips. "That's good to hear. At least we're in this together." He squinted his eyes from the glare of the sun off the water. "I'm just wondering what we're going to do about it."

"Wait," she finally said.

"For how long?" he asked.

"Nathan, I—I'll race you to that marker." She pointed to a red buoy about fifty yards away.

That wasn't what she was going to say at first. He knew it, but decided not to press the matter. "I'd better give you a head start," he drawled lazily. "I'm a good swimmer. I'll win hands down."

"Oh, you think so, do you?"

"I know so," he said confidently and grinned. "You've got until the count of three. One, two." He watched as Emily's small body dove into the blue water and took off, lengthening the distance between them quickly. She was a good swimmer. He wondered if he should let her win. No, he decided and started after her. His strong arms sliced easily through the water, first catching up with, then passing her.

Half an hour later they emerged from the water, laughing and dripping wet. Not bothering to dry with a towel, they both lay on the blanket and stretched out in the sun, their energy spent. After a few moments of resting, Nathan peered over the cooler that acted as a barricade between them and said, "I don't know when I've had so much fun."

Emily opened her eyes just enough to see Nathan's face. He was smiling at her. "Me either, but I know it's been a long time." She rose from her prone position and searched in her bag. "Here. Put some of this on," she said, and handed a bottle of dark tanning lotion to him.

"You do it," he said in a low-pitched, seductive voice, then closed his eyes.

Emily looked at his muscled back. He didn't have very much of a tan. If he didn't get some sun block on soon, he was going to burn and blister. And if she was honest with herself, she was dying to rub the lotion on his back.

Slipping on her shades, she crawled over to his side of the blanket. After making herself comfortable beside him, she poured a generous amount of the thick white lotion into the palm of her hand and set the bottle aside. The citrus smell of the lotion reminded her of Nathan's lemon scent. She slowly rubbed the creamy liquid between her hands before laying her open palms against his damp skin. His back was warm to her touch. The feel of his corded muscles beneath her hands sent ripples of desire through her. His moan of pleasure let her know he agreed with her feelings.

It seemed as if neither of them was in a hurry for her to stop, so she continued rubbing in a circular motion. The lotion made his skin feel like silk. The friction made her palms itch.

"How about a soda?" Emily asked, when it looked as if he might fall asleep on her.

"No, this feels too good," he mumbled. "I need some more lotion on my back."

Emily laughed and wiped her lips with the back of her hand and smelled the tanning lotion. "You just want a free massage. Come on, sit up. It's time for something cold," she said, and opened the cooler.

She gave him a cold Coke and then fished out one for herself. The drink was cool and refreshing.

"Do you know what today is, Nathan?" she asked.

He pretended to ponder over the question. "Saturday," he said, then grinned.

"Yes, but it's also a diamond day."

He laughed. "What is a diamond day?"

"A bright sunshiny day. A happy, carefree day. For long after Gary was killed I was so filled with pain and memories I couldn't enjoy anything in life."

"And now?" he questioned, holding his breath at her answer.

"Because of you, I have a chance at diamond days."

Nathan looked past Emily, down the beautiful sandy beach. Her words brought back a long forgotten memory about a woman who wanted diamond rings.

When they finished their drinks Emily and Nathan put on their shorts and walked back to the convertible. As they drove down the highway, Emily knew that Nathan was responsible for her diamond day.

A little past noon they stopped for lunch at a small seafood restaurant and enjoyed glasses of chilled wine and crisp shrimp salads. They lingered over lunch, waiting for the worst heat of the day to pass before leaving the air-conditioned sanctuary to continue their quest along the coast.

Once the afternoon journey had begun, they didn't stop again until Nathan suggested they watch the sun set before heading home. In silence they walked to the water's edge, leaving their footprints in the sand. The sea-green water formed beautiful white caps as it rushed into shore. The sun had melted into the horizon and filled the sky with hazy shades of mauve, coral and brown. A small area of the sky glowed like coals in a fireplace.

Nathan was the first to penetrate the hush that had settled around them after they sat down. "Hold out your hand," he said. When she complied, he placed a tiny seashell in her palm and closed her fingers around it. "Add it to your collection," he said in a low voice.

"What makes you think I have one?" She gazed into his arresting blue eyes.

Nathan looked away from her, picked up some sand and let it sift through his fingers. "I have a hunch you're the kind of woman who has a collection of little treasures from the sea tucked away somewhere."

Her hand tightened around the shell. He was right, and she liked the fact that he was. Emily laid her head on his shoulder and smiled.

A short time later they were on their way home. As darkness settled around them, Nathan switched on the headlights and the conversation ebbed into silence as the hours passed.

When they were a few miles from her home, Emily noticed that Nathan turned in the wrong direction. Thinking he had made a mistake, she quickly said, "No, Nathan, you were supposed to go left."

"The day won't be complete if we don't do a little stargazing. And I know just the place."

"I don't think it's a good idea." She hadn't forgotten how quickly his kisses could make her forget who she was, where she was, everything except his touch.

"Don't worry." He reached over and grasped her hand. "I promise we won't do anything but watch the stars. When I make love to you it won't be in the cramped backseat of a Mustang."

A few minutes later, Nathan stopped the car along the side of a dark road. When the engine died, Emily instantly heard the sounds of night. Crickets chirped noisily, and the deep, throaty cry of a bullfrog echoed in the distance. She brushed at her hair with her hands and wiped at her eyes, thinking she was glad it was dark.

"Pull up on the handle to your right and the seat will lie back like this," Nathan said. Suddenly his seat flew back and landed with a thud. After following his instructions, she also lay back in the seat and stared up at the tranquil night sky.

When she heard a faint chuckle come from his side of the car, she turned toward him. "What's so funny?"

"This makes me feel very young," he admitted.

"Mmm. I know what you mean." She sighed. "They are beautiful, aren't they? The stars. They look like diamonds sprinkled on a black silk screen."

"Do you like diamonds?" he asked.

Not sure why, she hesitated. His question made her suddenly uncomfortable. "I suppose," she answered.

"Did your husband buy you a diamond engagement ring?" he queried.

"Why do you ask that?" Her tone was defensive. She propped herself with her elbow and stared at him. Why would he want to know whether or not Gary had given her an engagement ring? His question was personal, and she wasn't sure she wanted to answer it.

"Settle down. Don't get upset. I only asked the question because I want to know more about you."

"Are you willing to answer as much as you ask?" It was too dark to see his eyes clearly, but she saw them sparkling.

"Yes."

"All right. No, I didn't get a diamond when we married. We were in our last year of college and there wasn't enough money for an engagement ring." She took a deep breath. "Did you give your wife a diamond?"

"Yes, but Michelle didn't like the one I bought. Not only wasn't it big enough, but it wasn't the right cut. When she saw it, she stuffed the ring back into the black velvet box and dragged me down to the jewelers to pick out the diamond she wanted."

"That must have disappointed you," she said, thinking that was a horrible thing to do to the one you loved.

Nathan chuckled lightly as he bent over the gearshift that separated the bucket seats. "That was only the beginning, and I never gave it a second thought until a few hours ago when you mentioned diamond days. I couldn't help but compare the woman who wanted diamond rings to the one who wanted diamond days."

Emily smiled and settled back into her seat, pleased with what Nathan had said. "Today was a diamond day. I wouldn't trade it for all the jewels in the world."

"Neither would I." Nathan reached over the gearshift and kissed her softly. His hands lightly caressed her shoulder and moved to the warmth of the back of her neck. "Emily," he whispered. "I can't explain how good it feels when I hold you and kiss you. It feels right."

"I know. I feel the same way." She rested her forehead on his shoulder while he continued to rub the back of her neck. His light massage felt wonderful.

She pulled away and lay back in her seat once again, feeling warm and content. "Tell me more about your wife. You've never talked about her or your marriage."

"It's not something I like to talk about."

"I can appreciate that. But you know so much about my husband I think it's time I knew a little more about you."

Nathan let out a sighing breath. "All right. When I was in college I became interested in politics and hoped to one day have a seat in Washington. A few years later, I thought it was the greatest thing in the world when I met a woman who was willing to work with me for a political career. I knew it would be a tough life for any woman. Michelle was young and beautiful, eager to be a senator's wife. She was great on the campaign circuit. Everyone loved her. But what I didn't realize was that she had a problem. A big problem. Cocaine."

Emily gasped. "How did you find out?"

"I won't go into all the details. But stress shows up rather quickly during a political campaign, and her dependency materialized close to the end. I found out that she'd started in college, kicked the habit once or twice, but never for more than a year or two at a time."

"What did you do?" Emily reached over and took hold of his hand, wanting to comfort him.

"I asked her— No, I begged her to check into a treatment center immediately. She wouldn't. She knew what that would do to my chances for election, and at the time I had a fairly good chance of winning. I insisted she cut back on the campaigning, and thinking back, I now believe that was a mistake. She sat at home with nothing to do and that made her problem worse, not better. I still don't know how, but a week before election, her drug dependency was leaked to the press. I didn't want to know who did it. It wasn't me or the election I was worried about, it was Michelle. I knew how fragile her mental condition was and that the announcement would put her over the edge.''

"What happened?" She was afraid to ask, but knew she had to hear the rest.

"The inevitable. I lost the election. And Michelle went into a depression because she blamed herself. For a long time I blamed myself because I didn't know how to deal with her drug problem or cope with her depression. I kept thinking if I'd done things differently she wouldn't have gone off the deep end that night. After a year of treatment she was better and insisted on a divorce. I wanted to make our marriage work, so she agreed to try. We spent another six months together. It wasn't any good. There was no love left, only guilt.''

Emily felt a lump rise in her throat. She felt sorry for the woman who had thrown her life away for an artificial high. "Where is she now?"

"Last I heard, she'd opened a dress shop somewhere in south Florida. As far as I know she's clean. I never thought we'd lose touch. But time passes.''

"So she's the reason you gave up a political career?" Emily asked.

"Yes. At the time I didn't want to give it up, but I knew if I continued Michelle's name would always be brought into any campaign. I couldn't do that to her, so I took the job with John Merritt.''

Emily moaned inwardly. Nathan would have been a good politician. She hurt for his lost political career. "Do you feel cheated?" she asked as she bent over him and looked into his eyes.

He laughed lightly and reached up and cupped her face with his hand. Emily turned her head and kissed his palm, wanting in some way to let him know that she cared, that she wished things had been different for him. "Cheated? No way. I'm as active as I want to be. John listens to my ideas, like the CAT project, and he respects my opinion. We work well together."

"And Michelle? Do you miss her?" she asked, wondering if she really wanted to know the answer.

"Not for a long time, Emily. My only regret is that I couldn't do more for her."

"I was just thinking. Even though it wasn't in the same way, we both lost a loved one. It's not easy, is it?" she asked.

"No, it's hell." He gently pulled her to him and kissed her softly. "Emily, I don't want to lose you. I don't want you to go to California and forget about me."

She tried to get closer to him, but the gearshift blocked her way. "I won't. Nathan, you're the first man I've been attracted to since Gary's death. There has to be a reason for that."

"I hope to God it's what I think it is."

Emily smiled. "What do you think it is?" she teased, but in the pale moonlight saw there was no humor in his face.

"I'm going to be the one who makes you forget about Gary Spencer."

Emily's chest tightened. She didn't know how to respond. She didn't know if he expected a response. "I don't know what to say to that."

Nathan straightened in his seat. "You don't have to say anything. Just don't forget what I said." He kissed her briefly and raised his seat. "It's time for us to go."

Chapter Nine

Because of delays, the flight to Los Angeles was much longer than Emily had expected it would be. After the young bellhop arranged her luggage, she smiled and thanked him, handing him a tip. When the door closed, she slid the chain lock into its holder and turned to look at the luxuriously decorated room on the second floor in the Beverly Hills Hotel.

Everything, from the walls to the carpet to the furniture, was in shadings of her favorite colors, coral and green. The bed sat between two large windows that showed a heavenly blue sky. In the far corner a sitting area had been tastefully arranged, enhancing the character of the room.

A closer inspection of her surroundings showed the hotel's age. The many coats of paint covering the wood and walls testified to its glorious years.

Emily walked over to the small cocktail table and picked up the card jutting out from a basket of fruit, cheeses and candies. The card simply read, 'Tad.' Letting go of the card, Emily watched it flutter to the table. What was she really doing in California? Janice had said she was working on the movie for herself. Nathan had said she needed to do it for herself. Why did they think that? She knew she was doing this movie for Gary, to preserve his memory.

Now that she was in Beverly Hills, she knew working on this movie was the right thing to do. It was more than just a duty to Gary's memory. She had to make sure this movie did not discredit Gary's name by showing him completely different from his true character. Smith had called him America's kind of hero, but had failed to show that in the book he'd written.

She picked up a red apple and rubbed it on the front of her blouse before sinking her teeth into the thin skin of the fruit. The tangy juice ran out the corner of her mouth and she caught it with the tips of her fingers. She looked at the hole left by her bite and breathed in the scent of the fruit. The spicy smell of apples was one of her favorites.

Biting into the apple again, she remembered her last conversation with Nathan. It was a shock hearing about his wife, his lost political career. Nathan could have gone into hiding, given up politics completely, but instead he had chosen to stay in the arena even if only as a press secretary and advisor to Senator Merritt.

Sighing, she realized that Washington would always be a second home for Nathan as long as he worked for the senator. Could she handle that? What was she doing? Why did she care if Nathan spent a lot of time in Washington? Because she knew she was falling in love with him. It wasn't just physical desire. She was sure of that now. There were many things about him that she liked, many things that impressed her.

Loving Nathan certainly had its drawbacks, though, she thought as she leaned back against the armchair and took another bite. Knowing he was at the beck and call of a popular senator would take some getting used to. And she still had the feeling that he had more to do with

CAT than he admitted. Why else would he have been pushing for her to join? He was happy to hear she would be doing all she could to help them. But working on this movie was all she could handle at the present time. Her real-estate career was going to suffer because of the movie, too. Before leaving town, she'd made arrangements to talk with Mr. Stobey when she returned home.

True to his word, Tad had a car waiting in front of the hotel at three o'clock that afternoon to take her to the studio in Hollywood. She felt very businesslike in her cream-colored suit and brown Victorian-styled blouse. In her briefcase she carried the script she had massacred with a red pen. In her heart she carried the knowledge she was doing what had to be done.

She was a bit disappointed when the driver didn't take her through Paramount's famous iron gates which showed the HOLLYWOOD sign in the distance. When she mentioned it, he informed her that those gates had been closed to traffic years ago and it was now only a pedestrian entrance and the only place on the grounds where cameras were allowed. She had never been on a studio lot, but she didn't expect to see so many buildings that looked like warehouses.

The driver was an excellent tour guide, pointing out places such as the park where Lucille Ball's children played while she taped the "I Love Lucy" show, the sets where "Cheers" and "Family Ties" were rehearsed and filmed, and Michael J. Fox's black Ferrari as they drove through the narrow streets.

At last they stopped in front of one of the metal warehouses, and Tad met her at the car. Inside the building she found the large room filled with all sorts of camera and lighting equipment. Tad didn't bother to introduce her to any of the people they passed as he directed her to a secluded corner.

When they reached a pair of director's chairs, he immediately turned one around and she saw the name "Clements" printed on the back of the canvas in bold black letters.

Emily smiled warily as she looked into his dark eyes. "I'm impressed," she admitted casually.

"One thing you'll find out about me, Emily, is that whenever I do anything, I do it right. And usually the first time."

Even though she didn't know him well enough to argue the point, she was tempted to do it just for the challenge. However, he spoke again before she came up with an adequate retort.

"Sit down, please." He held the chair out for her.

With a slight feeling of trepidation, Emily laid her briefcase on the table and eased into the chair. She supposed she'd never be rid of all her fears, never be truly comfortable in this new position.

"Now," Tad was saying, "I've scheduled the news conference for five this afternoon."

Emily's stomach knotted and her chest tightened. Was the inevitable only a little over an hour away? Why had she consented to an interview? Why had she let Tad talk her into it?

"Can't we make it later in the week? I'd like a chance to get used to things around here."

"Believe me, Emily, this is the best way to handle this. If we give the reporters an hour today, they will ask their questions, then go away, write their stories and forget about us until the first of the year, when the movie comes out."

Run and hide were always the first words Emily thought about when she heard the word reporter. She couldn't do that anymore. Nathan told her he knew she would handle herself very well. She didn't want to let him down, so she had to appear strong and confident. Maybe in time it would get easier.

"I know you're right, but that's not going to make me like it any better when the time comes."

"Don't worry. If I see you hesitate over a difficult question, I'll answer for you."

A few months ago she would have welcomed that statement. Now it only challenged her. Her eyes held steady. "I won't have any problem answering the questions," she confirmed. "I just wish I didn't have to do it."

"I'm sure," he agreed. "Tomorrow we start casting for the lead. The field has been narrowed a great deal, because I insisted on having an actor from the south. I abhor the job most people do trying to mimic a certain accent. I'd especially hate to see any actor do a injustice to an accent as lovely as yours." He smiled.

Taking his statement as a compliment, Emily smiled appreciatively, and said, "So would I."

"Do you have any questions about the script?"

She waited a long time before she replied, "Yes, quite a few actually." She opened her briefcase and took out the dog-eared pages. If he knew how many questions she had, he'd probably have a stroke. All that talk about his having final say over the script didn't mean a thing to Emily. He might as well learn the first day that she didn't intend to let anything pass that she was unhappy about. She'd fight him every step of the way.

Tad eyed the rumpled script with skepticism. "All right, we'll start on this and see how far along we get before we're called in for the interview." He scooted his chair closer to hers. "What's the first question?"

An hour and a half later, Emily walked into a crowded room with Tad at her side. Strobe and camera lights started the instant they walked through the door. Her arms hung loosely, but her hands made fists. The man who led the way showed them to a table littered with microphones and wires at the front of the room. Dozens of lights flashed continuously until they were seated. The moment she'd dreaded had finally come. Emily Clements had granted an interview.

Silently she wished Nathan was by her side instead of Tad. After all, he was an expert at this. She would have never agreed to this if Nathan hadn't been gentle with his encouragement. He was certain she would do fine. If that was true, why were her insides churning, her hands sweating and her head pounding?

Emily sat with regal straightness as Tad read a prepared statement that, in essence, said she would be working with him as a consultant on *America's Kind of Hero*. The lights shining into her eyes were exceptionally bright, and she forced herself not to squint. Continuing to remind herself she was going to make it through this event, she swallowed the lump building in her throat and took a sip from the water glass in front of her.

At last Tad finished his opening comments with, "And now, we'll take your questions."

Everyone spoke at once. Emily couldn't distinguish one question from the other until most of the reporters gave way to one man seated in the front.

"Mrs. Spencer, could you tell us what made you decide to work with Mr. Aubrey after you took him to court to stop production?"

Taking a deep breath, she bent her head and spoke directly into one of the mikes. "If this movie has to be made, I want it done right. I'm here to see that Mr. Aubrey doesn't make any mistakes." Her strong voice lent strength to her weakening self-confidence.

Emily stole a glance at Tad and saw him lift an eyebrow as if in protest that she would imply that he would do anything less. She turned back to face the crowd. The first question was over, always the hardest, Nathan had told her. It would be easier from here to the finish.

"Mrs. Spencer, could you tell us how much Mr. Aubrey is paying you for this?"

Emily moistened her lips and swallowed. If there was any way she could keep the press from knowing she had done this, she would. She hadn't even mentioned it to Nathan. Tad had accurately guessed why she had asked for the money and some sharp reporter would, too. "I go by the name Clements now, and yes, I asked to be paid one hundred thousand dollars for my services and that the check be made out to a charitable organization to be named at a later date."

"Will you receive anything else from Mr. Aubrey, Ms. Clements, and could you tell us why you're now using a different name?" the same man asked quickly, before another had the chance to jump up and bark a question.

"No." She answered his first question first. "Clements is my maiden name. The only thing I hope to gain from working on this project is a certain amount of satisfaction," she answered, feeling quite pleased with her quick response.

"Could you explain that?" The question came from a woman in the back row.

Would it be wise to tell the truth? Emily rubbed the back of her neck, wondering when they were going to get around to quizzing Tad. She didn't know if it was nerves or the hot lights, but her skin was already damp. "I'll have the satisfaction of knowing that I'll be a constant irritation to Mr. Aubrey."

Unexpected laughter erupted from the crowd of reporters. Emily glanced at Tad to see how he was taking her sudden attack on him. He was unperturbed, for which she was grateful.

"What do you have to say about that, Mr. Aubrey?" another man questioned.

Tad turned toward Emily and his eyes seemed to smile at her before he faced the reporters again. Her stomach tightened. "Look at her," he said in a low-pitched voice, deliberately thickening his European accent in order to be provocative, implying their relationship might be more than simply business. "Could a woman this lovely irritate anyone?"

More laughter. Emily pursed her lips. He gave as easily as he took. She suddenly realized that he was playing a part, trying to win the audience. Maybe he'd missed his calling. He should have been an actor, not a producer.

"Do you have anything to add to that, Mrs. Spencer?" someone from way in the back asked.

"Clements," she corrected in a firm tone that made her pleased with herself. "Ask Mr. Aubrey the same question this time next week and see if he has changed his mind." She turned to Tad, her confidence showing in the smile she wore on her face. He acknowledged it with a slight nod of his head and an expression that said, *"You asked for it."*

The press conference lasted exactly an hour, then the man who had showed them into the room stood and said there would be no more questions. With Tad again at her side, Emily walked out of the room as quietly as she had entered. Her back was ramrod straight, her teeth pressed so tightly together her jaw ached.

Emily felt drained from the constant questions about her relationship with Tad. The reporters didn't want to believe there was *no* relationship to talk about. She felt a stiffness emanating from Tad as he walked beside her. She knew he wasn't happy about the interview, either. In cold silence he steered her to the back door, away from everyone on the soundstage and outside into the shadows of late afternoon.

"Where have you been hiding your viper's tongue?" he asked as soon as they were alone.

Emily took off the clinging jacket of her linen suit and unbuttoned the first three buttons of her blouse. An hour under those hot lights had left her feeling uncomfortably sticky. She lifted her hair off her damp neck and met his cold stare. "You led those reporters to believe there was a romance going on between us," she accused.

"You wanted them to believe we're snarling adversaries tearing at each other's throats," he countered in the same angry tone of voice she had used.

"We are!" she snapped.

"What?" His eyes were no longer angry, but seemed confused for a moment. He looked at her with a curious expression. "What in the hell are we doing working together, if that's the case?"

"I've made it quite clear to you, Tad. I didn't want this movie to be made. I still don't. I'm here for one reason, and one reason only—to see that you don't discredit Gary's name in any way."

"If you're going to make it sound like a prison sentence, we'll call it quits right now. I don't need you hanging around here making my life miserable." He stuffed his hands into the pockets of his summer slacks, dropping his sophistication like a soiled garment. "One of the reasons I asked you to help was to get you off my back."

"What?" It was Emily's turn to be confused.

"Don't tell me you're truly that naive, Emily? I can make this movie with or without your help. I knew if I could persuade you to work with me, you wouldn't keep me tied up in the appeals court and possibly keep this production held up for years. This movie has to be made while people still remember your husband's name, and I intend to do it one way or the other."

Anger coiled tightly inside Emily. He'd made her think he needed her to make this movie a success! "You arrogant—" She bit her tongue to keep from saying the word.

"Bastard? From time to time," he admitted dryly.

A fire burned inside her, flooding her with its heat, its fury. Muggy air hung around her like a wet sheet. Her hands wrung the expensive jacket she still held.

"You do need *me*!" she declared prophetically. "You're a perfectionist. This movie won't be perfect without my guidance. You're reaching for an Emmy and you intend to get one from this picture. You can't do that without me!"

"Watch me." His tone was confident, his eyes cold.

Emily was shocked by her own words. They'd tumbled from her lips as if someone else was speaking them. She didn't know where they'd come from, or if they were true.

One corner of Tad's mouth slowly lifted in a disarming smile that not only brought a change in him, but in the atmosphere around them, as well. With that look he had maneuvered their argument to an intimate level. Emily took a step backward.

Tad folded his arms across his chest and chuckled derisively. "So this mistaken liaison between us has been reduced to its basest form. We need each other."

His words made her skin prickle. "I don't need you." Each word was formed with a hiss.

He watched her closely. "Really? Prove it. Walk away right now and leave me to make this picture however I see fit." His expression told her he was capable of letting her do just that. "Well, Emily? I'm waiting."

Emily searched his dark brown eyes. He had a point. No, more than a point—he was right. She wouldn't walk away. Never!

Taking a deep breath, she acceded. "All right, I guess we do need each other." She stepped closer to him, his height and size no deterrent to her words. "But don't you ever again, at any time, hint to anyone that I'm doing this out of a romantic interest in you or to earn your gratitude, as you implied to the press just now."

"Which you quickly shot down with your caustic barbs," he said in a deeply annoyed tone.

"Which I'll continue to deny at every opportunity," she insisted.

"Then you'll constantly have reporters snapping at your heels," he warned. "You gave the reporters the meat for their story. Hoping to quell their interest, you left them with the feeling 'the lady doth protest too much.'"

Realizing what he said was true, Emily felt a cold chill wash over her. She had played into the reporters' hands by being outraged at their probing insinuations about a love affair with Tad. How could she have let that happen?

"I had to deny it," she argued, her voice softening, her anger subsiding. "Their hints at romance were ridiculous, but they spurred a defensive mechanism I couldn't control. It seemed such a violation for them to suggest an involvement between us." She lowered dark lashes over pain-filled eyes. "How could something like that even enter their minds?"

"Emily." He said her name softly. "Surely you're not that naive. Whether it's true or not, romance sells papers and magazines. Your denial gave them exactly what they wanted. A good story."

"Do you think anyone will believe it?"

"Of course they will, because they want to. That's why people read the gossip section of the newspaper. The only person I'm worried about is a certain woman who happens to be very important to me right now. I'm afraid this will take a lot of explaining."

Emily thought of Nathan. "Yes, I know what you mean. It just doesn't seem fair."

"Life seldom is, but I'll play fair with you, Emily. And in return, I expect the same. I am not a modern day Lord Byron, as you suggested. I assure you my sexual exploits are not as *varied* or as *numerous* as you've been led to believe. And your statement about my dressing like a dandy set my teeth on edge."

Smiling to herself, Emily ran a hand through her damp hair. If it had bothered him, it had been worth the agony. "So, it's settled. You don't say anything about me, and I won't say anything about you." She was tired, drained, but determination spurred her on. "Tad, I'm not going to let you make a circus out of this movie."

Intense dark eyes stared at her. "I don't want a circus, Emily. I want an Emmy."

EMILY HAD COFFEE SENT to her room as soon as she returned to her hotel. For a while, she'd cut down on the amount she had been drinking, but the habit had resurfaced. Anyone else staying in the Beverly Hills Hotel would be heading for the Polo Lounge to see if any movie stars had gathered there for an early evening cocktail and the latest Hollywood gossip. All Emily wanted was a cup of coffee, a bath, and to hear Nathan's voice.

As she sipped the cooling coffee, she sat down on the edge of the window seat and looked at the burning blue sky of early twilight, wondering what Nathan would think of the implied romance between Tad and herself. Would he believe it? Would he be jealous?

She had called his apartment in Washington twice already. It was past dinnertime in the east, but Nathan still wasn't home. He could be at a meeting with the senator, or at a late dinner.

Emily drained her cup and let it settle on the saucer with a clatter. What was the matter with her? She couldn't start depending on Nathan. She had to get through this on her own. But that didn't keep her from missing him and wanting to talk to him.

I'm just tired, she told herself. She'd call again after she had a bath. If he still wasn't in, well—she'd wait and let him call her. He knew where she was staying.

Emily wasn't disappointed. As soon as she sat down in the tub of hot water the telephone rang. Certain it was Nathan, she hurried out of the water and grabbed a towel as she ran back into the bedroom, picking up the phone on its fourth ring.

"Hello." Her greeting was breathless.

"Emily, it's Nathan. How are things going in sunny California?"

Emily smiled. Hearing his voice made her warm all over. She tucked the plush towel underneath her arms and sat down on the bed. "I haven't even noticed whether or not it's sunny. Does that tell you what kind of a day it's been?"

"Sounds like a hectic one. There wasn't any mention of the interview on the D.C. news. How did the interview go?"

"Oh, Nathan, it was dreadful. I don't think I'll ever understand reporters. They seem to think I'm romantically involved with Tad." She picked up the edge of the towel and wiped at the water running down her arm.

"I can't say I'm surprised, Emily. Hints of romance sell papers. Reporters are famous for it. Unfortunately Hollywood and Washington, D.C. are their two favorite places. Don't let it worry you. I'm sure they'll forget about it in a week."

"You don't believe it, do you?" She didn't know why she asked, maybe she just wanted his reassurance.

Nathan laughed huskily, invitingly. "No. Not on your part, anyway. Still, I don't like the idea that others might believe you're involved with him."

"Neither do I. How could anyone believe I'd be involved with the man who was making this movie?"

"Just don't try too hard to convince them otherwise. If they think you're hiding something, they'll never leave you alone."

Emily sighed. "Tad said as much. I guess the main thing is that the interview is over. And I hope I never have to do another one."

"I know you did a terrific job, so don't let it worry you. Haven't I said you can handle anything that comes up? Just keep telling yourself you can do it."

Smiling she said, "You're very good for me."

"You're good for me, too," he answered in a low tone.

"Even with all my hang-ups?"

Nathan laughed lightly. "You've got a few of them, that's for sure, but I think we're taking caring of them one by one. You're giving interviews and talking to reporters. You didn't do that when we first met. You're helping CAT and working on this movie. I'd say you've come a long way, and I plan to be around when you get to the finish line."

His words made Emily's heart quicken. "I'm beginning to believe there's going to be one. I'll be home on Friday. Do you have to spend the weekend in Washington?"

"No," he answered. "I'll be heading home on Saturday. Are you free for dinner?"

"I was hoping you'd ask. My house at seven?"

"We've got a date."

EARLY THE NEXT MORNING, the driver of the car dropped Emily off in front of the studio. Tad wasn't outside waiting for her as he had been the day before. That didn't surprise her. After their argument yesterday, she knew he wasn't going to pamper her. And that was the way she wanted it.

When she walked into the warehouse-sized room, she immediately saw Tad in the far corner, talking with a woman not any taller than herself. In contrast to Emily's designer summer suit, the woman wore faded jeans and an oversize T-shirt with the Paramount logo printed on the front.

"Good morning," Emily spoke to the chattering couple as she approached them.

"Ah, Emily, you're here. Good." His eyes took time to look her over. "I'd like you to meet Angelique, our casting director."

Emily shook hands with the woman. Now that she was closer, she saw that Angelique was more than twenty years her senior. She had a pretty face, but her smile was forced as she asked Emily, "Are you going to help us with all the casting, or just the lead?"

"Just the lead," Emily assured her. She wished Angelique hadn't tried to hide her disapproval. Obviously the other woman thought casting was her job, and she didn't want any assistance. That was too bad, Emily told herself. As far as she was concerned, picking the man who would play Gary was the most important and the hardest thing she would have to do.

"Excuse us for a moment, Angelique," Tad said, and touched her arm affectionately. "We'll meet you in the casting room in a few minutes. I need to speak to Emily."

"All right. I'll get things rolling so we'll be ready as soon as you two come in." Angelique turned and walked away.

Tad turned his attention back to Emily. He studied her for a moment, then said, "You look absolutely stunning in that lovely suit, Emily, but a movie studio is not the place to dress for a board meeting. I think you'd be more comfortable in—" He gestured with his hands trying to find the right words. "In more casual clothing," he finally decided.

Emily looked around the large room and saw that she was the only person who wasn't dressed in slacks or jeans and T-shirts, most of them bearing the Paramount logo. She turned back to Tad and asked, "Why didn't you suggest this yesterday?"

"Actually I thought the reason you dressed so formally yesterday was because of the interview. As you can see, even I'm dressed for work today."

Emily stared at his faded jeans and T-shirt with New York's skyline printed on the front. She hated to admit it, but with his slim build he looked good in anything. "Thanks for the suggestion. I'll remember that tomorrow."

"Good. We can get you something more comfortable from wardrobe, if you like?" he offered.

She thought about the idea for a moment. Wearing the clothes movie stars had worn did have a certain appeal.

"No, thanks," she said, pulling off her jacket. "I'll just make do with this today."

"All right, let's get started."

He wrapped his arm around her shoulder so quickly that Emily was startled and jumped away from him. "Don't touch me." Her voice was high with surprise.

"What's wrong with you? I only touched your shoulder." He glared at her.

"I don't want you to touch me at all," she protested. Maybe she was overreacting but she didn't believe for a moment the reporters had all they wanted. She couldn't cope with a picture of Tad and herself arm in arm on the front page of a daily newspaper.

There was a faint trace of anger in his dark eyes as he swore between clenched teeth. "I don't bite," he remarked.

"Yes, you do," she argued. "And your bite is sharp." She took a deep breath when she saw his features soften. "Tad, I don't want anything to happen between us that could be misconstrued. Not even a friendly pat on the shoulder. This is a business relationship."

She saw reluctant sympathy in his eyes, and he acknowledged her words with a nod. "Very well, I won't touch you again. You have my word on it," he promised.

"Thank you," she murmured quietly, then pressed her teeth into her bottom lip. She noticed several people had stopped to stare at them. She didn't know why she was being so irritable about it. Nathan hadn't sounded like he was the least bit worried about her relationship with Tad, and what he thought was the only thing that really concerned her. And that, she feared, was part of the problem.

"Shall we go?" he asked as his hand swept out to point the way. "Angelique is waiting for us."

Emily squeezed her eyes shut for a brief moment, then followed Tad. This was going to be a long week. Silently she made a vow to be nicer to Tad. He could decide she was too much trouble to deal with and he'd be better off without her.

The casting room was small and dark, except for two bright stage lights that illuminated a platform on the far end. As Tad showed her into the room, she saw that Angelique was sitting at a table on the other side.

"You need only remember two things, Emily," Tad told her as they crossed the floor. "If you think the actor has possibilities for playing the part of Gary, mark a 'two' beside his name. If not, then give him a 'one.' We'll compare the marks at the end of the day and ask for callbacks."

"That certainly seems easy enough." Emily took a chair at the end of the table, leaving the chair in the middle for Tad. While he spoke to Angelique, Emily picked up the sheet of paper and glanced at the list of names. She didn't recognize any of the hopefuls as being big stars, which for some strange reason made her feel better. Her stomach wasn't feeling any better; if anything it was worse.

When Tad gave the sign indicating they were ready, the first actor stepped from behind a curtain and stood on the lighted platform and stated his name. She noticed that Tad held a résumé with a black-and-white glossy head-shot of the actor glued to the back. Very efficient, she thought. That was one sure way of seeing that the picture stayed with the right résumé.

Tad spoke briefly with the man. As soon as he'd finished, the actor exploded into swift dialogue. She recognized the words from the part of the script where Gary was talking to one of the hijackers, asking him to let the women and children go.

The script was so real, the man so earnest, that Emily felt her face pale. The butterflies in her stomach turned into a mass of knots, and her hands trembled. She quickly untied the bow of her blouse and opened a couple of buttons, allowing her to breathe easier. This was the hardest thing she had to do. Once they selected the actor to play Gary, she'd be all right, she thought. She had to be. Three minutes later, the man was through and another took his place. Weakly, Emily marked a one by his name and wondered how many of these she had to go through and if she would make it.

After twenty or so actors had graced the platform, Tad called for a break and Emily was more than relieved. Even though it was air-conditioned, the room had become stuffy and hot. She had long since rolled up the sleeves of her silk blouse and opened more buttons. The strain of hearing those same words over and over again had her whole body taut.

During the first few auditions, she had questioned her sanity in putting herself through this. Each man looked less and less like Gary, but the dialogue was so hard to bear.

"Well, Emily," Tad queried, turning toward her. "How many possibilities do you have?"

"Oh," she mouthed as she looked at the paper filled with nothing but ones. She ran a shaky hand through her hair and answered, "I don't have any possibilities so far."

It was clear Tad wasn't happy with her answer, and neither was the casting director. Out of the corner of her eye, she saw a smirk cross Angelique's face and it angered her. She knew Angelique would give Tad the "I told you so" look. Emily resolved not to let the casting director pick the man who would play her husband. She'd find the right person.

"All right, let's see what Angelique has." He turned to the older woman and asked for her score sheet.

Emily glanced at Angelique's paper. She didn't have very many twos, either. However, Emily couldn't help but notice all of them matched Tad's except one. Rubbing the back of her damp neck, Emily looked over the sheets. Was she fooling herself? Could she be objective about this? Of course, she could. When the right actor came on the stage she'd know. Taking a deep breath, she realized she had to find the right man.

Later that afternoon, when lunch had been cleared away from the small table, Emily looked up to see an actor approaching the platform. Her breath left her lungs and lodged in her throat at the sight of him. He looked just like Gary. The way he moved, the way he carried himself, with a slight swing to his shoulders. The bounce in his step was familiar, and the way he wore his hair. His smile, oh, God, his smile! Emily's heart felt as if it were going to beat out of her chest.

"Gary?" she whispered huskily. Her body trembled as she tried to deny what her eyes saw. It couldn't be!

When he spoke, Emily moved to the edge of her seat, not wanting to believe there was someone who looked and sounded so much like Gary. She wanted to get closer. She wanted to see his hands. Did they look like Gary's, too? She had to talk to him. She rose from her seat.

"Gary?" she whispered as she started toward him.

"Emily." Tad touched her arm, and she swung around to face him.

"That's Gary," she said breathlessly.

"No, Emily, he's only an actor." His fingers closed around her arm as he rose from his chair.

She shook her head. "No, it's Gary, I tell you. Let me go. I've got to see him."

She pulled away from Tad's hold and started toward the young man as he continued the well-rehearsed speech. Without warning, someone grabbed her arm and jerked her around. Tad's hands dug painfully into her flesh, and she winced. He was holding her back, keeping her from Gary. "No. Turn me loose. I've got to talk to him," she pleaded.

Tad grasped her other arm and held her tight. "Listen to me! He's an actor playing a part, Emily, you're confused. Come with me and sit down."

Emily looked back at the man standing on the stage. Gary had come back to her. "No!" She groaned and tried to pull out of Tad's restraining hands. "Let go of me."

Tad pulled her closer, held her arms tighter and shook her. "Stop this, Emily," he said roughly. "He's not Gary. You're confused. Look at him, he's not Gary, he's an actor. Dammit, Emily, just turn around and take a good look at the man!"

Slowly his words penetrated. Emily turned to stare at the man standing quietly on the stage. He was silent, and she could see he wasn't Gary. Oh God, Gary was dead. Tears filled her eyes, then tumbled down her cheeks. For a few moments she had thought Gary had come back to her. She was going crazy.

She knew Tad was holding her, staring at her, but she couldn't take her gaze off the actor. He looked so much like Gary it was frightening.

"Come sit down, Emily." His voice was gentle, and she responded to it.

Emily let Tad lead her back to the table. She felt completely drained, as she sat back in the chair. What had happened to her? How could she have thought Gary had come back?

Tad kept his hand on her arm. He looked up at the actor and said, "That'll be all for now. We'll be in touch. Bring some water," he called to someone in the back of the room.

Swallowing, Emily mumbled again, "That's him. He looks just like Gary. It's the way he sounds, the way he moves and smiles. I wanted to see his hands."

Emily watched the man walk away, and the knot in her stomach grew larger. She turned back to Tad. "It's him," she said, then corrected herself by saying, "He's the one we want." She couldn't control the quiver in her voice, no more than she could control the shaking in her limbs. He looked so much like Gary. So much! She reached for the water that had been placed before her.

"Emily, you overreacted. I think you should go back to the hotel and let us finish this."

All right, she might have flipped out for a few moments, but she'd recovered. She knew exactly what she was saying. But she was in control of herself now. She rubbed her forehead, the back of her neck and down her shoulder.

She looked up and met Tad's dark brown eyes. "No, it's already finished. He's the man we want."

"He does have passion in his voice, but his facial expressions aren't that good," Tad reasoned in a whispered voice. "I don't think he's what we're looking for," Tad said under his breath, as if he intended that to be the last word on the subject.

"Then you're looking for the wrong actor, dammit," she said angrily. She wouldn't back down on this. This movie was about her husband, and she intended to see that this actor would be the man who portrayed him. She couldn't let anyone else do it.

"I told you I'd have final say over any disagreement," he reminded her in a clipped tone.

"You also said I could change your mind," she shot back just as quickly.

"I said you could try," he responded in a low, clear voice that left little room for doubt. "You're not yourself, Emily. I think you should go back to the hotel and rest. I didn't realize how difficult this would be for you."

"I'm all right," she answered, but knew she was weak. Watching that actor had almost sent her over the edge. "You're only saying this because of the way I reacted to him."

"Emily—"

"It's true. Admit it." Her voice was still shaky, and that angered her. "I promise I won't fall apart again."

They stared at each other, neither backing down until Angelique coughed behind them.

"You go on back to the hotel. Angelique and I will discuss him, and I'll call you later."

Emily rose on shaky legs and picked up her purse and jacket. She was empty and aching. "He's the man we want. I won't agree to anyone else." She grabbed the pencil and marked a large two by the actor's name, then turned and walked away.

Chapter Ten

"I'm talking too much, aren't I?" Emily asked as she looked over the candle flame and stared into Nathan's midnight blue eyes.

"No, I wanted to hear about your first week in Hollywood and about the movie."

"But you didn't expect to hear so much about the actor." Emily sighed, brushing her hair away from her forehead.

Nathan slid his empty plate aside and sipped his red wine. "Your emotional reaction to him is understandable." His voice was dry.

Emily couldn't help but notice that Nathan deliberately avoided her eyes. She wondered what he was thinking. Was he really as calm as he appeared? Or was his stomach churning like hers? He should have a stronger reaction. She'd just told him that the actor looked so much like Gary that for an irrational moment she thought Gary had returned to her.

Maybe if she changed the subject, things would be better. "I didn't mean to spoil our time together with so much chatter about what I've been doing. How are things in Washington?"

"Nothing new in Washington. Same old rhetoric." Nathan pushed his chair away from the table. "Come on, let's go sit on the couch." He helped her with her chair, then wrapped his arm across her shoulder as they walked together into the living room.

There was a certain amount of comfort in his touch, yet the tension mounted between them as they sat down. "Actually I could say the same thing. Nothing new is happening. Tad is only dramatizing the same old story that's been whirling around in my head for two years." She sighed. "It's just that it was so much worse than I expected. That man looked so much like Gary I was forced to remember things about him I thought I'd forgotten. For a few moments Gary was alive again. It was a feeling I'll never forget."

Nathan grabbed her shoulders harshly, and Emily's gaze flew to his face. "Dammit, Emily, what exactly are you saying? Gary's dead!" His eyes held the hint of frustration, his hands the strength of anger.

Stunned by his physical reaction, Emily was momentarily speechless. What was she trying to tell Nathan? Her heart beat loudly in her ears as she found her voice. "I'm telling you what I felt at the time. For a few minutes the past seemed very real."

"Let me tell you how I feel." His fingers dug into her arms. "I'm jealous as hell. I don't like you spending all this time with Tad. I'm jealous of some actor whose name I don't even know, and it tears me up inside to know you're thinking about Gary and your love for him, when I want to be the only man on your mind." The longer he spoke the softer his voice became. "I can't take anymore. I need to know that I have a chance of one day being the only man on your mind."

She didn't want to be thinking of Gary. Nathan was real, here. "I want that, too, but I'm frightened," she admitted.

"Why? Of what? Me?" he asked.

She shook her head. Her eyes pleaded for understanding. "Of the past. I want to think only of you, but Gary is still so much a part of my life I can't let him go." Emily closed her eyes in a spasm of guilt.

"Open your eyes, Emily," he whispered huskily, and she obeyed. "Who do you see?"

"You," she answered.

"That's right. What do you feel?"

"Your warm hands on my arms."

"Do you see or feel anyone else?"

"No," she said softly.

"That's right," he whispered. "I'm the only one here. Now close your eyes and tell me the first thing that crosses your mind."

Her lashes fell, and she saw stars twinkling against the black backdrop in front of her eyes. "Stars," she whispered. "I see stars."

His hands tightened on her arms. "So do I." His voice was raspy. "Every time I look at you I see stars. Open your eyes and look at me, Emily." She did. "I'm the one who needs you. Right now, I'm so eaten up with jealousy I'm going crazy. I don't want *anyone* on your mind except me. Do you know what I'm saying? I love you, Emily."

Emily nodded, although she wasn't sure she heard past his "I love you." He did say that, didn't he? His hands still held her upper arms so tightly she was losing circulation. Abruptly he let her go and stood up, combing through his hair with his hands.

He faced her with a troubled look, a deep sighing breath on his lips. "I'm sorry. I didn't mean to say that."

Emily gasped, her eyes opened wider, and she stared at Nathan. "I don't understand." Her breath caught again on her words.

Nathan's mouth tightened. He sat on the edge of the sofa beside her and took her hands in his. His short laugh had a bitter edge. "What I meant was that I didn't intend to tell you that I love you until after this movie is over and done with, and you're free of it. I don't want to interfere with what you have to do, but I'll be damned if I'm going to sit calmly by and watch you get all starry-eyed about some actor who looks like Gary." He watched her closely. "I may have to share you with his memory, but I won't share you with some real-life look-alike."

"You're not," she whispered, placing her hands lovingly against each side of his face. "You're not sharing me with anyone or anything. The only man I dream about is tall with midnight blue eyes, light brown hair, and he dresses in dark blue suits."

"Dammit, Emily, don't play games with me." Anger returned to his voice and his eyes. "You know you'd help my feelings quite a bit right now if you admitted you love me."

"I think I love you," she answered too calmly.

Nathan jerked away from her and stood up. "Oh, that's great, Emily. I love you, I missed you like hell and I want to be with you, and all you can say is you *think* you love me." He didn't try to hide his irritation.

She rose to stand before him. "Nathan, I'm attracted to you physically, emotionally and sexually. I missed you. I want to be with you, but I'm not sure it's love. All I know is that I haven't come close to feeling this way about any other man except Gary."

Nathan grabbed her arms so suddenly it startled her. His eyes were intense. His hands held her with strength, but she didn't mind.

"I want to make you forget about Gary. He's gone and he's never coming back. You've got to let him go." His arms slid around her waist and pulled her close. "I want to be the only man in your life. He has to go."

"I know." Emily circled his neck with her arms and looked into his eyes as Gary faded from her mind. She lifted her lips to his and touched them reverently at first. A rising hunger, like nothing she'd ever known, grew inside her. Tonight had been a long time coming.

Nathan buried his face in her neck and kissed the hollow between her throat and shoulders, sending shivers up her spine. He moaned his approval when she cupped his face with her hands and sought his lips with her own.

"You're beautiful, Emily," he whispered against her lips. "I'm glad you're home. It seems so long since I've held you. Has it been months or years?"

Emily smiled as her hands moved up and down the width of his shoulders, exploring his muscled back. "It's only been a week, but it does seem like years since we've been this close."

"Mmm, you smell good. You feel so good, and you taste even better." When his lips touched hers, the kiss was possessive, seductive.

His breath was hot, moist, enticing her to encourage him. His lips found the pulse point of her neck, accelerated the erratic drum of her pounding blood, made her weak with desire for him.

Nathan's arms slid around her, taking time to caress the contours of her body before his hands met at her back. His kiss gentled, while his movements grew even more erotic.

"Emily." His voice was a husky murmur in the still room. "Let me show you how much I want you. Let me make love to you."

"Yes," she whispered. Their kisses turned into little hungry bites of pleasure.

Emily's senses were acute to everything about him. With every breath the clean scent of shaving soap, the scent that meant Nathan, surrounded her, drew her to him. Her tongue explored the depths of his mouth, tasting the intoxicating wine that clung to his lips and lingered on his breath. Giving her hands freedom, Emily kneaded the lean corded muscles of his back and neck. She returned his kisses with fervor; harder, softer, she couldn't decide which she liked better.

"I've wanted to do this since the first day I saw you," Nathan admitted between kisses. "You were so beautiful, so vulnerable."

Lost in his warmth, she savored his words of love. It was his lips that kissed her, his eyes that watched her, his hands that caressed her, slipping beneath her cotton sweater and finding her breasts. It was Nathan and no one else. There could be no one else when there was Nathan.

Emily pulled away. He questioned her with his eyes. "Not here," she said. She rose and reached for his hand. In one fluid motion, Nathan came to his feet and folded Emily's hand in his own.

The bedroom was bathed with soft, warm light from the hallway. Stopping in front of the bed, Nathan pulled her into his arms, crushing her breasts against his chest, arching her hips against his, and kissed her hungrily.

"I've wanted you for so long," he said softly, earnestly.

"I've been waiting for this a long time, too. I want to rush it and savor it at the same time. Can we do that?" she asked breathlessly.

Little raindrop kisses brushed her eyes and cheeks as he pressed her against his hardness. "I don't know. My body is telling me to rush it this time and savor it the next." He hugged her tightly. "Emily, you make me feel so damn good."

"Oh, Nathan," she whispered against his neck. She loved to bury her nose in the sensitive skin there and breathe in his scent. She couldn't get enough of him.

"Let me undress you," he murmured against her ear. "I know how beautiful you are, and I'm aching to see all of you."

Gently he released her. Nathan couldn't slow his breathing. He was too excited. This was too real. He took the hem of her sweater and carefully pulled it over her head and tossed it aside.

She wore the sexiest bra he'd ever seen, the color almost the same shade as her skin. The way it fit her breasts made his throat go dry. He wanted to rip it off and devour her, but he knew he needed to take it slower. Forcing himself to remain calm, he reached for the zipper of her slacks. Undressing her was sweet torture.

He followed the pants down her legs, helping her step out of her shoes, then the slacks. The pressure of her hands on his shoulders as she steadied herself warmed him.

A fine tremor shook him as he slowly wrapped his hands around one leg, caressing her soft skin all the way up to her panties. Did they have to be that lacy, that sheer, that tempting? He'd longed to touch her like this, to feel her silkiness.

"Oh," he whispered, huskily. "I don't know how long I can hold out."

Kneeling, he slid his arms around her buttocks and buried his face in the lower part of her stomach and breathed in deeply. She smelled sweet. He had to taste her. Kissing the silky skin of her inner thigh, he let his tongue leave a trail of moisture in its wake. A shudder passed through her, heightening his arousal. Her arms circled his head and her hands stroked his shoulders and back, sending him to the breaking point. He didn't want to rush it, but he had to go faster than this. He was dying.

Rising from his knees, he took her with him and laid her on the bed, settling his body over hers.

The sheets were cold to her back, yet the shivers shaking her had nothing to do with them. It was Nathan, all Nathan. His touch flamed through her body, heating her with anticipation, burning her with wanting. His body lay heavy, hot and hard upon her. She'd never known such wanting. Never.

When their eyes met in the dim light, he whispered, "I love you, Emily. I want to look at you. I want you to look at me."

"Yes," she whispered. "I want to see all of you. I want to touch you everywhere. I want to love you."

His fingers fumbled with the front clasp of her bra, and when it gave way, he reverently pushed the sides away from her breasts.

"You are beautiful, and I love you." His voice was intimate, sensuous and when he looked back into her eyes she knew he meant every word.

He loved her and at that moment she knew she loved him. All her doubts were gone. Suddenly she didn't want to wait any longer. With shaky fingers Emily unbuttoned his shirt, while he removed his pants. Their movements were frantic, urgent, demanding, until the last piece of clothing was cast aside. She didn't think of anyone but Nathan. She wanted only to touch and be touched, to love and be loved, to give and to take.

She welcomed him into her arms, into her body to become one with him. Her desire for him was so intense, the rapture of feeling him inside her so ravaging, she only said his name once before she shuddered with fulfillment. Nathan was only a second behind her.

A few moments later Emily lay wrapped in Nathan's arms waiting for her breathing to slow. It had never happened so quickly before. She had never known such desperation, such fierce ardor, and she'd never felt so complete afterward.

Even though her eyes were closed, she knew Nathan was watching her. She wondered if their coming together had shaken him to the core, too. It happened so quickly, there wasn't enough time for all the loving and touching she wanted. She didn't get to see and touch all of him. She wanted more. A smile crept across her closed lips. She was in love with Nathan and it felt wonderful.

"Why are you smiling, Emily?"

Emily opened her eyes and looked at him, letting her gaze travel down the length of his gorgeous, manly body before returning to his face. He was smiling, too. He lay on his side facing her. One arm under her head, the other across her waist. His eyes twinkled in the soft light.

"I do love you, Nathan," she answered.

"Oh, so now you know for sure, do you?" He grinned as his hand ran over her hip and down her leg and back again. "Did you have to try me before you were certain?"

"Now that you mention it, maybe that is what I was doing." She smiled sweetly.

"You're lying," he teased. "I know you would have never made love to me if you didn't love me."

"What makes you so sure of that?" She caressed his cheek with the back of her hand.

He caught her hand in his and kissed her palm. "Let's just say I know, and let it go at that."

She laughed lightly. "It was wonderful. Everything I expected and more."

"For me, too, and I'd say that's worth smiling about." He brushed a wisp of hair away from her cheek.

She wanted him to know how she felt. She wanted to know if it had been as good for him as it was for her. "It was wonderful. I've never felt so complete, so full—like nothing's missing."

"I knew it'd be that way between us, Emily. I knew it'd be worth the wait."

"The wait?" She teased, rubbing her hand up and down the smooth skin of his hip. "I thought we rushed it."

"We're not talking about the same thing." He smiled and kissed her temple. "I knew I wanted to make love to you the first day I saw you. But we took our time and got to know each other before we made love." He rolled over on top of her and looked deeply into her eyes. "I wasn't disappointed. I'm sorry I rushed our first time together, Emily, but I've been aching for months. I wanted you so badly I didn't take the time I should have."

The hardness of his body told her he wanted her again. She shivered with longing. "I didn't want to wait, either," she reminded him. Rotating her hips beneath him, she asked seductively, "We don't have to rush this time, do we?"

Nathan caught his breath as her hands slipped between them, to that part of him she was eager to touch.

"No, my love. This time, we take the whole night and savor it."

MONDAY MORNING EMILY LOOKED out the patio door of her condo and found a brassy sun floating in a cloudless blue sky. Nathan stood beside her. The silence between them had been stretched to the limit, still neither of them spoke.

The weekend had gone too quickly. She didn't want Nathan to leave. Not even for a moment. She loved him too deeply. How was she going to manage without him for weeks?

"So it looks like this is going to be a long-distance relationship for a while." Nathan was the first to speak. "You have commitments in California, and I have to be in Washington. In fact, I'll have very few free days between now and the time Congress breaks for the holidays."

Emily's stomach knotted, and she sank her teeth into her bottom lip. She was definitely unhappy about that. But her work on this movie was as important as Nathan's work, and he knew it. She also knew he'd never ask her to give it up, even though it troubled him.

"That will be about the time the movie is finished." She rubbed the back of her neck and walked away from the door, wanting to put some distance between them. Whenever she was close to him she wanted to touch him, to run her hands up his chest, over his shoulders, down his back. This was the time for goodbye, not for clinging.

"Maybe I can fly to Washington for a couple of days later in the month. We might get lucky and you can come to California, too." She made an effort to smile.

"I know I'll try. Emily, I don't want to leave you today. I haven't had enough of you to keep me warm until I see you again." His voice was low, a hint of regret in its tone.

"I feel the same way, but there's nothing we can do. Our responsibilities are taking us in different directions. I guess we're going to have to plan for some busy holidays." Her words were an attempt to lighten the mood.

"How about a skiing trip to Colorado? You said you'd like to learn how to ski. Can I make reservations for two?" He walked over, pulled her into his arms and rested his cheek against her head.

"Sure. I'm not going to let you go alone this year."

He had the warmest body. His heat surrounded her, making her feel protected, loved. Emily didn't want to believe it would be a couple of months before they'd have more than a weekend to spend together.

"What are you going to do about your fish?" He rocked her gently back and forth.

For a moment the gurgling of the tank's filtering system was the only sound in the room. "I'll call Janice later and see if she wants them. Being a schoolteacher, I'm sure she can find someone who'd like to have them." She snuggled closer to him. "The tough part comes in the morning when I resign from my job at Stobey and Ackerman."

"That's a big step, Emily. Can't you take a leave of absence?"

She looked up at him. "In reality that's what I'll be doing. I'll keep my licenses up to date so I can return to real estate after the first of the year."

"Sounds like this movie is going to be your life for the next few weeks." There was a touch of jealousy in his tone, but she didn't mind. It meant he cared.

Her gaze lingered on every detail of his face. "I'll think about you each day."

Nathan smiled. "And I'll be thinking about you and wishing we were together."

He kissed her with hunger. Her body responded. A tremor shook him. His lips left hers and brushed along her cheek before he turned and walked away.

"EMILY, COME IN," Mr. Stobey said as he removed his pipe from his mouth and laid it in the crystal ashtray. "I think I know why you're here, but I'll let you do the talking."

"Thank you, Mr. Stobey." When she had settled on the chair, she nervously took a deep breath. She felt good about her decision to leave, but that didn't make quitting any easier to do.

"I've decided to resign. As you know, I have a lot of personal matters to attend to right now, and I'm not doing justice to my clients. You haven't said anything about all the time I've taken off from work, and I want you to know I appreciate it."

"Yes, I was sure this was what you wanted to see me about," he said, watching her carefully. "I didn't say anything before because I felt sure you were going to realize for yourself that you needed to take a leave of absence." He shifted in his chair. "I had already made up my mind to say something today, if you didn't."

"I was hoping I could handle both the movie and my job here, but now I see that's impossible."

"Why don't we just put you on the inactive list. That way we'll continue to hold your license and you won't have to go to a lot of trouble if you decide to come back." He paused and picked up his pipe. "And I hope you do."

"I'm sure I'll come back to real estate someday, so yes, I'd like to keep my licenses here. I don't want them to expire."

For the first time, she really appreciated the fact that Gary's estate had left her well provided for. If not, she wouldn't be able to quit her job and accept this nonpaying position with Dreamstar.

"Good, I think that's the best thing to do for the time being. If you'd like, I'll have Melody mail you the status sheets each week so you can keep up with what comes on the market and what sells."

Feeling more at ease with the way things were going, Emily smiled at the older man. "That would be great, Mr. Stobey. I'd like to keep up with as much as possible." She hadn't expected him to be this nice and understanding. He'd never been the kind of man she could get close to.

"Now about the clients you're currently handling— have you spoken with them about your decision?" He picked up his unlit pipe and put it between his teeth.

"No, I wanted to talk with you first." Emily ran a hand through her hair. "Actually I only have one listing at this time. The Saxtons. If you remember, I spoke with you about their listing a month or so ago."

"Ah, yes. The one that Raymond handled for you back in the summer," he said.

"Yes, that's the one. I don't know what your policy is, when an agent resigns. Am I at liberty to give the listing to the agent of my choice?"

"Well, since Raymond has already worked with them, I think we should just let him take over, if the Saxtons are willing. Of course you'll receive the usual referral fee."

Having to give her last client to Raymond bothered Emily. Even his name left a bad taste in her mouth. She hadn't spoken with him since she had returned from California. He was the one reason she was glad to be leaving Stobey and Ackerman. She contemplated trying to change Mr. Stobey's mind, but decided she had too many other things to worry about. She would let Raymond have the Saxtons, but not before she told him a few things.

"All right. Then it's all settled. I'll clean out my desk." She rose from her chair. "Thank you for all your help, Mr. Stobey. You've been more than generous."

"You're a good agent, Emily. I hate to lose you. But I'm going to expect to see you again in here when things settle down."

She shook his hand. "It's nice to know I have a place I can come back to."

Funny, but she felt as if a weight had been lifted off her shoulders when she walked back into the main office. She had one more thing to clear up before leaving. Raymond Sanders.

He was talking on the telephone, so she went to her desk and started putting her personal things into a shopping bag. It was rather odd, but after having worked here for over two years she felt no sadness in leaving. There were no ties to bind her. She realized she had the same feeling for her condominium. She could move away today and never look back.

Raymond was still on the phone when she finished. Thinking maybe she could hurry him along, she walked over and sat down on the chair in front of his desk. He eyed her warily for a moment but continued his conversation for a while longer. There was something inside her that wouldn't let her leave without telling Raymond what she thought about him.

When at last he hung up he swung his chair around to face her. "Well, if it isn't my old pal Emily Spencer." He leaned over his desk and asked in a whispered voice, "What was it like sleeping with the famous Tad Aubrey? I hear movie producers have—ah—weird tastes. I'm sure you know what I mean." He smiled and sat back in his chair.

Emily gave him a sardonic grin. "Raymond, do you lie awake at night thinking of crude things to say, or do they just roll off your vile tongue?"

"They just ease off," he said in a lascivious manner, his tongue coming out to wipe his lips. "But Emily, what I read in the papers about you is much more exciting than anything I could dream up. I'm all ears. Tell me everything."

It was impossible to have a normal conversation with him. She should have known Raymond would find some way to get hold of Hollywood's society papers. According to the daily column, she was Tad's latest lover. What a laugh. They were barely on speaking terms.

"I expected someone like you to believe everything you read, or did someone have to read it to you?"

Raymond laughed. One of the things she disliked about Raymond was that he was too arrogant to be insulted.

"I wanted to let you know that I've resigned from my position here, and Mr. Stobey has asked that I give the Saxtons' listing to you. With their approval, of course."

His eyes shone brightly and he sat up straight. "Hey, this is big news. I guess you've really fallen for this guy. But let me give you a little advice, Emily." He leaned closer to her again. "These rich-and-famous movie-star types don't hang around very long. They get bored with the innocent type real easily, if you know what I mean."

She wished she didn't. "I'll be stopping by to see the Saxtons when I leave here. I'll tell them you'll be in touch." She rose from her chair. "Oh, and Raymond, there's one other thing I want to say before I leave. You are, without a doubt, the rudest man I have ever met, and you have no class or sophistication whatsoever."

Satisfied that she had delivered the most cutting words she would allow herself to say, she turned on her heel and walked away.

Before she was out of earshot, Raymond's racy laugh drifted past her along with the words, "I love it when you get mean, Emily. I'll be waiting when Tad's through with you."

Even though his crude comment made her shudder, she wouldn't dignify it with one of her own. She picked up her shopping bag and walked over to Melody's desk.

"Is that jerk giving you a hard time?" Melody asked.

Emily gave her an easy smile. "As usual. I've decided I'll speak to Mr. Stobey about Raymond before I'll come back in January."

"You can try, but I don't think it will do any good. Raymond makes sales and that's what's important to Mr. Stobey."

"I won't come back without trying." She cast her gaze around to Raymond. He was back on the phone. Good. Maybe she could get out before he decided he had something else to say to her. "I told Lucy Morrow that you'll be coming to the next CAT meeting, and she's pleased. Membership is so important right now."

"I want to be a part of it. I've supported MADD and SADD and a few other groups. But remember, you have promised to tell me all about Hollywood when you return."

Emily laughed. "I will. Keep your arm in shape while I'm gone." She reached over and gave Melody a brief affectionate hug before turning away.

Chapter Eleven

"Tad, I'd like your help with something," Emily said as she walked toward him, careful not to trip over one of the many camera cords littering the soundstage.

Glancing up from the script he was reading, Aubrey gave her a wary look. "Did I hear you correctly? You want my help? What's come over you, Emily?"

She'd never tire of his accent. It was so pleasant to the ear. He had reason to be cautious, though. She usually stayed as far away from him as possible.

"You've heard me mention CAT, the organization I'm involved with back in Florida."

"Mmm, yes," he answered, then looked back at the script booklet he held and turned the page.

He couldn't have appeared less interested. Really she couldn't blame him. She had avoided any attempts at friendship, preferring distance. They had worked together for six weeks. In that time, they'd had very little to do with each other outside the studio or the filming of *Hero*.

This wasn't easy. Taking a deep breath, she took the plunge. "I want you to help me give a fund-raiser for CAT."

He closed the script with a thump and gave her his full attention. His eyes studied her face. "You want me to help you give a fund-raiser for CAT?"

"Yes. I was hoping we could have it at your house in Beverly Hills."

"You want to have it at my house?" A look of incredulity crossed his face.

"Tad, you sound like parrot repeating everything I say." Her tone was edgy, but fear of rejection made her rush. She had to be nicer, if she was going to talk him into this. There wasn't a reason in the world why he should help her. That made it all the harder for her to ask.

He chuckled nervously. "I'm sorry, Emily. This has taken me completely by surprise."

She brushed a lock of hair away from her forehead. "I know, I'm not saying this well, but I don't know any other way to ask. I know we haven't been friends. The truth is, I haven't even been nice to you most of the time. But, Tad, this is for a good cause."

"Whose fault is it we haven't been friends?" he asked.

"Mine. I admit it. It's been so important to me that our relationship be circumspect, so the reporters wouldn't give us a hard time."

"Has it kept them from writing their stories?" he asked, his own tone impatient.

"No," she admitted reluctantly. "They still say we're lovers."

He gave a short laugh. "You amaze me, Emily. Did I understand you correctly? You want me to do something for you, based on a friendship we've never had?"

He was right. She did have a lot of nerve. "I guess I'm being a jerk for even asking, but this is too important to let pride stand in the way." She exhaled slowly and looked around the studio. It didn't appear that anyone in the crew had noticed that they were having an argument. She moistened her lips and continued. "I'm asking you to please host the fund-raiser. I think everyone I've gotten to know here on the set will come, but you know so many more people than I do, I was hoping you would invite some others."

He leaned a hip against a table behind him. "Let me see if I have this right. You want me to host this party and invite the guests? And you probably expect me to pay for it." His eyes grew wide, his brow puckered into a frown. "You're incredible."

"I know. Will you do it?" She would have never been this forward six months ago, but she'd changed. This was an excellent way to start the Los Angeles chapter of CAT. She had to talk him into it.

"No."

"Why not? It's for a good cause. You can't just say no without giving me a reason." She couldn't believe she was badgering him. Her heart was pounding in her ears, her hands were sweaty, and she had the nerve to continue. Suddenly she was very pleased with herself.

"I don't have time. I'm not interested, and I can name a dozen other reasons why I can't do it, if those two aren't enough." He threw the script on a small table and turned away.

"Tad, wait." She grabbed his arm and forced him to face her. Blood was racing to her head, making her hot. "Hear me out. I haven't given you all the details."

"Maybe you didn't hear me." His eyes darkened and his accent thickened. "I'm not interested in your little group, so go peddle your plan elsewhere."

"Don't be so stubborn that you won't even listen to me. There's something in this for you, too." She was grateful her voice remained firm even though she was losing.

Tad glanced at the tight hold she had on his arm, then their eyes met. She expected a look that could kill; instead he appeared amused. She turned him loose and wiped her hand down the side of her cotton slacks. A quick glance around the room confirmed that others had finally heard them, but Emily couldn't let that stop her. "At least give me the chance to explain."

He leaned against the table again. "All right. Go on, Emily. I want to hear what's in this for me."

She took a deep breath and realized her chest ached. Her stomach was jumpy. She wasn't quite sure why she was sticking her neck out for an organization she had become involved with just a few months before. Maybe guilt was the reason. The movie had taken so much of her time, she hadn't done anything for CAT. All her good intentions had been pushed to the future while she worked on *Hero*.

"First, as I said, this is for a good cause. Second, we plan to have reporters cover the event, which will mean publicity for CAT, the actors and *Hero*."

Pushing a camera out of his way, Tad leaned against the wall, supporting himself with one foot. "So this is what's in it for me. Publicity for *Hero*."

"Yes." The way he said it didn't make it seem like much. She had a feeling his attitude would be different if she'd been nicer to him from the start of their relationship. It had never occurred to her that she might one day need something from him.

He folded his arms across his chest. "And all I have to do is open my home to all these people and feed them caviar and champagne?"

"Yes."

He laughed heartily. "Emily, you have more brass than most American women I've met. I find that very exciting. Extremely attractive."

She swallowed hard. "Will you do it?"

"I'll tell you what I'll do, Emily." He hesitated. "I'll think about it."

"I need an answer," she said quickly, sensing that he was weakening. "Senator Merritt from Florida has already agreed to come, and I was hoping to get one of California's senators here, too. I thought the Saturday after Thanksgiving would be a good time because Congress will break for the holiday."

He shook his head as his dark eyes peered into hers.

"Have you left anything out?" he asked ruefully.

Emily moistened her lips. "I don't think so."

"Sounds like you have everything all worked out. Why even bother to ask me? Why not just show up at my house? I couldn't have been more surprised."

He wasn't taking this well. She hadn't expected him to be thrilled about it, but she had hoped he'd agree. "I know this is sudden. But the president of CAT called a couple of days ago and asked if I could pull it off. I agreed to try. Tad, you've got to know it hasn't been easy asking this of you."

"You could have fooled me."

"Oh, Tad." She felt like a first-class jerk. Why had she let Lucy Morrow talk her into this? Movie stars, directors and producers such as Tad didn't do anything they didn't want to do.

"All right. We need publicity for *Hero*." He rubbed his chin. "If I do this for you, you'll have to return the favor."

His words thrilled her and made her uncomfortable at the same time. "If you host the party, I'll have to do something for you in return?"

"That's the way it's always been between us, Emily." His voice lowered and he smiled. "Remember, we need each other."

Emily's skin prickled. She didn't like the sound of that. A chill crept up her back, and a vague feeling that they had been at this point before hung over her.

Clearing her throat, she asked, "What did you have in mind?"

"Publicity."

Funny, the word didn't scare her as it once had. It no longer bothered her when a reporter stumbled onto the set of *Hero,* or the papers ran an outrageous story. "What kind?"

"*Hero* will be airing in January. I'll arrange for interviews on 'Good Morning America,' 'Today' and maybe a couple of other shows. I think it would be impressive to have you hype the film about your husband. We usually use the star of the movie, but in this case I think a new twist is in order. What do you say? I'll help you with CAT, and you make the talk-show circuit. Do we have a deal, Emily?"

That old fear crawled up Emily's spine. Talking about Gary in front of the camera was the last thing she wanted to do. She wanted to help CAT, but could she go on national television and ask millions of people to watch the movie about her husband's death?

She looked up at Tad. He was waiting. He knew what it would cost her to say yes. She could see it in his eyes. "I—I don't know if I can do that."

"There's no hurry. Think about it." He smiled, then turned and walked away.

"Damn you, Tad Aubrey," she whispered to his back as her hands made fists. CAT needed that fund-raiser for the California chapter. People in the entertainment business were known for helping the homeless, earthquake victims, farmers and many more groups. She wanted to help CAT, but—Emily remembered Lucy Morrow's words that night she attended the CAT meeting at the university. *"I know the first thing you're going to say is, I'd like to help, but—"*

Emily closed her eyes for a brief moment and took a deep breath. "Tad?" she called.

He turned around. "Well, Emily?"

She walked toward him with outstretched hand. They had a deal.

OH, IT IS GRAND, Emily thought as she looked over the grounds behind Tad's twenty-room house sitting on a secluded cliff in the midst of Beverly Hills, California. It was definitely a scene right out of a Hollywood movie.

Already the place was crowded with reporters, TV personalities, movie stars, directors and probably a few hopefuls. She smiled at the chattering groups of luminaries as she made her way down to the pool. The mid-afternoon sun was playing peekaboo with light gray clouds that floated across the pale sky.

The pool had a beautiful crest of dark blue ceramic tile. Its kidney shape wasn't unusual; however in the curve of the kidney stood a statue of a winged cherub with a stream of water spewing from its mouth. Emily smiled. Tad did have a certain style.

"Welcome to my home, Emily. I'm sorry I wasn't at the door to greet you."

Turning to face Tad, her eyes lighted with friendliness. Since the day she'd asked him to host this party, their relationship had changed. They had had lunch together, had gone shopping on Rodeo Drive and had taken the Universal Studios tour together. Once she had gotten to know him, Emily had found Tad to be a charming man with a wonderful sense of humor. She enjoyed being around him. They'd truly become good friends.

She reached up and kissed his cheek. "Tad, this is all so beautiful. Your home is lovely. I'm so happy you agreed to hold this fund-raiser here. I know it'll be a big success."

"I think the reason you are so happy is because your lover will be walking through that door soon." He pointed behind him.

"That is probably ninety-nine percent of it." She'd checked the door every minute since she arrived. "It's been ten weeks since I've seen him."

"You should have gone to Washington the weekend we filmed in New Mexico," he chided her.

"I would have, but as you remember, Nathan couldn't get any free time."

"For you, he should have made time."

Tad wasn't going to let Nathan off the hook, but she didn't mind. "I want to thank you again for sending the limo for Nathan and the senator."

Tad laughed and settled mirrored sunglasses over his eyes. "What's a few more dollars? So what do you think? Did I do a good job?" His hand swept across the area.

A table was set up at one end of the pool, draped in white linen, and covered with hors d'oeuvres of various sizes, tastes and shapes. A portly man stood behind the table, impeccably and formally dressed, waiting to attend to anyone's wishes. Champagne flowed freely to every guest.

"You really know how to throw a party," she praised him. "I'm impressed."

"I hope you know I wouldn't do this for many people."

"I do." She smiled knowingly. "And I hope you know I wouldn't go on national television for many people."

Tad laughed. "Emily, you have challenged me from the moment we met. You are a very determined woman."

"When I have to be," she answered. "Tell me, will I get to meet your elusive lady friend today?"

A faraway look crept into Tad's eyes. "Not today. She couldn't make it."

Emily wasn't sure she should delve deeper into his private life, but curiosity prevailed. "I'm beginning to get the feeling she's hiding from me."

He grinned. "Not this woman."

"Does it have anything to do with the rumors that circulate about us?" she asked.

"We have many things to work out, but none of them has anything to do with you or with this."

"I'm glad."

"Well, it's time to mingle." He paused. "You look stunning in black. You should wear it more often."

Emily looked at her black silk jumpsuit with its sequined belt, then back to his darkly tanned face. She smiled, laughed. "You know, the first thing I liked about you was the way you dressed. Not many men can wear a white suit with a blue T-shirt and still look sophisticated."

He bent and kissed her lightly on the lips. "When your lover comes, find me. I want to meet him."

"I will," she promised.

"Here comes Belinda Brown. She stars in that new drama series set in the Middle East. You'll want to talk to her. Come with me. I'll introduce you."

Emily kept a watch on the door as she talked to the young woman, but Nathan didn't show. From Belinda she moved to the star of the current number-one sitcom. She tried to keep her thoughts on CAT, but she was beginning to worry. Nathan was over an hour late. Most everyone she'd spoken with at the party was interested in what CAT was doing and pledged generously. Lobbying for stricter laws for convicted terrorists seemed to be at the top of everyone's list.

At last her eyes were rewarded, the one she'd waited to see walked through the door. Senator Merritt was immediately stopped by the California senator and she saw Nathan scanning the crowd, looking for her. She started toward him. Her heartbeat speeded up. He was as handsome as she remembered.

Their eyes met, a few more steps and their hands met, and finally their lips in a brief, sweet kiss that tingled all the way down to her toes. She squeezed his hand tightly.

"I've missed you," she whispered, refusing to let go of him. His smile seemed to melt away all the weeks they had been away from each other.

He carried her hand to his lips and kissed the back of her palm. "How long will we have to stay here? I want to show you just how much I missed you."

Now it was Emily's turn to smile. Some of the longing she'd carried around with her for over two months was arrested by his presence. In its place came the reality that before this day was over she would be lying in his arms making slow, warm love. Regretfully she said, "At least a couple of hours."

"Tell me you're kidding." He cocked his head back without taking his eyes off her. "Two hours is a lifetime. I've missed you, I want to hold you and love you. Even if I have to do it in front of all these people."

Emily laughed. It felt wonderful being with him again. Her urgency matched his, but this time business had to come first. "I don't think Senator Merritt would approve of that, or if we disappeared too quickly."

He pulled her close, letting his hand roam up and down her back in slow, provocative movements. Her stomach contracted from wanting. He was right. Two hours seemed like a lifetime.

"I don't think he'd mind if we found a secluded spot and stole a few kisses."

"Oh, I think he might," she said and squeezed his hand before pulling away. "He's walking toward us."

Nathan turned around and looked. "Damn. He did say he was eager to meet the woman who convinced a hundred movie stars to come to a fund-raiser for CAT on a holiday weekend."

"I couldn't have done it without Tad." She felt obliged to remind him.

He rested his hand on the small of her back. "Let's don't talk about him right now. I'm jealous that he has just spent the last three months with you."

She laughed. "A little jealousy is good for you."

"You're right. It's going to make me give you one helluva loving when we get to the hotel."

More than two hours later, Emily was looking for Nathan. Earlier, she'd turned her back on him for a moment and he was gone. There were so many people, so many questions about CAT, that she hadn't seen him for more than the first two minutes of his arrival.

It was growing dark, and a bright half moon shone in the eastern sky. Even though it was cool, some of the guests had changed into swimsuits and jumped into the pool. The band had arrived and was playing a medley of Broadway show tunes. She found herself humming along with them as they played, "Don't Cry for Me, Argentina." Its haunting melody stayed in her head long after the song was over.

At last she spotted Nathan, and her breath grew short. He was watching her, waiting for her to see him. She wanted to run into his arms, but discretion forced her to walk.

He took her hand. "I've been looking for you. I don't think I can take one more smile or handshake. Can we leave?"

"I was looking for you, too." She tried to tell him with her eyes that she wanted him. Right now. "Yes we can go. Unless you want something to eat first?" She pointed to the buffet spread at the other end of the pool.

"All I want right now is to be alone with you, so I can touch you and kiss you and make love to you."

For the first time that evening, his voice was husky with passion, his breath thick. Emily's pulse quickened. His eyes roamed hungrily over her face. The passion he was showing thrilled her. She wanted to unleash it.

"Nathan, how's it going?" Emily looked around to see Bill Hadly, the reporter Raymond Sanders had introduced to her months ago, slapping Nathan on the back and shaking his hand. "It's nice to see you again, Emily." He reached for her hand, which she extended reluctantly.

"Bill, what are you doing so far from home?" Nathan asked.

"A special invitation from the senator. I happened to be talking to him yesterday and he mentioned this big bash. When I told him I was going to be doing a series of articles on CAT, he asked me to fly out here and cover the fund-raiser. Unfortunately I couldn't get booked on the same plane."

"I guess John forgot to tell me that he talked to you," Nathan said dryly.

"Hey, no problem. The senator's a busy man. I'm sure it wasn't intentional." He looked at Emily. "I hope you'll agree to give that interview we talked about the last time we met. Maybe we could include information about this fund-raiser."

After staging this extravaganza, she'd sound like a dope if she said no. However, she didn't intend to make it easy for him.

"If you want to interview me about CAT, I'd be happy to talk with you when I return to Florida. I'll call you the first of the year and we'll get together."

Bill laughed. "Oh, you're a sly one, Emily. I'm not going to get caught in that trap. Why don't I call you when I get back to work on Monday, and we'll go ahead and set up a time."

Anything to get rid of him so they could leave. "Sure, that will be fine."

"I'd also like an interview with you, Nathan. When are you getting back from Costa Rica?"

Emily went still. Nathan was going to Costa Rica? Latin America, Central America, South America, it was all the same to her. Why? She fixed her eyes on him. He was talking to Bill, but she couldn't hear what they were saying. The ringing in her ears was too loud. White heat seared through her. Why hadn't he told her?

Her throat was dry, she needed something to drink. Her legs were weak, shaky, she had to sit down. Watching Nathan's lips move, she learned that he was going the second week in December. He was going with John to Costa Rica the second week in December. Fear closed around her like a damp blanket. No, she wouldn't let him go. He couldn't go. She wanted to shout that he couldn't go, but her throat was too tight. This was madness.

What could she do? She turned away, blindly heading for the bar.

His voice was faint, but she heard Nathan ask, "Emily, where are you going?"

"I—need something to drink." She didn't know if she had said the words or only mouthed them. She was suddenly too tired to think.

She didn't wait for him, but kept walking on heavy feet. Nathan was beside her, but she didn't look up at him. If she moved her head, she was afraid she would lose her balance.

"Emily, what's wrong? You don't look well."

When she reached the bar, she leaned heavily against it. She moistened her lips before barely getting out, "Vodka tonic."

"Emily, you don't drink vodka. What are you doing?"

"Nothing. I'm thirsty." Still she refused to look at him. She didn't want to see him. She didn't want to have to face the fact that he was going to Costa Rica. Her hands were shaky when she reached for the vodka. Even though it was warm, she felt chilled. She immediately took a long drink and winced. It was strong. Nathan grabbed her wrist and the vodka spilled over her hand.

Their eyes locked together. Raw tension shimmered around them.

"What the hell are you doing?" Nathan was too tired and too ill-tempered to be gentle. He'd been fighting frustration since he had arrived at the party. No, for months now. The only thing he wanted was to be alone with Emily so he could hold her. Now here she was acting as if he wasn't around.

She didn't put up a fight when he took her elbow and guided her away from the bar, over by a section of shrubbery.

"Now tell me what's wrong?" he demanded when they were far away from the others.

"Why didn't you tell me you were going to Costa Rica?" Her voice was soft and breathy and she blinked rapidly.

He didn't understand. He shook his head in bewilderment. "Emily, I was going to tell you later, when we were alone. I haven't had two minutes alone with you. What's the problem here?"

The tears came into her eyes so quickly it stunned Nathan. She was really upset. Her face was shadowed by early evening twilight, but he could see something was wrong. She was more than upset. She was in pain.

"I don't want you to go," she whispered.

His eyes lighted with compassion. "Emily, love, I'll only be gone four days."

"Forget it," she whispered in a ragged voice and turned away from him. She put the drink to her lips once again.

"Forget it?" he asked harshly and swung her around to face him. "Don't give me that." He took the vodka out of her hand and threw it into the shrubbery. "Tell me what the hell's going on?"

She fixed wild, glistening eyes on him. "My husband was killed in Colombia. Do you know how close that is to Costa Rica?'' Her voice was so full of fear her words were slurred.

Nathan felt something sharp twist in his gut. Oh, God. Nathan covered his eyes with his hands for a moment. Guilt ate at him. He swore bitterly under his breath. ''Emily, I'm sorry I didn't make the connection. Come here.'' He tried to pull her into his arms, but she jerked away. ''Emily, it—''

''I can't believe you're even considering going.'' Her words were a challenge.

He cursed himself silently. How could he have not realized she would be upset about his going to Central America? He wanted to do something, say something to make it all right. ''Costa Rica is a safe country, the safest in all of Latin America.'' He spoke slowly and softly, trying to calm her.

''I don't want to hear it. Please, I don't want to hear it. Just go away and leave me alone.'' She sounded impatient.

''No way. We've got to talk about this, and we can't do it here.'' He tried to take her arm again, but she pulled away. Damn, her rejection hurt. But he knew she was hurting, too. ''We're going to the hotel. Do you have a car here, or do I need to call a cab?''

''No, I have a car,'' she whispered.

He wished she'd look at him. All he wanted to do was love her. He didn't want to hurt her. It was difficult to be gentle with her when he was so angry with himself. ''Where's your purse?''

Emily sniffled and wiped her eyes. She lifted her chin and said, ''I need to say goodbye to Tad.''

Her soft voice tore at his masculinity. ''To hell with Tad and the senator. We're leaving. Right now.'' He took her arm, even though she resisted, and after finding her purse they headed for the door.

Stopping for directions, they made it back to the Beverly Hills Hotel. Nathan had left his luggage with the limo driver, who promised to have it delivered later. The valet took the keys to the rental car and they walked through the entrance of the historic hotel. Any other time Nathan might have been a tiny bit impressed. He was too angry with himself for not realizing news of his trip would traumatize Emily.

"Which floor?" he asked, when they walked into the lobby.

"The second. I always take the stairs," she said, absently looking through her purse for the key.

Once inside the room Nathan watched Emily kick off her shoes, take off her belt, lie down on the bed and close her eyes. How could he take away the pain without giving up his job?

He stretched out on the bed beside her. Her heat drew him and he scooted over until his legs were touching hers. What could he say that would make her understand? He had to go to Costa Rica. Refusing to go would be professional suicide.

"Emily," he whispered gently and watched his breath fan her lashes. "I love you. I don't want to hurt you." He brushed her hair away from her slender neck. Her hair was longer now, long enough to gather in his hands and feel its silkiness. He watched her breasts heave with each troubled breath, loving her with his eyes. She was so soft, she smelled so sweet, she looked so innocent.

"Emily."

Her eyes, wet with tears, fluttered open and gazed into his. "Don't go," she whispered.

Nathan's stomach formed into a thousand knots. How could he comfort her, when he was the one hurting her? He'd give anything to take the fear out of her eyes. "I have to."

"You won't come back," she said softly.

"Yes, I will. I promise." With his lips, he wiped away a lone tear that rolled down her cheek. He threw his leg over hers and slipped his arm under her head, pulling her closer. He wanted her so badly his insides were trembling. He wanted to take the hurt away.

"Emily, listen to me. Remember when I told you John was appointed to the Foreign Affairs Subcommittee on Terrorism?" When she nodded, he went on. "Well, this trip to San José has to do with that." She stiffened.

"Emily, I'll be as safe in Costa Rica as I am in Florida. The country is a democracy. The main difference between their constitution and ours is it's written in Spanish. The country has a high standard of living, a high literacy rate and a large middle class." She looked doubtful. "I know it's hard to believe when it's stuck between Nicaragua and Panama, but I swear to God it's the safest country in Latin America."

Her eyes were luminescent. "I still don't want you to go."

"I have to. We need their help. If we're ever going to get a handle on terrorism, we've got to start somewhere." He was frustrated by her refusal to accept the inevitable.

"I'll worry about you every moment you're gone."

Nathan sighed. "Don't do that to yourself, Emily. I'd change this if I could. You know that, don't you?"

"Will you have protection? Will policemen travel with you?" she asked, her voice a throaty whisper.

Nathan sensed she was accepting it. He smiled. "Yes. The President has okayed a special team of Secret Service men to travel with us, as well as several others who'll arrive in San José a couple of days before we do. This meeting has been planned for months and San José is taking extra precautions, too. I'll be so protected no one will be able to find me."

"I couldn't stand it if anything happened to you." She turned into his arms and Nathan went weak. He hugged her so tightly he was afraid of cracking her ribs. Relief was so sweet, he trembled. For a few moments, he'd thought he'd lost her.

"Oh, God, I love you, Emily."

"I love you, too," she mumbled to his shirt front before looking up at him. "I've missed you." She slipped her arm around his neck and pressed close to him.

"I've missed you, too." He kissed her lips. Sweet longing filled him, and he ached to show her how much he loved her. With the tips of his fingers he lifted her chin and forced her to look into his eyes. He reached down and kissed the tip of her nose. "Don't worry about me. I promise you nothing is going to happen to me. I know you can accept this. Remember what I've told you, you're stronger than you think you are. Look at all the things you've accomplished in the past six months. You can do it, Emily. I know you can."

Emily moistened her lips and attempted to smile. "I guess I'll have to because I don't want to lose you."

"You won't." His lips came down on hers hungrily and nothing else was said that night.

Chapter Twelve

The tenth day of December brought a chilling wind to Tallahassee, Florida. The filming of *America's Kind of Hero* had been completed. Emily had left Hollywood when all that remained to be done on the movie was the editing. She hadn't wanted to hang around the studio for that.

She was busy, her first full day back at home. Her condo had been closed up for three months and needed a thorough cleaning, which took most of the morning. Next she had to go to the post office and get her mail, then run several other small errands.

Nathan would be flying back from Costa Rica tomorrow and she wanted to have everything finished so they could have the weekend to spend together.

When Nathan returned to Washington and left her in California, she'd done a good job of hiding her true feelings about his trip to Central America from them both. But deep inside she knew she'd never easily accept this part of the job.

In retrospect, her own intense reaction to the news surprised her. She had thought she was all over those fears. After the hijacking it had taken her a long time to overcome her fear of flying. Because of the way the media had relentlessly pursued her and hounded her for statements about Gary's death, it had taken even longer to get over her dread of the press. Now she had to learn how to deal with Nathan's traveling to the same part of the world that took Gary's life. That would be the hardest.

By the end of the day the house was clean, the wash completed, and all her errands accomplished. She looked for something else to do, knowing if she could stay busy she wouldn't worry about Nathan as much. When she could find nothing else to do, she went into the kitchen to make dinner. A tuna-salad sandwich sounded good, so she made one, took it into the living room and turned on the TV. Since working on the movie with Tad she had a greater appreciation for television and all the hard work that goes in to making a thirty-minute comedy look simple.

A few minutes later Emily was more interested in finding the tuna that had fallen from her sandwich onto the sofa than the program, until she heard the word car bomb. She looked up and realized the hourly news brief was on.

She listened. " . . . exploded outside the American embassy in San José, Costa Rica about two hours ago. No casualties are being reported at this time. More news later on this NBC station."

Emily was frozen in shock. A car bomb. Costa Rica. Nathan. He said it was the safest country in Central America. The safest! Nathan!

"No," she whispered vehemently, her insides shaking. What should she do first? Who should she call to get more information? Settle down, she told herself. The news said there were no casualties. That meant no deaths. Right? But did it also mean no one was injured?

Nearly knocking over the glass of iced tea, she set her unfinished dinner on the coffee table and ran to her desk. Her fingers felt cold and stiff as she looked for the number Nathan had given her before he left. Hands shaking, she dialed the telephone. "All circuits are busy. Please try again."

"No!" she whispered again, trying to calm her gulping breaths. This was not the time to fall apart. But her chest hurt. She couldn't stop trembling. She pressed the zero.

"Yes, Operator, I want to uh—I mean I'm trying to place a call to San José, Costa Rica, and I got a recording that says all the circuits are busy. Can you help me?"

"I suggest you try again later."

Her stomach tightened. "Operator, this is an emergency. I'm trying to call the American embassy in San José. This is an emergency," she pleaded again.

Something must have registered in her voice, because the operator said, "Give me the number you're trying to reach and your own number. I'll try to get through and call you back."

"Thank you," she whispered and gave the numbers, repeating each one twice before hanging up the phone.

Nathan knew how worried she'd been about his going to Central America. The news said the bomb exploded over two hours ago. Nathan would have called her if he could. She was sure of that.

"Oh, God, no," she whispered on a sigh. She'd known this was going to happen. Why hadn't she stopped him? Why!

What could she do? Wait? No way! She was going to Costa Rica. As she ran into her bedroom, her mind was going faster than she could work. She pulled the tweed-bound suitcase from under the bed and tossed it on top

of the coverlet, then ran over and switched on the TV
There could be another news break and she didn't wan
to miss it. She reached for the telephone to call the air
lines, but realized she didn't want to tie up the phone i
case the operator called back.

She hurried back to her closet and started pulling dow
clothes, not caring what she grabbed. With franti
movements, she did the same to her underwear drawe
and the shoe rack. At last, when the suitcase was full, sh
locked it, and carried it into the living room.

She looked at her watch. It had been ten minutes sinc
she called the operator. What was taking her so long t
get through? A chill shook her.

Pacing the room, Emily nervously rubbed her hand
together. Hadn't she'd been through this before? Wasn'
it two years ago that she paced the floor like this waitin
for news, praying everything would turn out all right?

Emily stopped and stared at the door. Fear trans
ported the past into her consciousness. It was a balm
August evening. Everything was quiet except for th
television. An airplane had been hijacked. Gary's plane
Wait! The demand for money and the release of th
prisoners had been made. Wait! The women and chil
dren were let go. Wait! A passenger was killed an
thrown out onto the tarmac. Wait! The doorbell rang. A
man telling her Gary was dead. No!

Dazed, Emily came back to the present. Was the ring
ing doorbell in her mind, or for real? She looked at th
front door and it seemed to grow bigger, stretching to
ward her. A loud knock sounded, and she jerked wit
panic. There was someone at the door. No! It couldn'
be.

She blinked rapidly, trying to focus properly on th
door. Another knock, louder. She had to answer. Emil

moved forward on sluggish feet. When she opened the door, she couldn't believe her eyes. Nathan stood in front of her. "Nathan!" She only mouthed the word. No sound came out. He wrapped her in his arms, picking her up off the floor and hugging her to him.

Tears fell from her eyes, even though she tried to keep them inside. He was here, safe, in her arms. She shook with heavy sobs, with relief.

"It's all right, Emily. Everything's fine. I love you." He kissed her hair and held her tighter.

"I was so worried. How did you get here so fast? Nathan, I—" Suddenly she pushed away from him. Her stomach was quivering and she was shaking all over. She sniffled and wiped the tears from her cheeks with the back of her hand.

He tried to take her in his arms again, but Emily backed away. "I left Costa Rica early this afternoon. I tried calling to tell you I'd be coming in, but you were out. I thought about calling when we landed, but because I was only twenty minutes away I didn't want to wait to see you. I heard about the explosion on the radio on my way over from the airport. I knew you'd be frantic. Let me make a couple of calls and see what I can find out about this. Then we'll talk."

Emily watched in silence as he went to the phone. She stood with her arms folded across her chest, her hands rubbing up and down her arms. She listened as he talked. No one had been injured and very little damage had been done to the outside of the building. As far as could be determined from the evidence gathered so far, the bombing had nothing to do with the senator's presence.

Finally he hung up the phone and faced her. "No one was injured."

"I heard." She was stiff, rigid. She didn't feel natural. In fact, she couldn't feel anything at all. She tried to move away when he walked closer to her, but she couldn't. His expression was gentle, but she didn't want to see it. Trembling inside she said, "I can't take this."

He stopped just inches from her and let his gaze sweep over her face. "Emily, you got upset for no reason. As you can see, I'm perfectly safe and so is everyone else."

"I'm happy about that, but this is the last time."

"What do you mean?" His voice was soft, his eyes peering deeply into hers.

She looked up at him with unshed tears glistening in her eyes. "I can't live like this. I—I want you out of my life." There, she'd said it. She heard the uneven leap of breath in his throat, and her heart started thudding crazily. Her stomach churned. The blood rushed to her head.

"Emily, I was already on a plane out of the country when that bomb went off." He stood patiently and watched her.

"I didn't know that." Her words were almost whispered. "Knowing you're safe now doesn't take away the agony I went through before I found out." She turned her back on him and walked to the other side of the room. Distance. She had to keep distance between them. If he took her in his arms, she'd give in to her love for him. He'd soothe her and talk her out of her fear the way he had in California. And she'd probably be all right until it happened again.

"Emily, I—damn."

Hearing him stumble, she turned and faced him. He'd bumped into her suitcase. Angry eyes looked down at her. "What's this?"

Her throat ached from holding back the tears that wanted so desperately to flow. She took a deep breath. "I was going to Costa Rica."

"Emily."

"No. Don't Emily me again." Her voice shook with emotion. "I don't want to be packing my bags every time I hear a bomb has gone off. I won't. I've been through this once and I can't go through it again."

He stared at her for a long time, as if trying to come up with the words it would take to comfort her. "That car bomb had nothing to do with the reason I was there," he said in a leaden voice.

"Is that supposed to make it all right? Does that take away the fear I felt at the thought of losing you?" She couldn't stop shaking.

He ran a nervous hand through his hair. "I'm not insensitive to your feelings. Emily, I love you. The last thing I want to do is cause you any worry or pain."

Her throat felt as if it had been burned. Her eyes itched and her nose was stuffy. "Then stay away from me." The words were like a knife in her stomach. Tears of anger, frustration and sorrow finally ran down her cheeks. "I won't go through this every time you go away. I can't."

"Emily, what this committee's doing is very important to finding ways to better deal with terrorism. It's my job. I can't give that up."

She rubbed her eyes again. "Don't make this worse than it is. I'm not asking you to give up your work."

"No, dammit, you're only asking me to give you up. And I'm not going to do it." His tone became less tolerant. "You've had a shock. You don't know what you're saying."

"I know exactly what I'm saying, and I know what it's costing me to say it. I've been through this before, remember?'' Her tone softened. "I want you out of my life. If I don't know where you are, I can't worry about you."

"You're not being reasonable." His voice turned angry.

"No, I'm being emotional, because I'm frightened."

He reached for her again, but she spun away. "Let me help you. You can't let this fear control your life. You can't hide from reality anymore. Terrorism is real, Emily, and it can strike anywhere, anytime and anyone."

"Stop it!" she screamed at him. "Just who do you think you're talking to? I don't need a lecture on terrorism. I've been a victim. But I refuse to be again." She took a deep breath, feeling calmer for the first time. "I'm not going to let this fear control me. That's why I have to give you up. I don't want to hear from you again." Tears stung her eyes and she blinked rapidly, her lashes feeling heavy.

"I won't let you do this. You're feeling sorry for yourself again, thinking you're the only one who counts. I have a say in this relationship, too."

She watched his lips, loving him. Yet, she had to send him away. "No. You don't have a choice."

This time he grabbed her shoulders before she had the time to flee. His fingers dug into the soft flesh of her arms. "We've been through too much. I'm not going to let you push me away." His eyes met hers and caressed her face with a loving glance. "I love you too much to give you up so easily."

"It's not easy. It's so hard I'm aching inside. I have to do it. Please leave."

"Do you think that by simply telling me to go away you're not going to worry about me, that you won't care what happens to me? Think about what you're saying."

"I have thought about it, and it's the only thing I know to do."

His face was twisted with anger. "What in the hell am I supposed to do with my love for you?"

Emily had no answer for him so she looked away.

"Just like that." He snapped his fingers. "You expect me to leave just like that." The hurt in his voice turned to bitter resignation. "All right, Emily. You've got it." He whipped around and strode out, shutting the door with a bang.

She was so cold. Her legs were still shaking. She felt empty. It was as if a piece of her was removed, leaving her not quite complete. But she had to do it, she told herself. She couldn't risk losing another man she loved to terrorists.

Sometime later that night, the telephone rang. The operator had the American embassy in San José on the other end. Emily refused the call.

NATHAN LEAFED THROUGH THE four-hundred-page booklet with interest. The information was concise and brief. He knew he couldn't go wrong in giving the project to Roger. Nathan laid the book aside and glanced up at Roger. "You did a good job with this. Did you send a copy to John?"

"No way," Roger informed him. "I wanted you to look at it first to see if this is what you had in mind. You were right. Most of this stuff was on computer files. It was just a matter of finding it, and then getting my hands on it. There's a lot more to terrorism than newspapers tell us."

A picture of Emily flashed across Nathan's mind and his stomach knotted. "You're right, Roger. Newspapers usually report only the terrorist acts, not the long-reaching ramifications of it. I'll read this over the holidays and get back to you if there are any changes."

"All right," Roger answered. "What's next on the list?"

Nathan chuckled and realized it was the first time he'd laughed in three weeks. "I wish everyone I knew had your enthusiasm for getting to a job and getting it done. Holidays and parties are the only things on the agenda for the rest of the year. Enjoy yourself."

He smiled. "Thanks. I will. You coming tomorrow night?"

Shaking his head, Nathan said, "No. I have other plans."

"Other plans?" Roger asked, shocked. "What could be more important than a party at the best restaurant in town? We work all year for this. Everyone will be there."

"This isn't something I can get out of," he explained. And he wouldn't if he could. He was going to see Emily tomorrow night. He hadn't seen her since the night he returned from Costa Rica. For days he told himself she would realize she made a mistake and give him a call, but after two weeks passed he knew she wouldn't.

It was time to set up the senate hearings on terrorism and John wanted Emily to head up the project. And John expected Nathan to talk her into it.

Nathan reached into his desk drawer and handed Roger an envelope. "John and I appreciate your dedication."

A smile stretched across Roger's lips. "Thanks. I was hoping to give Anne an engagement ring for Christmas. This will help."

A tinge of bitterness crept up Nathan's back. "Do yourself a favor and don't buy her a diamond. Make it a ruby or emerald."

"Why?" Roger asked.

Nathan ran both hands through his hair, angry with himself for trying to color Roger's happiness. He had no right to do that. "Don't mind me. I'm just rambling." He waved Roger away.

Roger rose and walked to the door. "Merry Christmas, Nathan."

"Merry Christmas, and I hope she says yes."

WITH CHRISTMAS JUST THREE days away, Emily dressed in a mohair sweater of red and beige and matching lightweight wool slacks. Her hair was casually styled, to hang loose about her shoulders with half bangs covering her forehead.

Just like her, the condo was decorated for the holidays; an artificial tree stood in the corner, brightly decorated with red, blue, and green bulbs and lights. A small candy-cane tree sat in the middle of the coffee table and a paper Santa Claus was taped to the front door. The mixture of cinnamon and clove that she'd heated in the microwave earlier still lingered in the air, giving the room a homey scent.

Nathan had called the day before and asked if he could stop by after dinner. Reluctantly she agreed. She hadn't seen him since the night of the explosion, but not an hour had passed that she didn't think of him. It wasn't that she didn't want to see him—she was afraid to see him. What would she do if he took her in his arms? She loved him so much she wasn't sure she could resist him if he touched her.

Emily took a dark blue ball off the tree. Holding it carefully, she looked at her distorted image reflected in the fragile ornament. Where was the smile that should be on her face? The movie was finished, Nathan was gone. But where were the happy, carefree diamond days she'd dreamed about? Telling Nathan to leave hadn't worked. It hadn't stopped her concern for him or erased the ache his absence caused.

Time, she told herself. She needed more time. It had only been a little over two weeks since she'd last seen him. Sometimes she would awaken in the night after dreaming about him and swear she could still smell his clean scent, feel his lips on hers, his body pressed close to hers.

Still holding the ball, she looked at her watch. It wasn't like Nathan to be late. She was eager, anxious, doubtful and apprehensive. Just the thought of seeing him again made her pulse race. She wondered what he wanted to talk about. Did he want to mend their broken relationship? Would she, if he asked? She'd been miserable without him, but could she hold up under the strain of his traveling out of the country? No, just thinking about it sent chills up and down her back.

When the doorbell finally rang, she jumped, then hesitated before walking to the door. He looked as handsome as ever in his dark blue suit. His eyes—had they always been that dark shade of midnight blue? She looked at the ornament she still held and knew why she was drawn to that particular one. It was the same shade as Nathan's eyes.

"Hello, Emily. It's good to see you."

Oh, God, it was good to see him, too. "How've you been?" she asked, closing the door behind him.

"I don't guess I have too much to complain about." He glanced around the living room. "I like your tree. It's very contemporary-looking."

Emily looked at the tree and realized she didn't like it. Just as she no longer liked her contemporary condo. She wanted a house with a fireplace and a live Christmas tree, where the tangy scent of cinnamon and cloves wouldn't seem out of place.

"Come on in and sit down. I made some spiced tea. Would you like some?"

"Sounds good."

She poured the tea into an earthenware cup. "Would you like a little brandy in it?"

"Why not? Sure."

Her hands were shaking, her stomach in knots and she felt as if the heat was turned up to ninety degrees. She handed him the tea, careful that neither their hands nor their eyes met, then sat beside him on the sofa.

"This is very good," he said.

"Thanks." She wasn't going to look at him, but she couldn't help herself. She'd missed him. Loving him was so painful she had to look away. She wished he'd go ahead and tell her what he wanted. Surely he knew this was tearing her apart.

Frustration forced her to be blunt, forced her words to sound angry. "Why did you come over, Nathan?"

He watched her for a moment, then replied. "All right, I'll get right to the point. John asked me to speak to you. When Congress reconvenes in January, the Foreign Affairs Subcommittee on Terrorism is going to hold a series of hearings on the effects of terrorism. He wants to know if you will be the key speaker and line up a group of others to come and talk to the committee on this subject."

"Me?" Her voice faltered, tightening her chest. Her hand flew to her throat.

"You have firsthand knowledge, combined with a claim to fame that few can match. The committee wants to hear what you have to say. They want to hear from the people who are behind CAT before they decide whether or not they'll support it."

"But why do they want me? Lucy Morrow should be the one they'd want. She knows so much more about CAT than I do."

"He wants you to head it up. I'm sure you can arrange for Lucy to testify, along with several others."

He avoided her eyes and fixed his gaze on the gold chain around her neck. "John was impressed with your efforts in Hollywood. We all were. Not just anyone could have gotten one hundred actors and actresses together to support CAT. The money you helped raise started several more chapters. But I'm sure you already know that."

"Yes. I received a nice thank-you note from John. Everything did go well with the fund-raiser, but Tad did most of the work." Emily turned away. She didn't want to think about California. It reminded her of the love she and Nathan had shared in the Beverly Hills Hotel.

"So, can I tell John you'll think about it?" he asked.

Emily had always known that Nathan wanted her to become involved in CAT for reasons other than for her benefit, but she didn't mind. "No, tell him I'll do it."

He chuckled under his breath. "It was easier to talk you into it than I thought it would be." He placed the cup of tea back on the table. His heavy-lidded gaze wandered lovingly, longingly over her face.

"I'm going to New York to do some publicity work for Tad in January, but I should be able to do both without too much trouble." She sounded breathless.

"Publicity for Tad?" He smiled. "That old fear of the press seems to be gone completely."

"No, it was a trade-off for his help with the fund-raiser." She looked at him. His presence left her wanting more of him. She wanted his touch, his embrace, his—

No. She brushed a hand through her hair and shifted on the sofa. "I'll never like the publicity, but as you once suggested I now use it to my advantage. I believe in what CAT's doing. I want the laws changed here in America as well as internationally, and I'm willing to do the work to see that it's accomplished."

"Good. I'll tell John." He paused. "We'd like to think that you'll also be willing to join John's reelection campaign."

They were talking as if they had never shared a kiss, let alone moments of earth-shattering passion. Never mind the passion, they had been in love. And here they were talking as if nothing had ever happened between them.

"I don't know. Lucy and I have talked about it. I know that supporting John means supporting CAT. I'll have to think about it."

"No hurry," he said.

"I guess you'll be leaving for Vail soon," she said, trying to keep her mind off how handsome he looked, how much she wanted to reach out and touch him, how much she loved him.

"No, I'm not going until the middle of January. Congress didn't recess until two days ago and I couldn't get away. My Dad and sister are happy I'm staying home for the holidays this year. How about you? Any special plans?"

"I'm going to spend a few days with my parents. Both of my sisters are joining us. So it should be fun." Fun? Who was she kidding? She wasn't looking forward to the holidays at all. At one time she and Nathan had planned to spend Christmas in Vail together. But that was before Nathan started traveling to Central America.

She ran her hand over the back of her neck and massaged the cramped muscle. Why didn't she just reach out and touch him? That's what she wanted to do. That and a whole lot more.

For the first time that evening, Emily looked into Nathan's eyes and he returned the caress. Yes, they were still in love. She was weakening. Something had to be done before she touched him.

Nathan's voice was husky, his breath thick, as he said, "I miss you, Emily."

Shoring up her strength, Emily returned, "Nathan, don't. We've said it all before. It won't work. I don't want to open old wounds again."

"I've given you time to think about us, to realize that we belong together. Emily, I can't let you throw away what we had, what we meant to each other."

An intense pain pierced her. "I have to. I won't put myself through that kind of torture again. It's wrong for you to ask it of me."

"When are you going to stop hiding from life, stop running every time something comes up that makes you the least bit uncomfortable?" His voice was filled with desperation.

"I'm not," she insisted, feeling as if he were closing in on her.

"Yes, you are. You were hiding the first day I met you and you're still hiding. Only now you have a different reason."

"That's not true. You don't know what you're talking about, and I don't have to listen to you." She jumped up. "I want you to leave."

Nathan grabbed her shoulders and pulled her close, forcing her head back. "Every time I say something you don't like, you're ready to throw me out. Listen to me. We'll get counseling for you. I'll go with you."

"No," she whispered. "I can't. You don't understand."

"Then help me understand. I told you I don't give up what I want easily."

"I don't, either," she shot back quickly. "But it's easier to live without you than it is to live with you."

"You don't mean that, Emily."

"Yes, I do," she lied. She had to. In time it would get easier to bear.

He let her go so abruptly she stumbled backward. "I guess that says it all." His voice was calm as he straightened the jacket of his suit. "Thanks. You couldn't have given me a better Christmas present."

He turned and started for the door. He was walking away. Was she going to let the man she loved leave once again? "Nathan, I—"

"You what?" he spun around and asked bitterly. "You're sorry you can't cope with the fact that I've got to go to Central America three or four times a year?"

His truthful words wounded her. "Yes," she said just as angrily as he had. "I'm sorry for a lot of things." Her eyes misted, her voice softened. "Most of all, I'm sorry for myself because I have to live without you."

"No. You have a choice." He challenged her. "Emily, we'll get help. We'll go to counseling."

The lump in her throat was so big she didn't know if she could speak. "It's not a choice I can live with."

"Merry Christmas, Emily." He turned and walked away.

EMILY STEPPED OUT OF the taxi. The cold January wind whipped at her cheeks, and she pulled her tweed coat closer. This wasn't her favorite time of year to come to New York. She looked at the horse-drawn carriages in front of the Essex House and Central Park. Tad gave the driver a twenty and told him to keep the change.

"Let's have breakfast before you go up to your room," Tad said as they waited for the street to clear before crossing.

She wasn't hungry, but she could use a cup of coffee. Joan Lunden had been very tactful, still her nerves were frazzled.

"I'm glad you let your hair grow long," Tad commented as they stood in the briskly blowing wind. "You wore it too short when we first met. A woman with hair as beautiful as yours should always wear it long."

"I like it better this way, too," she admitted and wondered why that comment should make her think of Nathan. If she was honest with herself, she'd admit that every comment reminded her of Nathan. No matter what she was thinking, Nathan was always at the back of her mind.

"Are you still nervous about the interview? You were wonderful."

She managed to smile. "No. I'm fine. The 'Good Morning America' crew are nice people to work with. But I'm glad it's over and I'm going home this afternoon."

Home? She used to look forward to going home, but not anymore. She looked to her right, then started across the street.

Suddenly Emily was shoved to the ground with a jolting force, the wind knocked from her lungs. The blaring of a horn followed her down. When her breath returned a moan escaped from her lips.

"Emily, are you all right?" Tad's concerned face loomed above her.

"Yes—I think so," she said, struggling to her feet with Tad's help. "What happened?" she questioned, brushing her coat.

"Emily, you walked out in front of that car." His tone was reprimanding. "If I hadn't pushed you out of the way—my God, I hate to think what would have happened."

"Hey, lady, you okay?"

Emily looked up to see the doorman from the hotel hurrying toward her. It hurt to breathe in the cold air. "Yes, really, I'm fine. I'm not hurt at all," she said, but knew better when she raised her arm to push her hair away from her face. Her arm and shoulder ached.

"Are you sure?" the man asked again.

"Yes," she said in an irritable voice. "Believe me, I'm all right." She turned to Tad. "Can we get some coffee?"

Tad kept his hand to her back as they hurried across the busy street. Along with her arm and shoulder, her hip hurt when she walked, but she wasn't going to let anyone know.

While they waited for the hostess to show them to a table, Tad helped Emily with her coat. Delayed alarm had set in, and she started trembling.

"Are you sure you're all right? Should we call a doctor?"

"No. I'll have a few bruises and be sore for a couple of days. You weren't too gentle with me."

His face was serious. "I didn't have time to be gentle."

The potency of his words drained the last of her strength. She opened her mouth to say she'd forget about the coffee, when the hostess appeared and showed them to a table. Gratefully she sank into the chair.

"Why don't you tell me what's wrong, Emily? You haven't been yourself this entire trip."

She rubbed her forehead and was surprised to see that her hand was still trembling. "I'm just tired. After three months in Hollywood, six days in Fort Lauderdale and four days in New York, I'm ready to spend some time at home. I'm tired of living out of a suitcase."

"There's more to your problem than that. Emily, you walked in front of a speeding car."

Oh, God, she'd almost gotten killed. "I didn't intend to," she snapped, fear forcing unintentional anger from her. Where was that coffee? Taking a deep breath to steady her voice, she said, "I looked, or I thought I did."

"What's bothering you, Emily? Tell me," he asked again.

She wasn't going to tell him she was thinking about Nathan. "I don't know. I told you, I thought I looked both ways, but I guess I didn't. It was an accident."

"That almost killed you."

"You don't have to keep saying that. Don't you think I know it by now?" At last the waitress appeared with the coffee. Not waiting for it to cool, Emily put the steaming liquid to her lips. Damn, it was hot.

Maybe she should talk. She'd do anything, if it'd make her feel better. "All right. I haven't been myself lately because I've broken up with Nathan, and I'm simply miserable about it."

"What happened? Was he playing around with another woman in Washington?"

Emily laughed with little humor. "No, it has nothing to do with another woman." She eased her coat off her injured shoulder and let it fall to the back of her chair. "From now on Nathan will be traveling to Central

America from time to time, and I just can't handle that. It's just too close to where Gary was killed."

"What can't you handle?"

She gave him a curious look. "The fact that he will be going to countries where there are terrorists and could very well be killed the same way Gary was."

"There are terrorists here in America."

"Yes, I know, but—"

"But what, Emily?" He gestured with his hands, not understanding.

"I couldn't bear losing another man I love to terrorists." Why was it so hard for people to understand that?

"Oh, I see. You could bear it if he suddenly died of a heart attack or in an automobile accident?"

"No!" She was shocked. The waitress came over and Tad waved her away.

"But isn't that what you're saying?" he continued when the woman was gone. "I can't bear it if he's killed by terrorists, but if it's a heart attack, I'll be okay."

"No! Stop it." She shook her head, furious that he would imply such a thing. "You're putting words in my mouth, and I don't like it. Tad, why are you being so callous?"

"The question is, why are you? Emily, life holds no guarantees for anyone. You could have been killed just now, and Nathan would be the one mourning you."

"No," she whispered. "I should have never mentioned it to you. You're confusing me. I don't want to think about it."

But she did think about it. She had almost been killed. Nathan wouldn't have known how much she loved him. Had she really been so foolish as to believe she could live without him? Tad was right. She'd be devastated if Nathan should die. How wouldn't matter.

"Do you love him?" Tad asked, breaking into her thoughts.

"Yes, yes! Very much." She suddenly realized how much.

"Then go to him and tell him you've been a fool and beg him to take you back."

Tad had the right idea, but it needed a feminine touch. "That sounds a little too dramatic."

"It's the truth." Tad laughed. "You American women. You need to be more subtle. So tell him you were wrong and you want to get back together."

Emily couldn't help it, she had to smile. "That sounds more like the way I'd say it." And she wanted to say it as soon as possible. She'd call as soon as she returned home. No, she'd call as soon as she went back to her room.

"You know, Emily, even though we started out as enemies, I think our friendship is going to last for a long time."

She reached for his hand and squeezed it fondly. "I think so, too. Tell me, when are you going back to L.A.?"

"Not today. I've decided to stay in New York a few days and look up an old friend. I want you to stop by my room when you leave for the airport. I have something for you."

She sipped the coffee again. "Oh, what?"

"A tape of *Hero*. I thought you might like to keep it or view it before it airs tomorrow night."

Emily suddenly felt warm. "Yes, I would like that. Thanks for thinking of it."

"I also have a check for one hundred thousand dollars to give you. I hope you don't mind, but I took the liberty of making it out to CAT."

A flush crept up Emily's cheeks. She had forgotten about asking for that money. "Tad, I'm—well, you don't have to do that. It wasn't right for me to ask for that money."

"A deal is a deal, Emily. Besides, I don't mind when it's for a good cause."

"You give a lot to good causes. Thank you, Tad. Do you think you'll get an Emmy?"

"It's out of my hands." He shrugged. "We did a good job on *Hero*. I'm pleased with the final cut. And when you see it, I think you will be too."

"I'm sure I will."

"So tell me, Emily, what are you going to do when you get home?" Tad asked, a boyish grin on his face.

Emily sighed and smiled. "Call Nathan and tell him I've been a fool and beg him to come back to me."

Tad and Emily laughed.

Chapter Thirteen

Nathan eased the cream-colored sheet away from Emily's warm body and crawled into the bed beside her. The black silk-and-lace gown she wore tantalized his senses to a fevered pitch. She murmured softly when he pulled her into his waiting arms. Feather-soft, her fingers played with the wiry hair on his chest.

"Oh, Emily it feels so good to hold you! Why have you waited so long to come to me?" He kissed the slender column of her throat, letting his lips glide down her smooth and silky skin. The exotic perfume she wore teased him with its scent and titillated his tongue with its bitter taste.

"I've wanted to so many times." She nibbled on the lobe of his ear, biting him softly, making him grow harder.

Nathan let his hand glide down her black silk-clad thigh, the feel of the material beneath his palm sending ripples tingling and dancing throughout his body. Through the thin silk he could feel every delicious curve of her body. The nightgown she wore was beautiful, provocative, but kept him from seeing all of her.

Her hair was soft and sweet-smelling. He wove his fingers through its silken length. Crushing the weight in his hands and lifting it to his face, he inhaled deeply. Everything about her turned him on.

He looked into her dark green eyes. "You are so beautiful, so warm. Sometimes I can't believe I'm so lucky. I love you, Emily." His body trembled with desire, with the emotion he was feeling because, at last, she was his once more.

"And I love you," she whispered in a low, sexy voice, her thumb lightly caressing his lips, her body moving temptingly.

His gaze slowly traced over her face and down her creamy throat to where her breasts were partially covered with black lace. Nothing could come between them now. He would take it slow and easy, and when he was through, she would know just how much he loved her and how desperately he had wanted her.

He glanced down into her gleaming eyes, which caressed his face with a loving look. Nathan shook with wanting. No other woman had ever aroused such passion in him. Her body lay against his so naturally, so perfectly, as if she'd been made especially for him. God had never been this good to him.

"There are so many things I want to do to you, so many ways to love you that I don't know where to begin." His voice was a raspy whisper as a trace of a smile lifted the corners of his lips.

"Start here," she murmured seductively, lifting his hand and placing it over her breast. "And here," she continued, brushing her lips against his with tenderness. Nathan groaned and pulled her to him tightly, arching, pressing—

The shrill ringing of the telephone ended the embrace.

Nathan opened his eyes. Stunned, he reached for the other side of the bed and found only empty air.

"Emily?" Sitting up in bed, he looked around the room. The phone rang again and he reached for the receiver, growling an irritated hello into it.

"This is the front desk with your wake-up call. The time is seven forty-five, and the temperature is nine degrees."

Nathan dropped the receiver onto its cradle and fell back against the damp pillow. "She was so real," he testified to himself as he rolled over, his body throbbing with frustration. He had smelled her perfume, tasted her lips, felt her soft skin with the palm of his hand. Squeezing his eyes shut, he tried to recapture the image of Emily lying so willingly in his arms.

A few minutes later the sheet was thrust aside in anger. Emily wasn't in bed with him. No amount of imagination was going to make her appear.

Jumping off the bed, he snapped on the TV, hoping a morning news program would force him to forget about the ethereal dream. While waiting for the picture to focus, he reached back and grabbed his flannel robe. Vail in January wasn't the place to stand around in the nude.

He swung back around, thinking to turn up the thermostat, when he caught sight of Joan Lunden and then Emily. Emily? He rubbed sleep from his eyes. Was that Emily on "Good Morning America"? A tightness formed in his chest. God, she looked good on television. Was her hair really that long, her eyes that green, her face that beautiful?

This must've been what she was talking about when she'd told him she would be doing some publicity for Dreamstar. He turned up the volume and stood back.

"What did you think about the actor who played your husband?" Joan asked.

"I was pleased with the way he handled the part. He was very professional."

Joan brushed a wisp of blond hair away from her face. "I heard that you're the one who picked him from all the other actors. You insisted that he be the one. Is that true?"

"Yes. That was a very emotional time for me. I took one look at him and knew he was the right man for the part. And he did an excellent job."

"There are a lot of true stories being made for television now. Would you recommend being a consultant to anyone who finds they're in the same position you were?"

Nathan's stomach tightened. He could see that the question surprised Emily. The camera held on her face. "Answer, Emily, you can do it," he coached her. "Just say what you feel and everything will be all right," he encouraged.

"I think it has to be an individual preference. For me it was the right thing to do. For others, it might not be."

"Great answer," Nathan said to the television.

"But isn't it true that at one time you tried to stop the production of this movie? Didn't you take Dreamstar to court over this issue?"

"Yes, that was a troublesome time, but now I'm very comfortable with the decision I made and pleased the way things have turned out." She didn't hesitate this time, and Nathan gave her the victory sign.

Joan Lunden thanked Emily for coming and reminded the listeners that *America's Kind of Hero* would be on the following evening.

That had worked better than a cold shower. Nathan pushed the button on the TV and the screen went blank.

He had known the movie was going to air in January, but not what day. Running his hands through his hair, he stared at the television. Tomorrow night? He wanted to be there for her in case she needed him. And here he was stuck in a ski chalet on a mountain twelve hundred miles away. Hell, what did it matter? She didn't need him or want him. She'd made that clear on more than one occasion.

Nathan let his hand slide down his face, the scratching noise as it ran over his beard indicating he hadn't shaved in several days. Would she be flying home or staying in New York? he wondered. Would she watch the movie with Tad?

He stalked into the bathroom and squirted shaving cream into the palm of his hand. The cool white fluff lay against his skin as softly as Emily's breast.

Damn, he was angry with her; angry because she gave up so easily, angry because she didn't have the courage to overcome her irrational fear of terrorists and Latin America, angry because she'd pushed him out of her life without so much as a thought as to what it would do to him.

Why couldn't she understand that she couldn't keep him safe all the time, any more than he could keep her safe? What would it take to tear her away from the unrealistic fear that had gripped her? Giving up his job—would that change things between them? Would that make her come back to him?

Maybe she just didn't have enough love or courage to build a solid, lasting relationship with him. Maybe the death of her husband had scarred her so badly she'd never be comfortable with love again. He knew she was stronger than she realized. But he didn't know how to make her see that. He'd tried for over a year with Michelle, and to this day he still wasn't sure that she believed in herself.

Nathan remembered the last time he had seen Emily. He'd said some of the same things to her that he'd said to Michelle years ago. "You can break the habit. You can cope with your fears. We'll sign you into a hospital. We'll go to counseling." But in the end his words hadn't helped Emily anymore than they'd helped Michelle.

Nathan couldn't remember the number of times he had told Michelle she was strong enough to overcome her dependency on cocaine. How many times had he told Emily she was strong enough to handle the reporters, strong enough to work on the movie, strong enough to cope with his trips to Costa Rica? He couldn't do anything more for Emily. She had to do it herself.

Lathering his face with determination, he decided the best thing to do was forget about Emily. That was what she wanted. Let her come to him if she needed him. He was through trying to make her see how unrealistic and irrational her fears were. If he thought it would do any good he'd try again, but Michelle had taught him it wouldn't.

He knew better than to get involved with her in the first place. Hadn't he told himself that she had too many problems for him to deal with? Hadn't he purposely kept all his relationships lighthearted since his divorce from Michelle? He knew better.

Maybe her dependency wasn't drugs, as Michelle's had been, but Emily had her own hang-ups that were just as hard to cope with. He was tired of it. He was tired of falling in love with and trying to help women who kept hiding from reality. When it came down to the bottom line he hadn't helped Michelle with her drug problem, and now he'd failed Emily, too.

"Damn!" He'd nicked himself with the razor. He threw the disposable into the sink and took a hard look at himself in the mirror.

EMILY'S BEIGE SILK robe swished around her legs as she paced across the living room floor in front of the TV. The black-faced clock told her that *Hero* would be on the air in less than an hour. She didn't know why she was so nervous. She'd been there when every scene was shot. She had the tape Tad had given her yesterday and she could view it at any time. The truth of the matter was that nervousness had nothing to do with the movie. She'd been trying since yesterday afternoon to get in touch with Nathan.

She'd made the first call while still in New York. His secretary said she couldn't give out his number in Vail. However, she would see that Nathan received the message Emily had called. When she hadn't heard from him by late morning, she called his office again and got a recording that all federal offices were closed due to an overnight snowstorm that had paralyzed the capitol. She didn't know whether or not Nathan had gotten her message.

If she'd known where he was staying, she would've taken the first flight to Vail. She only hoped he'd give her a chance to explain that for a short time she really believed her fear of terrorism would leave with Nathan. And yes, she'd tell him how much she loved him and missed him, and what a fool she'd been to think she could live without him. She tried to put aside the nagging fear that he had received the message and refused to return her call. No, she couldn't think about that possibility.

She should have agreed to let Janice come over, she thought as she continued to pace. With Janice around, maybe she wouldn't feel so alone, so empty. Who was she kidding? Nathan was the only one who could fill her, make her whole once again.

Why had she thought she could live without him? She couldn't. She loved him too much. He believed in her even when she didn't believe in herself. How could she have pushed him away?

In time, she'd learn to cope with his traveling to Central America. Maybe someday she'd have the courage to go with him and put her fears to rest for good. It wasn't easy coming to the realization she had been wrong to let him go, and now she was eager to make amends.

She looked at the television once again and groaned. In a few minutes a tribute to Gary would be airing and all she could do was think of Nathan. She needed a cup of coffee.

As she headed for the kitchen, the doorbell rang, startling her. "Janice," she whispered. "Bless you. How did you know I didn't want to be alone tonight?" She picked up the skirt of her robe and raced to the door, wanting to envelop her friend in a bear hug of thanks.

Cold winter air stung her cheeks when she opened the door and looked into Nathan's midnight blue eyes. If anyone had asked her to guess who would be at the door, she would have said a thousand names before Nathan's. She was so stunned, so unsure as to why he was there, she couldn't speak. He must have felt the same way because for a long moment they just stared at each other.

She closed her eyes for a brief second as her heart threatened to beat out of her chest. She didn't know how or why, but he knew she needed him and he'd come to her.

"Nathan." She spoke his name softly, reverently and rushed into his arms. "Thank God, you got my message. I'm so glad you're here. I've missed you so much."

His arms closed around her like a loving vise that halted her breathing. He buried his face in her hair, his hands caressing the length of her back. Emily's arms slipped through his open coat and circled his waist, her hands locking together at the base of his back. She was in his arms and it felt wonderful, like heaven. She didn't want to ever let him go.

The chilling wind from the open door nipped her bare feet, but she ignored the pain. She inhaled the clean, heady scent that belonged to Nathan. The scent she'd come to expect, to want, to love.

Opening her eyes, she saw that the night was filled with billions of twinkling stars, shining like exquisite little diamonds against black velvet. The heavens had never looked more beautiful than they did at this moment.

"I didn't get a message from you," Nathan whispered against her ear. "I just took the chance that you needed me. I knew I had to try one more time."

She raised her head from his shoulder and looked into his eyes. "I do need you. I always have." She was conscious of how loudly her heart was pounding, of how the wrong thing said now could tear them further apart, rather than bring them closer together. Surely his showing up at her door meant he still loved her. She turned him loose and stepped back, inviting him inside.

Nathan took off his coat while they walked silently into her living room and sat on the sofa. Emily took his hand and held it between both of hers. Her heart hammered in her chest.

"I have so many things to say to you, I don't know where to begin." She was so afraid of rejection that she trembled. Her feet were cold, so she pulled at the hem of her robe and tried unsuccessfully to cover them.

Nathan realized what she was doing and said, "Here, let me warm them for you." He swung her legs up on the sofa and took one of her feet in his hands and started massaging it.

Gasping, Emily clutched at the front of her robe as Nathan's hands glided over her foot. His hands were so warm, so soft, his touch felt so good that she couldn't breathe properly. Her heart was beating too fast, her palms were sweating. Did he know what he was doing? Did he know how enticing his hands felt on her feet?

He was driving her crazy. How could she think straight, say the things she needed to say with his hands so warm upon her? She pushed her hair away from her face and cleared her throat. "I left a message with your secretary that I wanted you to call me. You didn't get it?"

"I haven't talked with her in three or four days. She's pretty good about not bothering me when I'm on vacation."

Her breath leaped again as his fingers slid between her toes, lightly caressing. "Y-your offices were closed today—a big snowstorm."

He nodded. "I know. I heard it on the news."

Watching the circular motion of his hands caused her stomach muscles to tighten. The peaks of her breasts were taut with wanting. "Ah—why did you come, I mean, if you didn't get my message?"

"I saw you on 'Good Morning America' yesterday. You did a good job, handled yourself well. I was proud of you." His hands found her other foot and started the same ministration, causing the same euphoric sensations.

"Thank you." Her voice was breathy.

Suddenly his hands stopped and he looked directly into her eyes. "Emily. When I heard that *Hero* would be on I had to come to you. I guess I thought if you were ever going to need me, it would be tonight."

"I do need you, but not because of *Hero*. I need you because I love you and I've missed you."

His hand tightened on her foot, his eyes probed hers. "I still have the same job, Emily. Nothing's changed." His voice was soft.

"I know. I've been such a fool. I was so selfish, so worried about me and what I was feeling, that I didn't realize what I was doing to you, to us. I can't begin to explain what I was thinking. I just went crazy when I heard about that car bomb. I thought I was going to lose you the same way I lost Gary. I know now how irrational that was, but at the time all I could think about was what it would do to me to lose you to terrorists. In my overwrought state I couldn't comprehend that losing you by simply giving you up would be just as painful."

"And now?" he asked.

"Now I've come to my senses. I finally have things in perspective. From the day we met and talked in the diner, I knew you were good for me. I sensed that you understood what I had gone through but you wouldn't accept my self-pity. You were there for me when I needed you. I don't believe I would have ever accepted the movie if it hadn't been for you. I was depending on your strength to get me through, and when I thought I was going to lose you I snapped." She moistened her lips. "I've never stopped loving you."

"Come here," he said, pulling her gently into his arms, surrounding her with his warmth. "I'm going to do my best to see that nothing happens to either one of us. I love you, Emily Clements."

Emily buried her face in the soft material of his sweater, rubbing her nose against the firm muscles beneath it. "I was so afraid of losing you to terrorists that I couldn't see that it would be just as hard to lose you by sending you away."

"And now how do you feel?" he questioned.

She swallowed hard. "Like I'm going to conquer this fear that's been eating away at me. With your help, I know I can." She clutched at his sweater and buried her face in his neck.

"Oh, Emily, I want to help. I want to erase all your fears, but it's not going to be easy when I'm the one causing them." He pushed her hair away from her cheek and kissed her forehead. "What's going to happen when I go back to San José in March?"

Emily lifted her head and with a calm voice said, "I'm going with you."

"Emily!"

"No, I mean it," she responded quickly. "I've got to, Nathan. When I was afraid of flying I had to force myself to get on a plane. I was afraid of reporters so I forced myself to meet with them. Now I have to go to Central America. With or without you, I have to go. Do you understand?"

He caressed her cheek with the back of his palm, and smiled. "Don't worry. You won't be going alone. And this isn't something we have to settle tonight."

She looked up into his eyes and whispered, "I've missed you. I love you."

"I love you," he said as his lips captured hers in a passionate, burning kiss.

When at last his lips left hers, he cupped her face with his hands and said, "It's time for the movie." His voice was husky, his breathing ragged.

Emily wiped at her eyes. She was about to conquer another obstacle on the road to a full recovery from Gary's death. "I don't want to watch *Hero*. It represents my past. You are my future, and that's all I want to think about right now."

Nathan's hands trembled on her cheeks, his hot breath fanned her eyes. "Emily, do you mean that?"

"Yes. I've never tried to hide my love for Gary from you. But Nathan, he's now tucked away in a corner of my heart as a beautiful memory. I've finally put him to rest. I love you," she whispered.

"And I love you," he answered.

Emily melted into the circle of Nathan's arms as shivers of desire ran through her. He slid his hands around her waist and pressed her tightly against his chest. Their lips met and passion blossomed between them. She loved him and he loved her. Fresh confidence surged through her. Nathan's love had given her a second chance and she felt glorious. She wanted him to see love in her eyes, feel it in her touch, in the way her body responded to his.

Gently he pushed her back against the sofa, covering her. They moved and shifted until a moan of satisfaction passed Nathan's lips as their bodies finally fit together.

"I thought I'd lost you. I don't know what I would have done tonight if you'd asked me to leave."

"Don't even think about that," she said and covered his lips with her own.

Nathan lifted his head and looked into her eyes. "Emily, if I kiss you again, I'm going to want the whole night."

A smile spread across her lips and her hands slid up his chest. "I'd be disappointed with anything less."

THE NEXT EVENING, humming John Denver's song, "Some Days Are Diamonds and Some Days Are Stone," Emily stepped out of a tub of warm water and wrapped a forest green towel around her petite body. It was wonderful to once again feel the thrill and expectancy that comes from being in love.

She dusted her body with a lightly scented bath powder and applied a little shadow to her eyes and blush to her cheeks. From her closet, she pulled a royal blue sweater dress and slipped it on over her pale blue lingerie. Once she slipped her stockinged feet into her beige pumps, she was ready to go stargazing.

Nathan arrived a few minutes later, looking handsome in his dark brown slacks and the Harris tweed jacket he wore over a brown pin-striped shirt. They spoke briefly at Emily's door before going to the Mustang. She had such fond memories of the last time she rode in it she was looking forward to their evening together.

When they turned onto a deserted road, Emily looked at Nathan and smiled. Eyes sparkling, she turned to him and said, "I don't believe we're doing this in the middle of January."

Nathan reached across the gearshift and caressed her knee with his hand. "Stargazing is no respecter of seasons."

When he stopped the car, Nathan got out and let the top down. Emily shivered as the cold night air whipped through her light wool coat and chilled her.

"Come on," he said with a pleased grin, "let's get in the backseat. I don't want the gearshift between us tonight. Besides, I have to hold you close and keep you warm."

"That sounds like a good idea," Emily said as she crawled into the small backseat with good humor. She didn't mind a little cold air, especially if Nathan was going to keep her warm. In fact, this romantic side of Nathan was one of the things she loved about him.

Nathan pushed the two bucket seats up as far as they would go, then climbed in beside Emily. She went eagerly into his waiting arms and brushed her cold nose against the warm skin of his neck. The lemon scent of his shaving soap was tantalizingly close and she breathed in deeply.

"Mmm, you smell good," she whispered and kissed him just beneath his jawline. He smelled so good, she stuck her tongue out and tasted him. Tangy but delicious, she thought.

"I wish you weren't wearing this coat," he said and proceeded to unbutton it and slip his hands inside. Pulling her close, he sighed with contentment. "Ah—that's better."

"I can't see the stars," she complained lightly.

"There aren't that many out tonight anyway," he protested when she tried to pull away from him. Instead, he lifted her face to his and tenderly kissed her.

"Emily, I know we were only apart a little over a month, but I couldn't have missed you more if it had been a year," he said as she settled her head on his shoulder, their arms wrapped comfortably around each other.

"I feel the same. I'm sorry I was such an idiot."

He laughed. "You weren't an idiot. You were mixed up. But you did scare me. You can be tough when you want to."

"I know. And I promise it won't happen again." She kissed him, slipping her tongue into the warmth of his mouth. It was wonderful to be close to him once more. When the kiss ended, she watched moonlight dance off his hair and thanked her lucky stars that she had Nathan back.

"Emily, you understand that I spend a lot of time in Washington, don't you? I'm not going to be the kind of man who comes home every evening. How do you feel about that?"

"I don't like the idea that you spend so much time in Washington, but I do understand. I know you have to do it."

"How understanding would you be if you were married to me?" he asked, a grin on his lips.

Emily looked into his eyes and smiled. "I'm not sure. I know I would want you with me every night."

"Will you think about it?" he asked as he let his lips brush over hers. Emily moved her hands up his neck until she felt the roughness of newly growing whiskers. The bristles titillated her and sweet love filled her.

"Yes, I'll think about it," she answered, enjoying the light, teasing banter.

Nathan reached for her hand and slipped something on her finger. "Will you wear this while you think about it?"

Emily brought her hand out into the open and looked at it. On the third finger of her left hand was the most exquisite diamond she had ever seen. It glittered and glimmered in the moonlight. She gasped.

"Oh, Nathan, I love it. It's the most beautiful ring I've ever seen!" She glanced up at him, her heart swelling with love. "But I don't need a diamond."

He closed his arms around her protectively. "I never stopped loving you. I want you to marry me."

Emily's eyes loved him. "Yes, yes. I love you, Nathan. I'll marry you," she said passionately, kissing his eyes and cheeks and finally resting warmly, briefly on his lips.

Nathan chuckled lightly, his warm breath turning to smoke as it hit the cold air. "Do you remember what we talked about the first time we came here?"

"Yes." She looked up at him, a lump forming in her throat. "Diamond rings and diamond days," she answered.

He nodded. "And I wondered how I could be blessed with a woman who only wanted diamond days. Emily," he murmured, lifting her hand to his lips and kissing it. "It's easy to give diamond rings. What I want to give you is diamond days, but they're not as easy. I can't promise all your days will be filled with happiness and sunshine, so I want you to wear the ring for the ones that won't measure up."

As his gentle words reached her, tears of joy filled her eyes. She cupped his warm face with her cool hands. "Nathan, I love you. Knowing that you love me is all I need to make me happy. You're the one responsible for my diamond days." She circled his neck with her arms and met his lips with loving tenderness. She slipped her tongue into his mouth to taste his sweetness. The temperature was close to freezing, the wind blew hard, but for a few breathless moments neither of them noticed.

"It's not going to be easy for us, Emily," he said between kisses. "I do a lot of traveling back and forth between here and Washington. I literally have two homes."

"Then I'll have two homes," she assured him. "Nathan, I'm not worried. We'll find a way to make it work. I'll be in Washington when the senate hearings start. And I'm sure there are other things I can do for CAT in Washington. If you don't have any objections, I can put off going back to my real-estate job for a while and get to know the capitol."

"Do I have any objections? You've got to be kidding! You don't have to go back to work until you want to. If you decide you want to do something else, that will be okay, too. Oh, Emily, I love the idea of you coming to Washington with me. It's so cold there and you are so warm." He snuggled the base of her warm throat and moaned his pleasure.

"I love it, too. When I'm in Washington with you, I can visit the Smithsonian and all the other museums. That should take a few weeks."

"That could take forever. There's so many things to see and do in Washington, you may never come back to Florida." He hugged her tightly.

"I love you, Nathan. I want to marry you. I'll live wherever you live," she said softly before they kissed again.

He smiled. "I think it's time to put the top up and take you home," he murmured.

When he started to move away from her, she held him and asked, "Are you going to stay the night?"

She stared into his dark blue eyes, highlighted by moonlight. His hand came up, his thumb lightly caressed her lips. "Tonight and every night for the rest of our lives."

Emily's chest tightened with the love she was feeling. She circled his neck with her arms, her hand coming around so that she could see the sparkling, glittering gem on the third finger of her left hand, the gift of Nathan's love. Diamond days would always be more important to her, but this diamond ring ran a close second.

Back by Popular Demand

Janet Dailey
Americana

A romantic tour of America through fifty favorite Harlequin Presents, each set in a different state researched by Janet and her husband, Bill. A journey of a lifetime in one cherished collection.

In July, don't miss the exciting states featured in:

Title #11 — HAWAII
   Kona Winds

   #12 — IDAHO
   The Travelling Kind

*Available wherever
Harlequin books are sold.*

**THIS JULY, HARLEQUIN OFFERS YOU
THE PERFECT SUMMER READ!**

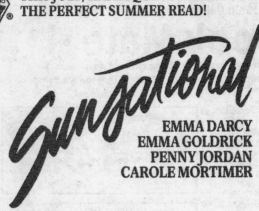

Sunsational

**EMMA DARCY
EMMA GOLDRICK
PENNY JORDAN
CAROLE MORTIMER**

From top authors of Harlequin Presents comes
HARLEQUIN SUNSATIONAL, a four-stories-in-one
book with 768 pages of romantic reading.

Written by such prolific Harlequin authors as Emma Darcy,
Emma Goldrick, Penny Jordan and Carole Mortimer,
HARLEQUIN SUNSATIONAL is the perfect summer
companion to take along to the beach, cottage, on your
dream destination or just for reading at home in the warm
sunshine!

Don't miss this unique reading opportunity.

Available wherever Harlequin books are sold.